Perilous Passage

RICOCHET TITLES

The Crime on Cote des Neiges by David Montrose

Murder Over Dorval by David Montrose

The Body on Mount Royal by David Montrose

Sugar-Puss on Dorchester Street by Al Palmer

The Long November by James Benson Nablo

Waste No Tears by Hugh Garner

The Mayor of Côte St. Paul by Ronald J. Cooke

Hot Freeze by Douglas Sanderson

Blondes are My Trouble by Douglas Sanderson

Gambling with Fire by David Montrose

The Keys of My Prison by Frances Shelley Wees

The Pyx by John Buell

Four Days by John Buell

The Damned and the Destroyed by Kenneth Orvis

The Ravine by Phyllis Brett Young

I Am Not Guilty by Frances Shelley Wees

Perilous Passage by Arthur Mayse

Perilous Passage

ARTHUR MAYSE

Introduction by
Susan Mayse

A
Ricochet
Book

Véhicule Press

Published with the generous assistance of the Canada Council
for the Arts and the Canada Book Fund of the Department
of Canadian Heritage.

Canada Council   Conseil des arts
for the Arts   du Canada

Canadä

Ricochet series editor: Brian Busby
Adaptation of original cover: J.W. Stewart
Typeset in Minion by Simon Garamond
Printed by Livres Rapido Books

Library and Archives Canada Cataloguing in Publication

Title: Perilous passage / Arthur Mayse.
Names: Mayse, Arthur, 1912-1992, author.
Description: Series statement: A Ricochet book | Previously
published: New York: W. Morrow, 1949.
Identifiers: Canadiana (print) 20210240156 | Canadiana
(ebook) 20210240210 | ISBN 9781550655841
(softcover) | ISBN 9781550655926 (HTML)
Classification: LCC PS8526.A88 P47 2021 | DDC C813/.54—dc23

Published by Véhicule Press, Montréal, Québec, Canada
www.vehiculepress.com

Distribution in Canada by LitDistCo
www.litdistco.ca

Distribution in the USA by Independent Publishers Group
www.ipgbook.com

Printed in Canada on FSC certified paper

Telling the Story
Arthur Mayse and *Perilous Passage*

SUSAN MAYSE

When my father wrote *Perilous Passage* as a seven-part series in *The Saturday Evening Post* in 1949, he was well established as a West Coast short story writer selling to magazines in the United States. He was Canadian to the bone, but he didn't then call himself a Canadian writer. From the start he intended to make his living by writing. As Arthur Mayse—to his friends and family he was always plain Bill Mayse—he sold his first short story at twelve to *The Star Weekly*. It took dozens of rejections before he sold another story, but he was determined. He came of age in the depths of the hungry thirties; the only way to get where he wanted was under his own steam.

His father, Will Mayse, was a pit lad who'd escaped the Yorkshire coal mines for the Boer War and a new life as a Baptist minister in Canada, where he married Elizabeth Caswell, an Ottawa Valley girl whose family tilled stony fields to raise fine airs and little else. His parents sojourned as missionaries in rural Manitoba for the birth of their daughter Shirley and son Arthur William Caswell Mayse at St. James Mission among the Swampy Cree. Arthur Mayse was named for his mother's ne'er-do-well uncle; as Bill Mayse he was his father's son. The family lived by oil light and travelled by wagon or sleigh under bison robes; radio and automobiles were distant luxuries.

His first memory was of hanging in a moss bag from a branch among other babies while a young boy held up a brace of ducks that he'd shot with his bow and arrow. His wet nurse was a Cree Métis woman, Maggie Flett, whose uncle had followed Louis Riel. My dad spoke fondly of people on the Peguis Reserve, told me their stories and never ceased to miss their quiet presence; I still have his moss bag and first moccasins, faintly scented with smoke from their tanning. Every spring when I was little he showed me how to cut a whistle from a fresh sap-swelling willow bough as one of Maggie Flett's relatives had shown him. Toward the end of his life, he missed Manitoba's springtime chorus of frogs peeping in the green roadside ditches.

In the early 1920s the family moved to the West Coast. Bill Mayse's school and work history was a grand tour of early twentieth-century British Columbia. His first job as a kid was picking strawberries for a Japanese Canadian farmer near Vancouver. At twelve, he won a Cowichan fishing derby with one of his mother's silver spoons hammered into a salmon lure, fishing from a dugout canoe given to him by a Khowutzun First Nation shaman who liked his father.

At tough, multicultural Britannia High School in East Van, not fast enough to compete on the track team, he ran as a "rabbit" to set the pace for a black friend. (The black student missed an athletic scholarship because the school principal decided not to notify him.) Britannia was one holiday after another; students booked off classes claiming to be Sikh, Chinese, Japanese, Jewish, Protestant, Catholic or Greek Orthodox. Between holidays, friends' mothers stuffed skinny Bill Mayse with perogies, grits, tamales, souvlaki or anything they could spare. He sold stories during high school to *The Province*, many about his fishing summers with his father on the Oyster River north of Courtenay on Vancouver Island. After the degraded and often privately owned streams of England, the astonishing freedom to fish the lovely West

Coast waters and camp on their banks made Canada a paradise. On the river or in town, Will Mayse and Bill Mayse remained close friends for life.

Poor boys and men were riding the rails looking for work by the mid-1930s, but it was a chancy life. Bill Mayse stayed in BC and borrowed a friend's name for job applications, since W. Cook had already landed work. The deception got him hired on a northern Vancouver Island logging operation based at Menzies Bay. The first year he worked as a whistle punk, running a signal device out to the fallers; after that he walked the woods alone all summer as a timber cruiser, making camp wherever dusk caught him, to assess the value of standing timber. On trips to town, other loggers made him their banker; his speed as a track-team rabbit saved him at last call in the beer parlours when he outran them to preserve their wads of cash. Logging and his prize money from poetry awards paid his way through university.

It was an exciting time to be young in the growing city of Vancouver, but Bill Mayse yearned to be on Vancouver Island or upcoast. The university year at UBC was only a wet-season distraction from the logging camps and fishing camps he loved and increasingly wrote about. When Bloedel, Stewart & Welch offered him a management job at its Franklin River camp, he turned it down with mixed feelings. But as his paid-by-the-inch freelance "string" of newspaper stories grew too long, *The Province* saved money by hiring him as a full-time reporter.

At *The Province* Bill Mayse trained with legendary reporter Torchy Anderson and travelled BC by train and car, fishboat, and horseback, to cover the news. He outran a forest fire and dodged a forest ranger determined to press him onto the fire lines. He fished streams around Cumberland with blacklisted coal miners and got to know wildlife bounty hunter Cougar Smith. At a Sointula dock he found himself eye to eye with a shotgun barrel; the utopian Finns didn't like strangers coming ashore. When he covered the police beat, he packed an illegal handgun. The cops turned a blind eye; they liked to have him along because he noticed details at crime scenes. He climbed Mount Waddington in the Coast Range with a crate of his newspaper's carrier pigeons on his back, only to see a hawk pick off his last bird. He had to hitch a ride by tugboat to file his story on the first successful ascent to *The Province*.

In 1940, Bill Mayse married his childhood friend and sweetheart Winifred Davey, a telephone operator he'd met on the Oyster River. He got drafted, or joined up, or joined up one jump ahead of the draft; the story sometimes shifted. The army flagged him as a good shot and trained him as a sniper until they discovered his old TB scars. He took a medical discharge rather than sit at an army desk as a censor. Unemployed, Bill and Win caught a train to Toronto, where he found work as a writer at a trade magazine and later at *Maclean's*.

After hours, pounding away at his second-hand typewriter in their small brick house on Halford Avenue, he wrote short stories, which he began to sell steadily to magazines including *Maclean's, Collier's, Country Gentleman*, and his favourite, *The Saturday Evening Post*. In 1947, they adopted their three-year-old son Ronald. I was born a year later. Soon afterward Arthur Mayse left *Maclean's* and took the leap into freelance writing. As with any great change in their lives, Win and Bill never hesitated and never looked back. In 1949, *The Saturday Evening Post* bought his serial "Perilous Passage," a thriller set in BC's Gulf Islands and the American San Juan Islands. William Morrow published it as a novel in 1951.

Perilous Passage was sold as a mostly American story to an American magazine and an American book publisher. My dad always liked working with Americans, he told me. They were hard-nosed, capable, and courteous; they treated him well, and most importantly, they paid decently. Several European publishers also picked up and translated *Perilous Passage*. The book brought him to the attention of reviewers and other publishers and got him an agent. It was the kind of story that he liked best, not only adventure and suspense set on the West Coast, but a hard-luck love story with young characters and a happy ending. He would repeat this theme of a poor boy and a slightly better-off girl—or occasionally a rich girl—more than once in later short stories and novels. After all, it was his own story, and he knew it spoke to the lives and struggles of Depression-era and post-war readers.

In my dad's view there was no Canadian publishing industry worth noticing. The few novels and short stories identified as Canadian fiction, he felt, were anaemic works written in subservient imitation of English writers of the time. He wanted no part of their pretensions. Even his fly-fishing friend Roderick Haig-Brown sold to UK and US markets. Instead, Bill Mayse followed the respect and the paycheque. It was honest work, and he never wanted to be counted among the second-raters. If a man couldn't make his living by writing, was that man really a writer?

Man, not woman. Most of the women and girls in his stories were feisty characters whose strength and courage drove plots and deepened their significance beyond the obvious. Bill Mayse held many women fiction writers in high regard—including Daphne du Maurier, Naomi Mitchison, Joyce Carol Oates, and Dorothy Dunnett—but some he regarded as flutterbrains. As a girl, I met some of them; maybe they acted like flutterbrains faced with the low opinion of misogynistic male writers. Later my dad worked happily with women editors and directors, but

11

perhaps because my non-writing mother deferred and demurred, being a woman of her times, he never fully appreciated women's capabilities. Naturally, he aired his views to me; naturally, I challenged them as malarkey. We would argue frequently, but an hour later be friends. In time he grudgingly acknowledged the virtue of equal pay for equal work and other women's rights.

Eventually, he also grudgingly acknowledged the rights of working people. He'd been "fired on the job"— deprived of his beat, his desk, and his typewriter—for helping to organize the first union local at *The Province*, and so went to work for *The Vancouver Sun*. In his own perverse fashion, he'd blamed the labour movement, not *The Province*'s management or the former friend who ratted out the fledgling union and was subsequently rewarded with a management job. It wasn't a totally misguided aversion; in the late 1930s union members and especially organizers were still blacklisted or worse. But in time he came to accept the rights and dignity of workers like him who'd hauled themselves up from dire poverty by their bootstraps.

His mild misogyny and classism were ironic in some-one who'd always been essentially free of racial prejudice and religious bigotry. I saw him tell a Texas senator to leave our house after he told a racist joke. I never heard my dad make a racist comment. As a teenager, I fre-quently misunderstood others' words and needed to have derogatory terms explained to me. He occasionally told a questionable joke, but strangely, in a dialect that puzzled me for years. I finally asked why he always told jokes with an Irish accent. The question shocked him; he was unaware that he slipped into his Irish Canadian grandmother's storytelling voice. Nonetheless, in his 1940s and 1950s writing he displayed a then-common insensitivity to race and gender by using language that would rightly shock today's readers.

British Columbians in exile eventually find their way home. Both my parents had grown up mostly in Vancouver, and they missed the slow, cool rainy springtime and the warmth of family. In 1951, with nothing to keep us in Toronto, we drove west in our shiny new maroon Studebaker, ending up in a waterfront house north of Victoria. My dad set up his typing table in front of his bedroom window, looking ten kilometres across Haro Strait to the dry hills of San Juan Island in Washington state. There he wrote many short stories, a handful of novelettes and his two adventure novels, *Desperate Search* and *Morgan's Mountain*.

Our family lived on Arbutus Cove from 1951 to 1972. There, as a girl, I learned to fly-cast on the back lawn, tie a Royal Coachman, shoot a .22, pound a typewriter, plant a garden, and row a boat. We lived with exceptional freedom in a marvellous place. Always there were wants and worries, but I realized only long afterwards how few people could ever lay claim to that charmed life.

A child's view of a writing parent is shaped by self-interest. My dad was the one with all the good white bond paper that I coveted for drawing. He was the one who paid fifty cents an hour to dig Netted Gem potatoes, wore his old high-top logging boots till they fell apart, knew mysterious old-timers, made herring rakes and salmon landing nets, and could repair almost anything. Most especially he was the one who told stories. I heard many stories about my father's childhood, but fewer about my mother's. Win Davey came from a big, noisy, happy family of engineers and inventors, so it may be that she felt less need to tell stories. Many of my dad's earliest short stories had happy family endings, as he recreated his own experience of crushing poverty and troubles in sunnier ways. Win's stories leaned to history and science, sparking my interest in the natural world.

My brother Ron, always on the go, didn't hang around for anyone's stories. Both my parents had their noses in books whenever possible. Without TV, we gathered most evenings in the living room to read, or in Ron's case, to build models.

Perilous Passage, and *Desperate Search* and *Morgan's Mountain,* were our unseen companions. It never seemed odd to speak of the characters as real people; in fact many of them originally had real-life inspiration in people that Bill Mayse knew. He never made a reporter friend's mistake, though, of giving characters the names of people working in his newsroom. One day, the city editor exploded in a rage when he discovered his name adorning an unsavoury short story villain, who as my dad told it, looked like an angry monkey with a bald head and red hair-tufts in his ears. The fiction-writing reporter had forgotten to find new names for his story characters.

My dad told me about the pilots, fishermen, sea-men, prospectors, miners, and farmers that inhabited his books while they were still on the drawing board. Sometimes he asked my mother or me what a character might do or think at some turn of the story, but he didn't incorporate all our suggestions. My mother and I gave him a sounding board but not necessarily an answer. As often as not I had my own questions. When I was old enough to struggle through *Perilous Passage,* I asked what happened afterward to Clint and Devvy. As always, my dad thought before he spoke. He said they got married, had kids, and fixed up their island stump farm, and sometimes Clint worked on the fishboats. And then what? I demanded, disappointed at the lack of further skullduggery and peril. From then on my dad would answer this question, "What do you think?" and leave me to spin out my own adventures for the characters he'd fanned to life.

Having grown up largely in a world of early pre-industrial technology, my dad was a medieval thinker with a Renaissance love of learning and language. His upbringing was intensely Christian with a minister father and visits from famous tent evangelists including Gypsy Smith, who taught him how to tickle a trout. Still he would put out a dish of milk on our back step for the little folk that he said followed our families from Ireland and Wales; if a stray cat or a raccoon drank the milk instead, that was the way of the world. One of his cousins had seen the banshee weeping beside an Ottawa Valley road. He passed on his sense of the many layers of human habitation and experience on the West Coast and anywhere else he travelled. He liked Europe, but he couldn't stay long in the great cathedrals because of all the silent voices.

Bill Mayse was a good if quiet companion to other men, from hunters and fishers to the Catholic bishop next door; the two of them would stroll along the road or beach, hands clasped behind backs, one in black broadcloth and the other in a waterproof tin hat and coat. He gave his second-best leather jacket to Leung Foon, who lovingly improved our garden, and when he knew he was dying, Leung Foon gave his garden tools to my father. I used his hoe yesterday.

My dad wrote every weekday morning, hilled his fine spuds in the afternoons and did business on Saturdays. In the fall we nestled our seed potatoes into straw from our neighbour's orchard in our root cellar, and in the spring we cut them up to plant. Will Mayse had been a great vegetable gardener, like his own father, eking out a mine-worker's wages by planting his tatties in the dank plots behind narrow houses in Sheffield or Leeds.

Living at Arbutus Cove, my brother and I graduated from one school to another. My dad sold movie rights to *Desperate Search*, and we all drove into Victoria to see the premiere. Our garage held a maroon Studebaker, then a green Studebaker and finally a sporty black Studebaker coupe with a red interior, one after the other. It was a struggle to make ends meet sometimes, but we had a roof over our heads, a good clam beach, a boat for salmon fishing and a big vegetable garden. Every year we went camping up-island at Bennett's Point north of the Oyster River. Our black Labrador Paddy frisked around our wildlands and beach, then grew grey-muzzled, then died. Another Lab puppy and a deranged black cat called Cleopatra arrived. Life would always stay about the same. Then it changed.

Television steadily encroached on the glossy magazines that published short fiction, Bill Mayse's mainstay, and his markets dwindled one by one. Always willing to adapt, he recast a short story about a boxer as a half-hour TV drama and sold it. But every year there were fewer magazines on the market, and my dad sold fewer stories. My mother mended her clothes. My toes curled under as I outgrew my one pair of shoes. My brother started doing odd jobs for neighbours. We bought our year's heating oil later and later each fall. Finally my dad went back to the newspaper work he'd abandoned twenty years earlier, and a new-old byline appeared in the *Victoria Times*. Arthur Mayse wrote features, then the BC Legislature column, then a general interest column. For ten years he was often too tired to write fiction.

In 1965, I learned to drive the last Studebaker, and one day I was driving my dad into Victoria when we got a flat tire. Dad got out to fetch the spare and the tire iron, but he lingered at the rear of the car so long that I went to check. I found him bent over the trunk, white-faced.

"Don't tell your mother," he ordered. "I had a little pain in my chest. I'm hunky-dory now."

We changed the tire and drove on. I didn't tell, but I should have. His pains and indigestion got worse and more frequent after I left home to make my own way. A newspaper job had been great fun for a young fellow in the 1930s, but for an older man in the 1960s it meant long hours of pure stress. The *Victoria Times* job was killing my dad.

In 1972, Bill and Win Mayse did what they'd done before; they walked away from their beautiful house on Arbutus Cove without a backward glance. My dad was sixty, five years short of a pension that he forfeited. Neither of them had a penny. The sale of their house raised just enough to buy a tiny former floathouse up-island on a beach north of Oyster River that had once belonged to Cougar Smith. To pay the taxes, my dad sold weekly newspaper columns to the *Victoria Times*, which waswere reprinted in the Campbell River *Upper Islander* and a few other papers. This brought in a pittance. When my parents reached their mid-sixties, they talked about not applying for Canada pensions—after all, they could make their own way—until I pointed out they'd paid for their pensions throughout their working lives. They lived on about nine hundred dollars a month, which wasn't much even in the 1980s. A vegetable garden, a clam beach and steady supplies of salmon and cutthroat trout kept them going. They volunteered at the Campbell River museum, learned some Kwak'wala and joined outdoors groups, having been lifelong environmentalists before the word found common use. In their seventies they lay down in front of a bulldozer brought in to raze trees in Strathcona Park on northern Vancouver Island. For twenty years they were unreasonably happy.

Meanwhile, in the long shadow of Expo '67, Marshall McLuhan, multiculturalism and Pierre Berton's engaging books on Canadian history, the unthinkable happened: a new generation of publishing and television production appeared that was proudly, exuberantly Canadian.

Bill Mayse experimented again with television writing and sold a script to a new drama with a West Coast setting, *The Beachcombers*. Later, Win Mayse joined him as a script adviser. She'd always given him ideas and feedback, but now it was a paying job, her first since she lost her switchboard job at BC Tel by marrying. No one seems to have an exact count of the *Beachcombers* scripts Bill and Win Mayse created—at least twenty, probably more. *The Beachcombers* was nominally a comedy, but my parents used its humour to explore their serious concerns: the injustices faced by BC's Indigenous peoples, the threatened BC environment, adoption, women's issues, and perhaps most remarkably in a time when few people openly discussed it, the wrongful treatment of Japanese Canadians during World War II.

My dad's writing life came full circle when he sold his young adult novel *Handliner's Island* in 1989 to Howard and Mary White at Harbour Publishing, a BC company dedicated to West Coast stories in fact and fiction. Finally, he was happy to be a Canadian writer selling Canadian stories to a Canadian publisher. In 1992, Harbour accepted his last book, *My Father My Friend*, a memoir about Bill Mayse's fishing life with his father Will Mayse. The day my dad died in the Campbell River hospital, he was happy about his new contract. My mother died two weeks later.

On my dad's death, a few writers noted that he'd been a clear, powerful voice of an earlier British Columbia. My husband, Stephen Hume, wrote much the same in his obituary, which ran in the same issue of the *Upper Islander* as Arthur Mayse's last newspaper column. People commented that he was a writer's writer, a beautiful stylist who wrote otherwise untold stories of the West Coast. I rediscovered how seamlessly he wrote as I made minor revisions to his prose while editing *My Father My Friend*. For years I heard from his old friends and the many people he'd quietly given a hand up in writing or in getting through rough patches of life. Win and Bill Mayse are remembered with respect and affection by islanders.

So why is Arthur Mayse now an unknown name farther afield? One reason is that Bill Mayse never sought the limelight and didn't like it when it happened to fall on him; he didn't apply for awards, fellowships or grants, since he didn't need them. He avoided interviews. The concept of platform for a fiction writer—experience and background that lend credibility to one's writing—would have scandalized him. He had no interest in boosting his income by writing, as he saw it, overstuffed epics or magazine puffery. On his own terms he wrote honest stories. He was proud of his work, but he felt it spoke for itself. He was a working writer who paid his own way.

Another answer is simple snobbery, I believe, not only other people's but his own. Bill Mayse did what other people couldn't do, selling scores of short stories and five books, mastering new media and crowning his lifetime writing career with success. He never diminished anyone else's efforts, but he knew his own achievement.

After the University of Victoria opened in 1965, he met members of the English and writing departments. A few sought him out and asked for his comments on their work. He gave straight answers, often suggesting they beef up plot and character to make their story serve its purpose instead of striking a pose.

Some dismissed him as a regional writer, and worse when that was still unfashionable, a genre writer. My dad was amused that men and women who'd published one or two stories in small journals would look down on his success. He could quote Chaucer and Thomas Wyatt and Chidiock Tichbourne with the best; his prose sang and struck home. For his part he regarded his critics with polite scorn. Literature was changing in ways that he didn't appreciate, including admirable and ambitious ways, and it put other writers in the limelight that he'd avoided so long. In an era of television that conferred fame and glamour, that mattered to readers.

Perhaps most importantly, his career was ending just as the internet came into existence, so his work went unrecorded in ways that readers could easily access.

In his last years he thought of selling his papers to the Special Collections Library at UBC; other Canadian writers were receiving tens of thousands of dollars or more for their archives. But the academic who assessed his work valued his papers at eight hundred dollars. In his pride and disdain, instead he gave away his lifetime's records. UBC didn't want everything. I have a few of his papers now, and nowhere to take them but the landfill.

Bill Mayse chose to be a quiet and courteous man who fitted easily into an Indigenous big house, a CBC producers' meeting or the Lieutenant Governor's levee. Kindly as he was, on the rare occasions when he showed anger in a cold stare, people would take a step back. His natural courtliness led some to think he was born to privilege; he used to say our family had *oblige sans noblesse* and we would do well to remember it. My dad didn't court anyone or strive to impress. Time after time I watched young visitors find their way to him and ask questions or ask for a story. Dogs followed him happily. He didn't love cats, especially after one time our ferocious Cleopatra clawed his sunburned feet, but cats always found him and made themselves at home. He patiently accepted the honour until he could get free.

In *Perilous Passage*, his first book after many published short stories, his gift of observation and his ear for language were keen. His writing grew smoother and more subtle over his later books and stories, but his first book carried a sense of freshness and excitement in his world.

One summer evening when I was a kid, as the swallows looped and twittered outside, I sat side by side with my dad on the tweed chesterfield in our Arbutus Cove house to leaf through *Fifty Centuries of Art*. Dad wanted to show me something important from the section on Greek pots, but he couldn't find the right image, so instead he told me.

Inside one handle of some amphorae and water jugs, you might see a small human figure leaning, arms often crossed, to watch the world around him. A writer is that figure, my dad said, not taking much part in the activity of the day but quietly observing everything. And that is what we do.

THE VOICE BROUGHT HIM UP from some darker pit than sleep. By degrees he became conscious of a dull, unfocused ache and a weariness that turned even his bones fluid. He was in a boat and its gentle rocking was utterly familiar; but where it lay and how he came to be in it were questions his mind refused to answer.

He forced himself to think about that, and for a moment he almost had it. Then the half-memory of fighting and fire and blood wavered out of reach like a stone sinking, and he was glad to let it go. The thing that had happened was not to be remembered—it would tear him apart if he ever remembered. But the fear stayed, forcing itself from his throat in a wordless cry.

"Don't try to talk," the voice said. "Lie still. You're all right now."

A girl, cut off at the waist by the edge of the bunk on which he sprawled, was bending over him. Her golden face was too sullen for prettiness. She had gray-green eyes with lights in them like the sun wheels in deep water.

"Lie still," she repeated, and went away, leaving him alone with the ache and the tiredness, and the fear that was part of both.

After a timeless interval he saw her feet in scuffed sandals on the companionway and her long brown legs as she came down to the cabin. The girl wore faded blue jeans, copper-riveted at the pockets and rolled above her knees. Her hands, he saw as she bent to him again, were small, and the nails were cut short. They were not soft, smooth hands as a girl's should be, but roughened, with calluses at the roots of each finger. But they were cool on his hot face, and the wet cloth they plastered on his forehead eased the ache.

He would have been content to rest like that, not moving or thinking or trying to remember, but other feet were on the companionway now. Man's feet, dirty and broad across the toes, with frayed corduroy pant legs above them. They angered him, appearing like that so stealthily; he wanted to let the girl know, but could only lift his chin, trying to warn her with his eyes.

That was enough. She stooped, and when she straightened and turned away from him, he heard a click that was sharp as a spoken "No!"

She said, "If you come down here, Joe, I'll shoot you."

"You'd do it, too."

The new voice above was a grin in words. It was familiar just as this boat was familiar, and it worked like acid upon the dimmed negative of his memory.

Boats heaving fender to fender in a long, slow swell. Faceless men, the tearing sound of a knife in flesh, and this voice above him where he lay afraid.

Stung now by the knowledge of danger, desperate to escape, he caught recklessly at the misted impression.

There had been three of them, he and two others, in a boat. This boat. Then the faceless men had come aboard, and there had been fighting and a thing worse than fighting. Something so much worse that, knowing it, his life could never again be quite the same.

Only he didn't know. The negative had blurred out. At the companion head, the heavy, lazy voice went on:

"I don't want your damn' old hulk, Devvy." Then, amiably, "Say, you look nice with your shirt off. You're gettin' to be a real big girl."

"Never mind how I look," she said. "You get off this boat."

"Sure, Devvy. You'd better too. She's near sunk." The

feet shifted. He wasn't coming down. Farther away now, the grinning voice said, "I'll catch you without that gun sometime, Sweetheart."

It was part of the fear too, this heavy padding of feet above his head. The boat lurched as someone dropped overside. He heard a spaced plashing, and the diminishing creak of rowlocks.

Not turning, the girl said, "He may come back. You'd better get up if you can."

The weight of his legs was enormous, as if they were sheathed in lead. He worked them off the bunk and half slid, half tumbled to the floor. His head began to pound again at the shock, and the girl steadied him with her free hand. He gave her a crooked, vaguely shamefaced smile.

"I'm okay. Just kind of woozy. Cracked my head on something, it feels like."

"Maybe," the girl said. "Or maybe someone tried to beat your brains out."

Her gun, he saw, was a short-barreled .22 with a scarred and flimsy stock. Once in some other life he'd owned a rifle like that. They gave them to you for peddling perfume door to door. He'd kept it a week, then the old man found it before he even got to shoot with it, and broke the stock over his knee, and licked him.

"I'll go up first," the girl told him. She moved with a hunter's wariness toward the steps. "I'm pretty sure Joe's gone, but he's tricky. You'd better stay here till I call you."

He waited, steadying himself with a hand against the bunk. The face that peered back at him out of the foot-square, cracked mirror on the bulkhead was also familiar; and he thought wryly, It should be. It's mine, I've lived with it all my life. Rough brown hair badly in need of cutting. Blue eyes screwed to a squint by sun glare on salt water. Flat cheeks with a small scar under the left cheekbone, and a wide, tough mouth. He wore a tan workshirt that looked like Army surplus, dirty khaki dungarees, and a Texas belt with a fancy buckle. He studied his face again, wondering what name went with it, but because of the fear, not trying too hard.

There was a brown smear under the mirror against the white bulkhead paint. It could be a handprint, he thought, palm and fingers in dried blood. His own, like as not—the top of the sleeping bag in the bunk was stiff with blood. That would be from his nose. It was swollen and he touched it gingerly, hoping it wasn't broken.

After what seemed a long time, the girl's voice came down to him:

"All clear."

He climbed into dazzling sunlight and a west wind that struck cool against his face. Astern of the gas boat he saw the white and blue of a narrow bay between sidehills of fir and red-limbed madrona, with bald limestone outcroppings above. Half a mile—perhaps a mile along the south shore, a dock stuck into the bay. Behind it a sawmill burner lifted its rusty, bullet-shaped dome. There were no other docks, and the only boat out was a green flatbottom which squattered through the chop in the direction of the mill. The man in it rowed longshore fashion, facing forward; he was only a toy figure at this distance.

"That the guy you were talking to?" he asked.

The girl nodded; she continued to watch the skiff until it disappeared behind a rocky point.

A growl so low that one sensed rather than heard it troubled the air. Tidewater boiling through a narrows. He was still among the islands, then, somewhere north of Seattle on the Inside Passage to Alaska.

The boat lay snug in the gut of a creek that twisted back through saltgrass flats like a crippled silver snake. She was an offshore troller something between forty-five and fifty feet long, with slender spring poles upright on either side of her mast, and bull poles of peeled fir that projected rakishly beyond her bows. He knew every inch of her. Just yesterday he had run a new steel-wire salmon line onto the second of her portside power gurdies, the gurdy that sometimes kicked out of gear when you set it turning against a heavy chinook. Under her flank rode a white dinghy with an outboard cocked on the stern. The girl's, he guessed.

"What happened to you?" she asked him.

He said, half-apologetically, "I don't know. We were heading in off the Swiftsure Bank and someone boarded us. There was a fight. I guess I got slapped around."

"I can see that. What were you carrying?"

"Fish. What else would we have?" He didn't like the way she stared at him. The rifle rested carelessly across her forearm; but the muzzle pointed directly at his stomach, and the blue-steel hammer was at full cock.

"There's a lot of things go down these passes," the girl said. "You're sure it was salmon?"

"I'm not sure about anything. Right now I couldn't even tell you who I am."

"I can tell you that," she said. "You're Clint Farrell." *Clint Farrell* ... and he knew who he was then, and everything about himself. Up to a point. Beyond that point a vagueness set in like Pacific fog, and somewhere in the fog was the business that his brain refused to touch, skirting it and shying away from it so violently that his stomach churned and his palms went clammy damp.

"If you know that much, maybe you can tell me what I ran into last night."

"You could have tangled with a government boat. Or you could have been hijacked."

"So you figure I'm a smuggler, eh?"

"I don't know what to figure." The girl lowered the rifle hammer. She frowned at him, standing on the hatch

27

cover with feet braced apart. She looked to be sixteen or seventeen. Her fair hair was short and raggedly cut as if she'd done the job herself, and her tan was deep and even. The salt-bleached jeans had seen hard wear; a blue bandanna was knotted casually across her small breasts.

Thinking was still an effort. He asked her, "How'd you know my name?"

"You told me two weeks ago when you were in here with your partner. Portland's your home town but you fish out of Vancouver—in case you don't remember that either."

She didn't have to be sarcastic about it. He remembered Portland well enough. The narrow downtown streets and the big gray river, and the Swan Island yards where the old man had welded tankers for Kaiser once, and come home on paydays with six brands of liquor helling around inside him. He was Clint Farrell, and he wondered if the Oregon cops were still looking for him.

He asked, "Where'd you pick me up?"

"Halfway to Martinez Island," she said. "You were drifting into Boss-Foreman Narrows. I couldn't hear your engine and the boat was low in the water. So I ran over and towed you clear."

"They're pretty skookum, those narrows, aren't they?"

She said gravely, "You'd never have come out of them." Still watching him, the frown between her eyes, she said, "Somebody tried to sink you. The plug's been knocked out of your garboard strake and there's a tarp jammed in the hole. What happened out there? Where's your partner? Did he get off in the tender?"

"I don't know," he said. "Don't ask me. Something's wrong in my head. All I'm sure of is I'm in a jam."

She nodded. "I guess you are. By the look of the boat, someone got killed on her." Suddenly her voice lost its steadiness. "I don't like this. I'm scared. Can't you

28

remember how the blood got here? I don't think you've killed anyone, but you *have* to remember."

He'd washed down the cockpit after the last fishing. They'd always washed down. But the hatch cover was filthy now, fouled in irregular, gummy patches with the same dreadful stain that he'd seen beneath the doghouse mirror. It would take a lot more than a bang on the nose to account for a mess like that.

He said, "Don't. For Christ's sake, don't ask me!" The fear flooded back, sapping the starch from his knees, pushing him to the deck. He sat with head knuckled between his fists.

"You'll get it straight later," she said. "You've had a bad time, Clint." She was speaking to him much more gently than before. "When you do remember, we'll call in the police."

"We?" He lifted his head. "This isn't your grief. Stay out of it. I've got to keep clear of cops."

He was crying, the tears were running down his nose and he couldn't stop them. Out of the shame of that knowledge he flung at her viciously, "Get to hell off and leave me alone. I'd as soon be down those narrows as have you pester me. Go put your shirt on—if you've got one."

She had a temper; it flared instantly, darkening her cheeks and bunching her square little hands into fists. "All right! I'm through pestering. You can explain to the police how you left here with a partner and came back without one. Maybe you can tell them what a Canadian troller is doing on the American side. Try telling *them* you don't remember!"

She whirled and scrambled over the side. Dismay grew in him as he heard her clattering in the dinghy— she was the nearest approach to a friend he'd got; he needn't have popped off at her like that when she'd saved his life and been worried about him.

29

He called to her, "Hey!" watching her wind the starting cord around the outboard's flywheel. What was her name anyhow? "Hey, Devvy." She didn't look up, and the motor coughed in answer to her pull. It hiccuped twice, then died.

"I'm sorry," he said. He couldn't remember when he'd last told anyone that. She wound and tugged again, and got only a string of belches from the outboard.

Clint jumped down to the dinghy. "Let me try," he said. "Maybe you've flooded her." She clung to the cord and he said, coaxing her, "I didn't mean that, Devvy. About your shirt and all. You look swell."

"You sound like Joe Peddar," she told him waspishly. "I should have let him come down. He'd have liked to meet you again." But she glanced up, shaking her short blonde mane back, and he saw that she was grinning. "Are you quite sure I'm decent?"

His ears tingled. In awkward silence he rewound the cord, gripped the wooden toggle, and yanked. The motor coughed and caught, and Devvy reached past him to grab the tiller.

"We'll tow her on up to my landing," she shouted in his ear above the motor's racket. "Tide's high enough now." There was something about her triangular face with its high cheekbones, something familiar in the way she'd torched up at him. But whatever it was, it lay over the edge of memory, close to the place in the fog where the sick, sweating fear lurked for him.

SHE CRAMPED THE DINGHY IN ON THE troller's portside and Clint swung back on board. Stepping carefully over the blood patches, he went forward. He dropped the bowline, and Devvy caught it and hitched it expertly around the middle thwart. The ancient outboard fidgeted as the line came taut, then buckled to its work with a tinny popping, and the troller gathered way. She towed heavily from the weight of water in her, but the tide, running fast into the creek now, helped shove her along. Clint stood on the bows with a pike pole. He didn't have to use it, though—Devvy seemed to know the involved channel to a hair. Bullheads and flounders scudded across the sand of the bottom, routed by the troller's sharp advancing shadow. Devvy never looked around. Almost, he wished the boat would hang up so she'd need his help; but the keel touched only once, scraping gently over a bar.

A hundred yards farther up, the channel kinked sharp to the left. They inched ahead against a stiffening current; and the flats were behind, and they rode now in a basin with gravel bottom and low rock walls. Open timber screened it, scrub fir for the most part, with here and there a twisted madrona flaunting its tropic red and buff and metallic green.

Devvy cut the motor. With the last of her way, the troller ghosted alongside a jerry-built landing. Clint dropped to the splintery planking and made fast.

"What do we do now?" he asked.

"I don't know." She secured her dinghy, and they stood together on the landing, the quiet strange in their ears. Presently Devvy reached to the hip pocket of her jeans and brought out fine cut in a red-and-white package. She rolled a cigarette as a man would, with a neat economy of tobacco.

"Smoke?" she asked, and Clint took the makings from her gratefully. His stomach was hollow with hunger, but right now he wanted tobacco more than food.

They sat on the end of the landing, their legs aswing over the green water. Devvy's face, animated for a while there, had settled into its guarded sullenness again.

"This is a swell place . . ." he started to say, but she cut him off with a frown and an impatient lift of her chin.

"It used to be," she said. "Don't talk, Clint. I'm trying to think what to do with you."

"Okay," he said. Then, under his breath, "Boss."

She heard him, and turned her head. The look she gave him was serious and faintly puzzled. "If you haven't done anything wrong, why must you keep clear of the police?" He looked down into the water, wanting to tell her, but with the habit of caution holding him back. She was a girl, and girls were queer. You couldn't tell how she might take a business like that. It occurred to him then that he had very little to lose. He dropped his cigarette butt into the tide pool, and half turned to face her.

"I did do something, a couple of years ago. My old man swung on me once too often. This night he swung with a beer bottle in his fist. I'd fought twice in the Golden Gloves and sneaked two-three pro fights under a phony name. I let him have it. He cracked his head on the stove, going down. They took him to hospital and tossed me into reform school, and the old man made good and sure they kept me there."

"Your mother let him?" Devvy was looking down too, worrying a splinter with her finger.

"She ran out on him when I was sixteen. I don't blame her."

"My father wasn't like that."

Clint shrugged. He didn't like to go back to those days. Now that he'd started he wanted to get the telling over with. "The day I went in, I told them I'd jump the fence first chance I got. But I had to wait eighteen months for it. I worked in Spokane a spell, then in Seattle, but I kept running into kids I'd known. So I lit out for Canada." That part he remembered very well. He had lammed out of Seattle on a bus. Maybe Washington cops wouldn't worry too much about a kid on the loose from another state, but he wasn't taking any more chances.

He'd felt that if they hauled him back now it would kill him. He was through with guards and fences, and doors that didn't open from the inside.

He got off the bus at a town called Blaine, a place that sat almost on the border. Canada was less than a mile north. A colored boy in the Spokane woodyard had been across plenty of times; had told him you could get a job up there without any finagling about Social Security cards. Maybe he could just stroll across the border, give the immigration cops a phony name and get away with it. But they might ask for identification, and if they did he was straight out of luck.

He loafed down the main street. Got himself a cup of coffee and a hamburger—he still had money from his last fight in Seattle, but for what he was going to do, he wouldn't want the burden of a heavy meal in his belly. The night was as dark now as it was likely to get. He left the main drag and angled down to the waterfront, not hurrying, whistling as he strolled. It was quiet here, and the sea was flat calm. Even if the tide was against him, it shouldn't be too hard.

He didn't know what he might run into in the way of patrols; that chance he'd have to take. He crossed the railway tracks and slid down a brushy bank to the beach. There in the shadows he stripped, and stuffed shirt and shoes inside his pants. He secured the top of his pants with his belt, knotted the legs into a loop for his neck. Then, bundle on his back, feet flinching from the broken clamshells and sharp-edged, dry seaweed of tideline, he walked down and in. He wasn't afraid of water; he couldn't remember how or when he'd learned to swim; he always felt good in deep water, confident and free, as an otter must feel, or a seal in a tideway.

Chest-deep, he turned on his side and swam straight out. There wasn't much tide, and what there was drifted him north, the way he wanted to go. When

33

he was sure he was beyond danger of being spotted from shore, he settled into an easy overarm. He was between the points of a wide bay. When he turned his head he could see a distant huddle of lights, and other lights in a long, straight string, running out from shore. A dock and a town on the Canadian side. It was hard to judge distance here in the water, but he guessed it shouldn't be more than two miles.

He stroked on, a kind of peace stealing into him, almost a dreaminess. No worries out here. Two miles or five, it didn't matter. He could swim as long as he had to in the deep, kind water.

When the end lights of the pier pulled level, he was only pleasantly tired. He stroked another quarter mile, on past the town, then turned in for shore. The shallows ran far out, but he paddled till his legs were scraping sand. Then, not hurrying, not splashing, he waded to a gently curving beach very much like the one he'd gone in from on the American side.

He could see the glow of a beach fire farther along the curve. Kids at a wiener roast, maybe; and just for a moment he was distressed and lonely. They were having a good time down there; he could hear radio music and voices singing. Fellows and their girls. It was two years since he'd had any of that; he felt suddenly as though he'd always been on the run, hadn't ever been a kid, and the peace of the deep water faded out of him, leaving him worried again, and grim, and obscurely angry.

He wrung his clothes out and put them on, then plunged into the brush and scurried across the railway tracks. There was a highway on the other side. He tramped north till dawn, and by that time he was pretty well dried out. Not long after sunrise, a cross-border transport slowed for him.

The trucker was a big brown guy with a friendly face. He said, "Early for walking, Mac. Hop in."

Clint swung up to the cab. After a while the driver brought out cigarettes. They were some Canadian brand, straight cut and stronger than American, but it was good to the point of luxury to have a smoke again.

He stuck with the transport to Vancouver. They had cops in Vancouver, not Mounties as he'd expected, but ordinary city cops in blue uniforms. So he was cautious that first day, and extra polite when he asked directions.

A city this size, there'd be fighters and managers. In a one-ring gym he found a dry, thin Scotchman by the name of Killick. He was watching without favor while a couple of ham-and-eggers pushed each other around.

The Scotchman wore racetrack tweeds, but he used words as if they cost him a buck a throw. He nodded at the colored boy in the ring and said, "Can ye take him?" Clint watched critically for a minute, then said, "Sure." Killick went with him to the locker room downstairs. Not taking any chances, Clint thought. The shoes were too big for him and God alone knew when the sleazy red trunks had last been washed.

He carried the brown boy for a couple of minutes, then opened him up and pulled the trigger on his left. Not hard, but hard enough. The boy peered at him from the canvas, mildly surprised. He slipped his mouthpiece and mumbled, "Mistah Killick, I bin hit!"

Killick studied Clint with a shade more interest on his boiled red face. He grunted, and said, "Ye'll do. I'll slip ye into a Friday night card. What name?"

"Ryan. Bill Ryan." He'd used that one in the wood-yard.

"Where from?"

"Toronto," Clint told him promptly. His Canadian geography was vague, so he'd keep it safe. "My old man has a farm out of town a ways."

"North or south?"

"South."

35

"South of Toronto," Killick told him dryly, "is a large body o' water called Lake Ontario. God hates a liar, but it's His concairn, not mine. Fifty to win, twenty-five if ye lose, and ye'll split seventy-five for a draw. Ye'll be a wee bit shaded in weight."

Shaded wasn't exactly the word. The boy that Killick put him in with Friday night was stacked like a truck and had anyway fifteen pounds on him. His name was Bernie something-or-other. He had no class, but his crouch made him hard to get at, and he had a worryingly long reach.

Clint put him down twice. Midway through the fourth round he stopped a hard one on the mouth. He got mad then—his temper had been growing progressively more brittle these last months—and went in slugging. Bernie was willing and the customers loved it, but a matter of seconds before the bell, Bernie gaffed him with a solid roundhouse that came out of nowhere. His head bounced hard on the canvas, and he stayed down.

Funny. His memory had kind of blanked out that time too, because the next thing he recalled was waking in a skidroad room with twenty-five bucks, his share of the fight money, safe in his pocket. He'd gone down toward the waterfront feeling rested and good, and he'd met someone there . . . *met someone* . . .

Devvy said sharply, "Why don't you go on? What's the matter?"

"Nothing," he mumbled. But he'd been close to something for a minute. "Let me roll another, will you?"

She handed him her tobacco. His fingers were uncertain, and Devvy reached out and took the paper away, and made him a cigarette.

"You'd better not try too hard," she told him. "How about Joe Peddar? Do you remember running into Joe before? You were scared when he started to come down."

"It was the way he talked. His voice. I'd heard it somewhere."

"Where, Clint?"

"Don't know. Who is that guy anyway?"

"Our local wolf," Devvy said. "He was my hired man for a while last spring. I fired him."

"You?" Clint turned his head to give her a skeptical stare. "You aren't old enough to fire people."

"I run my own farm," she said matter-of-factly. "Somebody had to after Dad died. Joe Peddar didn't think I was old enough either."

"Why'd you fire him?" Clint asked idly. It was good to loaf here in June sunlight filtered by the madrona leaves, their dry music in his ears. He was very tired. Time to think and worry later, when his head stopped aching.

"He caught me in the hayloft," Devvy said. She added with a certain dour relish, "I bit him. Then I fired him. He's working at The Retreat now for Doctor Morse."

"What's that?" Clint asked. "The Retreat?"

"The sawmill," Devvy told him. "It shut down years ago. Doctor Morse is fixing the headquarters building and the staff bungalows over for a missionaries' rest home. He used to be a missionary himself." She swung her legs, looking down at the water.

Clint was still thinking about that hayloft. He'd never run into a girl like her; he tried to imagine how she'd stack up in a dress and high-heeled shoes, with her hair done right in a beauty parlor. But the picture wouldn't take shape. When she'd grinned at him there in the dinghy, her whole face had lightened. Right then, she'd been pretty enough for anybody, with her fair hair flung back and the golden flecks dancing in her eyes.

"I don't blame that Peddar guy," he said experimentally. Devvy drew on her cigarette. She said calmly, "Since then, I carry a rifle. I don't like wolves, local or otherwise. So don't start that again."

He could only guess what she meant, and what, if

anything, she wanted of him. Her face told him no more than a mask would. She said, "You can stay on my farm till you … till your head gets better. Or you can leave. It's up to you, Clint."

"Which do you want me to do?"

She looked away from him, across the basin, her mouth stubborn. "Maybe it would be better if you didn't stay."

"I asked what you wanted," he said, stubborn too, wary and tough and puzzled.

"That's up to you," she repeated. She bent her head, and for a moment there was a disturbing, half-remembered sweetness to her, a childishness about the nape of her neck and in the way her short hair curved past her ears. "Maybe when you see the farm you won't want to stay. You're a city boy. You'd get lonely."

"Hell with cities," he said vehemently. "I've had enough of cities. But any cop sees me, he's liable to take me in. I'm trouble. You don't want me around, Devvy."

"That's short for Devise," she said. "Devise Callahan. It's a stupid name, but Dad liked it."

"Well?"

"I want you around." She looked him full in the eyes, and she was smiling again. "We'll fight a lot, and you'll probably get ideas about haylofts too. But I'd sooner you stayed, Clint."

He felt an absurd triumph. "Okay, if you put it that way." Grudgingly he added, "Thanks."

"Always afraid of an angle, aren't you?" Devvy got up, stretching so that her ribs showed white through the coffee tan of her sides. On her left forearm was a diamond-shaped scar. She must have had a bad break there, a compound fracture. "You can help Paddy Burke finish the haying. I won't be able to pay you except maybe a dollar or two till August, though. I get Dad's insurance check then."

"Forget it," he said. "You don't have to pay me. I won't be staying long. All I want is a place to hide out for a spell till I know the score."

"You'll get paid." She said it almost fiercely. "I don't take anything for nothing. Now, we'll go on up."

Clint asked her doubtfully, "What about the boat? I ought to hose her off. Anyone sees her all bloodied up like that . . ."

"Joe Peddar's already seen her," Devvy said. "No one else is likely to come around here. She stays like that till later."

"Till you bring the cops in, you mean?"

She nodded. "Yes. If there's anything in her you need, you'd better get it."

"I haven't anything. It's all Aleko's."

"Aleko?" She had started off the landing, but she halted now, and looked at him over her shoulder. "Who's Aleko? Was he your partner?"

Clint stared back at her blankly. Aleko. Aleko Johannsen. The name had come to him out of nowhere.

"Damn. That's funny. I guess he was."

Devvy said, "You do have something. When you came ashore at Martinez Cove you had brown slacks and a white sport shirt and a leather jacket. Go get them."

He didn't want to set foot on the troller again, but he boarded her and ducked down to the cabin. Devvy was right. The clothes were in a locker under the portside swing-out bunk, the bunk where he'd lain on the bloodied sleeping bag. They were new, folded and stowed away carefully. Besides slacks and shirt and jacket he found brown oxfords and a patterned tie.

There should be a white handkerchief—the little old man in the skidroad outfitter's had given him one for luck. He lifted the jacket pocket flap, and the handkerchief was there. He straightened; and smoothly and with no effort

39

of recollection, Aleko Johannsen returned from the place on whose edge memory flinched and cowered back.

Clint stood very still. Sunlight patterned the cabin, but he felt no warmth from it, and the impulse was strong upon him to turn and escape. This boat was the *Maiija*. This was Aleko's troller, his cabin; and if there were ghosts, Aleko's would be here. Hell, if he closed his eyes and opened them again slowly, the big Finlander would be hunched on the bunk, shiny brown skull and drooping mustaches, concertina gripped upon his knees.

Devvy's impatient call cut through to him. "Hurry! I haven't all day."

He crammed his shoregoing clothes into a dunnage bag and mounted to the landing. There was no *Maiija* in neat black letters on the troller's bow. Name, number and home port had been painted out.

"You ran into something down there," Devvy said. "Something else came back. You'd better tell me."

"No." He didn't like to lie to her, but he had to be careful, careful! "I just had a time finding my shoes."

"No, you didn't. You were standing still. Tell me, Clint."

She'd pry it out of him sooner or later. "All right, then. This Aleko Johannsen. He owned the boat. Her name's the *Maiija*, means Margaret in Finnish."

"I know what it means," Devvy said. "You met him in Vancouver?"

"Yes. The day after the fight. Right after I'd bought these clothes. I drifted into a beer parlor and he was alone at a little table off to one side. The joint was crowded so I took the chair across from him. Next thing I knew, one of those big Scotch cops they have up there was pointing at a sign on the wall and asking how old I was. He wouldn't believe me when I said twenty-two."

"I wouldn't have either," Devvy said.

"Well, he asked my name, and I couldn't think of the phony I'd used the night before. We got into an argument, kind of, and he was going to take me in. Only this old fisherman across the table, he spoke up for me. He said he was Captain Aleko Johannsen, and that I was his fishing partner. The cop bawled him out for bringing a minor into a beer parlor, but he let me go."

"Did Captain Johannsen offer you a job, or did you ask him?"

"I hit him up for it. He wasn't fussy at first, but when he knew I was in wrong with the law, he said he'd give me a break. We sailed that same night."

"After salmon."

"Yes. After salmon. You don't have to keep asking me."

The frown deepened between her oddly flecked eyes. "Look. You weren't carrying fish, and you didn't meet a government boat. I think you were running some kind of hot cargo over the border or in from the high seas. Whatever it was, someone wanted it enough to kill your partner and try to kill you." Her voice was careful, a little too casual. "It wouldn't be the first time that's been done around here."

He said grudgingly, "You could be right."

"If I'm not, there's only one thing else, Clint. I'd sooner not believe that."

"You mean I could have knocked Aleko off?"

"Yes."

"And wrecked the troller? Does that make sense?"

"There's half a case of aquavit in the wheelhouse, and three empties. If you'd drunk enough of that stuff, anything could make sense."

"Yeah. But you don't know I drank any. I hate that Swenska whisky."

"It was on your breath this morning," she said gloomily. "But we're not getting anywhere. What else do you remember?"

41

"Nothing. Why are you so interested, Devvy, any-how?"

"I want to help you, if I can."

"Why?"

"Because you were good to me at Martinez." She turned away from him, and started off the landing, toward the narrow, grassed-over lane that climbed through the timber. "But if you don't remember that, there's no use talking about it."

He could feel the sweat gathering in his palms again as he followed her up to the lane. The fear was like a beast waiting to spring on his back; but he knew now that he had to remember all of it. For his freedom and perhaps his life, he had to remember.

Half a mile of ups and downs, then the lane angled toward the creek between brown rock bluffs and thinning woods. Ahead, a sapling gate sagged across the twin ruts. Rusty baling wire held it together; it was weathered the silver gray of a hornets' nest. Clint judged his distance, ran in, and scraped over the top rail in a western roll. He should have cleared easily—he'd lost his dizziness and most of his headache, but his legs must be weaker than he'd thought.

On the far side he waited for Devvy. She lifted the bar from its brackets, edged through and dropped the bar back into place, something almost prim in the way she did it.

"Grow up!" she told him. But her eyes said she'd like to cut loose and jump a gate that way too.

The gate opened into a narrow hayfield hugging a curve of the creek. The hay was tawny in the hot June sun; a man worked in it alone, singing, up near the far end where stumps poked through a pink froth of fireweed. He saw them and straightened, waiting for them with the scythe gripped in both hands across his thighs. He was short and very wide. His head was tipped forward, giving him an air of truculence; black hair stuck through holes in his beat-up felt hat like the eartufts of a horned owl, and his rocky face was scorched red.

He said, staring hard at Clint, "Would you look what our cat's dragged in ... Devvy, where did you find the like of that?"

Devvy said, "He was drifting into the pass. He'd been beaten up."

"So one can discern. He was in a boat, then?"

"An offshore troller."

The little man was staring hard at Clint. "Wrecks and strays and castaways," he muttered. Then, abruptly. "You. What's your name?"

"None of your business," Clint told him; but the wide-shouldered little man puzzled him. He looked limber and tough as a chunk of sea kelp, and he had a scarecrow jauntiness. Humor lines were grooved at the corners of mouth and bright black eyes.

"His name's Clint Farrell," Devvy said.

"You let people call you Clint?"

"Sure. Anything wrong with that?"

"Plenty, plenty! Begob, the Clint throws it all out. Clinton Farrell, now, there's a good round lucky name."

"This is Paddy Burke," Devvy said. "He's a numerologist. He can tell about people from their names—he says."

"Do you doubt it?" the broad little man challenged her. "I've revealed yourself to you, and it has worked out to a hair. Or will you be telling me it hasn't?"

"You told Joe Peddar his name would hang him. That didn't need numerology," Devvy said. "I thought you weren't to sing that song any more."

Paddy Burke grounded his scythe. His black eyes twinkled at Clint. "For the sake of her ears I sing it in French," he said. "It is a marching song of the Bat d'Af. It has to do with women."

"If you sang less," Devvy told him, "you'd get more work done. Remember, Paddy, I want this field cleared by Saturday."

She nodded at Clint. "He's going to help you. I've hired him."

Clint could feel the shrewd black eyes sifting him, shaking him down. "You've inquired into his antecedents, I take it, Devvy? You've learned how he comes to be adrift in an offshore troller with blood on his shirt?"

"He can't remember," Devvy said. "All he knows for sure is that he went fishing out of Canada with someone called Johannsen."

"So." The hard, bright gaze swung back to Clint's face. "Johannsen, is it? He would be a Finn, Devvy, a compatriot of yours on the distaff side."

"He could be," Devvy said. Then to Clint, "Come on. He'd talk all day if I'd let him." But she hesitated, and when she spoke her voice was careful. "Is Aila home?"

Paddy spat. "She is not. She's hitchhiked into town with the parson, the darling. Aila will have a word to say about this one."

"She'll be in no state to say anything about anything." Devvy shrugged one brown shoulder. "Anyway, I don't care what she says."

"'The witch from over the water,'" Paddy said. "'The fay from over the foam.'" He told Clint, "The reference is to Mary O' Scots. She had the Widow Callahan's long slanty eyes, I've been informed."

"Shut up," Devvy said sharply. "Get on with your work." She said to Clint, "I've fired him twice but he won't go away."

"Why don't you bite him?" Clint suggested. He'd found that he liked making her look fierce like that.

Paddy chuckled, and drew a hone from under his harness-strap belt. "Well, I'll instruct the young gaboon in the art of haying, Devvy, if it's your wish. But you'd

44

best fatten him first, I'm thinking."

They left him whetting his scythe, singing again.

"What's he mean, the Bat d'Af?" Clint asked.

"Some kind of prisoners' battalion in the French Foreign Legion," Devvy said. "He was probably in it. He's been just about everywhere, one time or another." She didn't speak again till they had gone out of the hayfield by an upper gate and were jogging on through the narrow valley. Then she asked, "What do you make of him?"

"He's all right, I guess." Clint nipped a grass stem from its sheath and chewed on it. "But he's no labor stiff."

"What makes you think that?"

"Way he talks. Way he looked at me. What is he, a broken-down bottle fighter or something?"

"He's a good hand with a bottle," Devvy said. "He told me he knew my father overseas. That's my house, up ahead."

"Big place," Clint said. He glanced back over his shoulder on the way they had come. The hayfield was empty.

THE FARMHOUSE HAD STARTED AS CAPE COD, then climbed a story and gone mildly Colonial. The cupolas over the front porch, the octagonal bay windows and the round-butted shingles that overlapped like a bird's breast feathers beneath them, added a touch of Victorian. Its cedar siding was weathered to match the gates and snake fences of the farm, and it had a look of belonging here, comfortably at home behind its unmowed lawn, at ease with its tall hollyhocks, its rhododendrons and its overgrown flagged walk. On either side of the house, huge madronas lifted their glossy green helmets higher than the roof.

"Dad built it," Devvy said. "He kept getting new ideas as he went along." She spoke defensively, and the glance she gave Clint was half a frown, as if she expected, and was ready to challenge, any criticism he might make.

Clint said nothing. If she wanted to pack a chip on her shoulder, let her. She was a queer girl. He didn't know yet for sure if he liked her, but she woke a subtle excitement in him. Her sunstreaked hair had brushed his chin once, coming through the last gate. Irritatingly, he wished that would happen again.

"I don't think you'd have got on with him," Devvy said. "He wasn't like you at all. He'd spend a day making a box kite for me when I was little, or inventing a life preserver that nearly drowned him. He liked stumps with huckleberry bushes growing on them, so we wasted a day planting huckleberry bushes on stumps in the pasture. He should have been butchering pigs that day."

"Is Aila your mother?" Clint asked her.

"No!" There was scorn in the sharp denial. "He brought her back from England after the war. Her and her children."

He followed Devvy around to the back, past borders of half-wild wallflower and California poppy. Behind the house was a truck garden, weeded and hoed, its peas and cabbages and potatoes set in orderly rows.

"I put that in," Devvy told him, and he could tell she was proud of it.

There was no back porch, just a stone stoop and a door that opened directly into a large, low-ceilinged kitchen. It was cool inside, and dusky after the strong sunlight; the floor was of smoothly laid flags such as Clint remembered seeing once in an old book from the reform school library.

"Another of Dad's ideas," Devvy said. "It's cold in winter."

But the stove was American enough, a big old-fashioned range sitting on splayed lions' feet with a woodbox beside it. The box was almost empty and the top of the range was spattered with egg yolk. Its scrolled and curlicued nickel-work was dull for lack of buffing.

Devvy clicked her tongue. "Aila," she said, as if that explained everything. She stuffed the firebox with cedar kindling, opened the drafts, then went to the cupboards by the sink, reaching high to tug at warped firwood doors.

"Sit down," she ordered Clint over her shoulder. "I'll fix you something to eat. Then you'd better sleep."

He sat with elbows planted on the worn oilcloth of the kitchen table while Devvy put on bacon and eggs, and pumped water into a dishpan. The sink was piled high with dirty dishes. Aila, he gathered, didn't shine as a housewife. He should give Devvy a hand, he thought; but the laziness in him held him there, and anyway, she didn't look as if she wanted help.

With hair like that, she could be a Scandihoovian of some sort. She was supple-slim as a dancer. Dress her in girl clothes and her legs would be worth a whistle in any league.

"Look," he said. "You say I was in here before. You could tell me about that."

"I didn't say you were here." She'd filled two plates. She brought them to the table and set one in front of him. "You were at Martinez Cove across the channel. And if you don't remember, I'm not going to remind you."

The glance that went with the words was frosty. She went back to the stove and lifted off a graniteware percolator. Her sandals made a light clicking on the flags; apart from that slight sound, the house was very quiet. But still in a friendly sort of way, Clint thought. People had been happy in it ... you could learn a lot about a room or a house just from the feel of it.

He was ravenous, and ate greedily. Devvy, her own lunch half finished, poured him another cup of coffee and handed him her package of fine cut. It bothered him, not having his own tobacco, but she did it casually, as a man might.

She was left-handed. He saw the diamond scar again, white against the sun-darkened skin of her forearm. That one must have hurt.

"How'd you bust it?"

At once she turned her hand palm up, hiding the scar. She told him curtly, "Jamming it into other people's business."

"Okay, I just wondered."

He rolled his cigarette. She was watching him—he could tell even without looking up. But she didn't speak again till he had finished his coffee.

"You don't have to work this afternoon," she said then. "I'll fix a room for you. You can lie down on my bed for now."

He followed her up the spiral stairs with their worn carpeting. The rooms above were laid out on either side of a straight hall that traversed the house from north to south, giving it vaguely the look of a barracks. One door was ajar; he saw blankets and sheets tumbled in a pile on the bed, underwear and a green silk housecoat on the floor, a dresser with a silver-backed toilet set, and a clutter of perfume bottles and make-up gear.

Aila's room, he knew, even without Devvy's quick frown to tell him so. Her own room was larger, and bare to the point of being severe. Dresser, chiffonier and bedstead were of heavy golden wood, furniture that must have cost somebody a pile a long time ago. There was a bottle of cologne on the bare dresser top, the kind the kids used to lift from the five-and-ten for their girls, a pair of military hairbrushes and a comb and nail file beside them. Nothing else, except the big bed with a red point blanket folded across its foot and one pillow plumped at the head.

"I wasn't sure she'd have it made," Devvy told him. "She must have decided it was time for another snoop."

"Sounds like my old man. He was all the time spying on me."

"She goes through my things. But she's clumsy about it, and I always know."

"You don't get along, eh?"

"Get along?" Her laugh was short and mirthless. "She hates me, but she's scared of me. That's the only reason she does any work around here."

"Funny," Clint said. He turned to her, leaning his shoulders against the wall. Outside she'd seemed almost as tall as he, but looking down, close to her like this, into her triangular face with its firm mouth and strangely flecked eyes, he realized she was a good deal smaller than he'd thought. And older. Eighteen, anyway. That would make her a year younger than himself.

"What's funny?" she asked him.

"This. I knew what your room would be like."

She gave him a hard look, at once suspicious and ready to be tough with him. "What do you mean?"

"Well ..." He could feel a tingle of heat in his ears and on the back of his neck. Damn her anyway, it wasn't a thing you could explain or lay out all orderly, like a row of cabbages in the garden she was so proud of. "Like you. Hell, I don't know. Not flossy like hers, I guess." He plunged on doggedly, while she watched him with her considering gray-green eyes. "But you'd know it was a girl's room just the same."

"Thanks," she said dryly. "Paddy told me that too. Only he put it a lot better."

"All right," Clint snapped. "I didn't mean anything." It was strange how just with a word she could make him torch up. "If you think I'm on the make, forget it. I don't even like you."

He saw her temper wake, flushing her high cheek-

49

bones. "Good," she said. "I'm glad to hear it!" She turned on her heel; her sandals clicked down the hall and rustled on the stairs. The back door banged and the house was altogether quiet except for a yellow jacket droning drowsily in a window corner.

Clint flattened the pillow with vicious punches. Say something nice to her and she practically told you where to go. And it wasn't fair, throwing something at him that she might just have made up for all he could tell. Martinez Cove meant nothing to him but a squiggle on a chart. He couldn't dope her at all. One thing, though: she was right when she'd said they'd fight.

But he couldn't stay mad. He was too sleepy, and everything about the room soothed him—the stirring of the crisp white curtains in the breeze, the buzzing of the prisoned yellow jacket and even the room's clean emptiness that still kept something of Devvy in it. He buried his face in the pillow, and almost immediately he was asleep.

Once somebody, a small boy, he saw in a fuzzy half-wakening, came to the door and stood watching him for a while, then went away again like a shadow. Once he heard a stirring belowstairs and a hearty voice that he knew was Paddy Burke's got through to him. He heard the kitchen pump creaking vigorously, and the rattle of dishes, and once Devvy laughed. But he couldn't rouse, and when Devvy came in quietly to stand over him, her voice barely reached him.

"Want supper?" she asked, and he muttered "No," without turning his head on the pillow.

There were other voices downstairs, much later, when the room was dim and the curtains stirred in the night breeze with a ghostly flicker. Devvy's and a woman's. Their words were lost, but the woman's was loud with a shrill anger, and once a scraping cut across it as if someone had shoved a chair back.

That woke him; and this time he stayed awake. He'd been dreaming, but it was like no dream that had ever come to him before. Devvy had been in it, but not quite as she'd bent over him today. She'd been wearing a white, short-sleeved shirt open at her throat, and she'd had her hair tied in a blue bandanna. And it had been night, not morning, and a different place. On a landing somewhere ...

It wasn't a dream.

He'd remembered—another part of it, anyway. It had come back to him, not violently, but easily and quietly in his sleep.

But it was confused still, like a tangled skein of fishline, hard to figure where in the snarl lay the end and the beginning. Somewhere in it was disappointment and anger, and a curious grief. Sure, he'd run into her before, her and the man she called Joe Peddar.

Don't rush it . . . think it through. If he only had a smoke it would help. He considered getting up and going downstairs, bumming the makings from her or maybe from the blue-jawed little Irishman whose voice he'd heard below. But better not take that chance. The memory was there, some of it, perhaps all of it. He daren't jar it. Stay here in the cool and the quiet, work it out ...

Aleko again. Aleko in the *Maiija's* cabin, setting his concertina off his patched knees and looking across with humor in his pale protruding eyes. They'd been far out, north and west of the Swiftsure's cauldron, with the smooth, slow swell from Asia lifting the troller's hull. The spring poles were triced inboard to the mast, and the little bronze bells at their tips tinkled drowsily in the late evening.

"Tomorrow," Aleko had said, "I think we take a run inshore. Washing every day like you do, Clint, we use too damned much fresh water, and now our tank iss almost dry."

He'd gone into one of his long silences. Then, as the *Maiija* rose again with her lovely, easy lift, "We will put in at a Yankee port because that iss closer. For fresh water, by sea law, they let us put in anywhere."

Aleko was wearing a white cotton cap with green visor, tipped back on his bald brown skull. He fed a rare of snoose under his lip, tongued it into place and said, "A few more trips and I think maybe I sell the *Maiija*. Get for myself a seiner, something big, seventy-eighty tons. Then I will be a real captain, an important man on this coast."

Clint glanced up from patching the latest rip in his shirt. "Sign me on?" he asked casually, half-kidding.

"No." Another lengthy silence, long enough for him to rethread his needle and sew a puckered inch. "I think maybe I set you up on your own. Sell you my *Maiija* cheap. You would like that?"

"Sure," Clint said. The troller with her gear would be worth twenty thousand anyway; the old boy was ribbing him, and ribbing was something new for Aleko. It was as if one of the smooth-skulled hair seals that followed them when fish were around should up and crack a joke. The old man was in a good mood today, as if he'd finally resolved whatever had been weighing his mind.

Next morning Aleko set a course southeast, and in the late dusk they were among islands again, chunking down a calm sound toward a Pleiades cluster of lights on the horizon.

"That the port?" Clint asked.

Aleko nodded, one hand on the wheel, and shot snoose juice through the wheelhouse window. He said, "Martinez Cove."

The troller plugged against an ebb that swept down strongly from the north. A humming crept into the evening air, a drone which was distinct from the pulse of the heavy Diesel below, and the faint vibration of the hull.

Clint, lounging beside the binnacle, turned his head to Aleko. "What's that noise?"

"A narrows. Boss-Foreman Pass."

"Do we run her?"

Aleko said, "We stay out where it iss healthy. Most narrows you can run safe with a goot boat at slack water. But that one, no. In Prohibition days, even with eight-hundred horsepower and a government boat chasing, we did not run the Boss-Foreman."

Clint looked at him curiously. "What were you then, Aleko? Rumrunner?"

"Ya." Aleko's chuckle rumbled in his chest. "That game you would have liked, such a wild boy as you. But a man grows old, and I am damned glad now to be yust a fisherman. I got from rumrunning my stake to build the *Maiija*, I ever tell you?"

The lights were close now; they opened the cove, and across flat water that lay dull in the afterglow, Clint saw a dock with a cannery behind it on the sidehilly shore. He left Aleko at the wheel and ducked out to the cockpit. Waiting there, line in his fists, he watched the lane of open water narrow between hull and dock. The *Maiija* was a lot bigger than any of the clutter of inside trollers and workboats tied at the string of floats below the dock. Clint felt proud of her, possessively so; and he wished the old man hadn't been just kidding him about taking her over.

It was always a kick, coming in like this from the offshore. There'd be a company store, and he could hear dance music from somewhere up past the cannery buildings. Saturday night. People had a lot of fun away from the cities, down here among the islands. They'd come from all over hell's half acre to a Saturday night dance.

Aleko sidled the troller in to the end float. A kid in a white shirt stood there in the early dark. It was the same at every landing, there was always a boy or two hanging around. Clint whistled and tossed the sternline.

He saw, too late, that the kid was a girl. "Watch it!" he called, but late again; her head was turned shoreward, she didn't see the line coming and it whacked her on her bare legs under her knees. She went back a pace but didn't cry out, just stooped for the line and hauled the loop over a bollard.

Clint threw a hitch around the mooring bitt and scrambled forward to drop to the float with the bowline. "Say," he told her, "I didn't mean to land it on you. Hurt?"

Cannery girl, he guessed. Her hair was tied in a blue kerchief and she wore blue denims with a boy's belt around a slim waist.

She said, "Forget it." But there was a wet shine on her cheeks.

"You're crying."

"No I'm not." She turned away from him abruptly. "Mind your own business."

Aleko poked his head out of the wheelhouse window. Clint said, hardly knowing why except that she was a girl and the first he'd spoken to for a long time, "Don't go away."

She heard him, all right, but she walked on down the float string.

From above, Aleko said, "So soon?"

Clint grinned in the dark. "Need me around?"

"No. I will take the dinghy and go to call on a friend," Aleko said. "Then we fill our tanks and head out. Please to keep yourself out of trouble here, Clint."

"Sure." The girl was already climbing the gangway to the dock. He followed her and caught up with her at the top. She kept on toward the lighted buildings above, and he walked beside her, cramping his step to hers.

He asked her, "What's the matter? Boy friend stand you up or something?"

"Let me alone, will you?" By her voice, he knew she was still crying.

"Okay. You don't have to get tough about it. Only you'd better blow your nose." He fished out his handkerchief, hoping it was reasonably clean, and she took it. She said, "Sorry. I'm all right now."

In the dark it was hard to tell if she was pretty or plain. But he liked her low voice, and it was good just to be with a girl again. He said, "I guess you'll be going to the dance," and she turned her head and gave him a quick frown.

"Like this? When I go dancing I dress for it."

"Heading home, then?"

"It's no concern of yours, but I'm going for a walk."

"Can I tag along?"

She said crossly, "I can't very well stop you."

A dirt road led up from the dock, past the cannery offices and the brightly lit company store. The dancehall was west of the cannery somewhere—the music sounded better than it probably was, filtering through the soft summer night like this.

She'd stopped crying. He said, "You work here?" and she answered, "No."

That much conversation carried them another quarter mile anyway, to the top of the hill and around a bend in the road.

Suddenly, startlingly, she laughed. Her laugh was low too; it surprised him into an abrupt "What?"

She said, "Half an hour ago the last thing I thought was that I'd be walking with a boy I'd never seen before. You can talk to me if you want."

"All right. Why were you crying back there?"

"Feeling sorry for myself."

"That doesn't help. It just makes things worse—I know."

She didn't answer, and he said, "Why? What happened to make you feel that way?"

"Nothing. It's just that I haven't been to a dance for I

don't know how long. Hearing the music did something to me. I should have gone home. I came over from Cultus Island for groceries and hung around. The longer I stayed the worse I felt."

He could understand how it was with her—he'd felt that way often enough, these last two years.

"There's nothing wrong with how you're dressed," he said. "Not for a hole like this. Let me take you."

She said, "I wouldn't care about my clothes. But there's someone at the dance, a boy I'd sooner not meet. We'll just walk."

He reached for her hand and she let him take it. After a while he asked her, "Feel more like Saturday night?"

"Yes."

"Me too. You're not the only one gets lonely. You get that way, fishing. Take that thing off your hair, will you?"

"Why?"

"Something I want to see."

She reached up and tugged the kerchief loose, and gave her head a shake. Her voice was questioning. "Well?"

"You should have black hair," he said. "I'd doped out a Saturday night girl for myself. She had shiny black hair in one of those shoulder bobs. Except for that, she looked sort of like Rita Hayworth and was just about as good a dancer."

She laughed again. "I'm sorry," she said. "I'm a streaky blonde and I don't dance very well. Tell me more about your girl."

He told her. There was a sympathy of loneliness between them; telling her was almost like thinking out loud. She let him talk, not interrupting. He told her his name and where he came from, and he'd have spilled more except for the wariness that had become second nature. It was a long, long time since he'd shot off his face like this to anyone, least of all to a girl.

The lights were away below them. The girl said, "We'd better turn back, Clint."

"Do you have to? How about a cigarette first?"

There was an orchard on the seaward side of the road—he could see spaced avenues of trees, still with a scattering of blossom. They waded through long grass to the orchard fence, and Clint put his hands around her hips and swung her to the top rail. He climbed up beside her and they perched there, smoking in silence. He could see her dimly; she'd pushed her fair hair back; she was watching him, frowning a little.

She was going to speak; he guessed it would be something about heading for home. He bent and kissed her on the mouth. She hadn't been expecting that; he felt her surprise, and for an instant thought she'd pull away from him. But she didn't, and he kissed her again, knowing now that she wanted it too.

"We'll go back," she said, and he slid off the fence and reached up for her. She was inside the circle of his arms, and he held her there, searching her lifted face.

She read the question in him. She said, "No. Don't spoil something nice, Clint," not trying to free herself, just standing quietly, in the long grass, inside his arms.

He said, "Even if you haven't got black hair . . ." and took his arms away. She stepped past him, walking out to the road, and he could see she was smiling.

"I'm glad you came," she said. "I like you, troller-man." He took her hand again, swinging it lightly as they walked. He should be disappointed, but he was happy in a cockeyed sort of way. "I'll put in again sometime," he said. "Next time I'll take you dancing."

"You won't be back," she said. "I wouldn't want you to come back. I'll go down to your boat and you can kiss me good-by, and that's the end of it." She looked up at him, walking the road beside him. "I guess we were both pretty lonely. I'll remember you, Clint."

They went on down toward the cannery. The band was giving out with square-dance music now. At the store steps Clint halted. He said, "Saturday nights you buy your girl a present. Come on in."

"No!"

"Wait here, then," he told her, and went inside.

It was like every other cannery store. Work clothes and fishing gear. Bulky Siwash sweaters in piles, bright kerchiefs and shawls for the Indian trade. In a showcase of cheap jewelry he saw something maybe she'd like, a totem pole of dull beaten silver on a thin silver chain.

She was waiting at the foot of the steps, and he grinned at her and slapped his pocket.

"What is it?" she asked. "Can I guess?"

"No. You get it at the boat."

Aleko was still away. The troller rocked gently in the last of the ebb, her fenders squeaking against the edge of the float. He wondered, glancingly, what she'd say if he asked her aboard; but he shoved the idea aside. In a way he couldn't explain to himself, she'd become the girl he'd thought about in the long, clear days on the offshore banks, loafing on the *Maiija's* hatch cover, watching the gulls, hearing always the sleepy tinkle of the little bells on the spring-pole tips.

She was right: no use spoiling it. He took the flat box from his jacket pocket and stepped close to her. She stood quietly while he put the thin chain around her neck and fumbled with its tiny stiff clasp. Her neck was warm under his fingers; he was clumsy about it, and her hands came up to help him. He dropped the totem inside her shirt.

Her laugh was soft, with a note in it that called to some happiness newborn in him since he'd kissed her up there by the orchard.

"I still don't know what it is," she said. "I won't look till I get home."

She gave him a quick, light kiss. "I hope you find your girl with the shoulder bob," she said, and turned, and walked swiftly across the float. He heard the rattle of a mooring ring and saw her step down into a dinghy which rode dim white against the black-oil glint of the cove water.

Outboard rig; the motor popped and he called, "So long!" and she waved to him once as the dinghy curved out toward the mouth of the cove.

He watched her go, a little sad now, fishing for cigarettes.

Red and green running lights were moving in from the channel. Clint squinted through the dark, trying to make out the hull under them. Not much beam to her, and she sat low to the water. But she was long, longer than the *Maiija*.

A plank creaked behind him. He turned, and knew it was trouble even before the big guy swung at him.

The punch glanced off his cheekbone, weight enough behind it to break his neck if it had landed square. He blocked a left automatically, and drifted back.

She'd said something about a boy she'd sooner not meet …

Keep out of jams, Aleko had warned him, but this kind of trouble you couldn't duck. The man moved after him like a cat, but he came wide open. Clint slipped another looping right over his shoulder, stepped in and shot a short stiff left. It connected with a satisfying jar, and he kept after the man, tipping his head back with a two-handed flurry of short jabs, flummoxing him off balance.

With the float's edge a yard away, he uncorked his left from the hip. The big guy hit the water on his back. He bobbed up, sputtering and blowing.

The inbound boat was close now, almost alongside the float. Speedboat or express cruiser, he couldn't be sure. But she had the *Maiija's* tender astern, and Aleko was bawling at him from her cockpit. He waited, watching while the man who'd jumped him shook his hair out of his eyes and swam with a clumsy dog paddle for the float.

If he was coming back for more after that last belt, he was really tough.

Aleko hit the float in a heavy jump. He was snorting mad—but time for Aleko later. The big guy had hauled out and was catfooting toward him again, and this time his right hand was clenched rigid in front of his hip. Something in that fist. He'd pulled a knife.

Aleko plowed between them, facing Clint, shoving his arms down.

"Got damn, I told you no trouble. Get out of here. Perikelte! Get to hell on board!"

Voices above them now too, on the dock. Cannery people—if a battle started in the middle of a desert, somebody'd turn up to watch it. He told Aleko savagely, "The bastard jumped me. Let me finish this."

Aleko hung onto his arms, and the big guy was trying to circle him. Clint got mad then, really mad, and gave Aleko the point of his shoulder, jolting him violently in the chest. "I'll murder you," he snapped. "Lay off!"

From the night, from the shadowy cruiser, a disembodied voice said quietly, "Joe, leave it."

The big blond guy stopped in his tracks. Something clicked in his hand. He turned like a well-trained dog, and padded down the float, and swung aboard the cruiser. From her foredeck he said, thick-voiced, "I'll see you again, punk."

Clint stepped over the troller's side and went down to the cabin. Aleko had been mad enough to pop a valve, but he was too sore himself to care. So she'd had a boy friend after all. He wished now that he hadn't bought her the silver totem, hadn't taken her word for it in the long grass at the orchard's edge. She'd made a monkey of him—what you could expect when you got soft, stopped playing it tough. That wouldn't happen again.

Aleko called him topside when he was halfway through his second cigarette. The cruiser was gone and their tender rode astern. He couldn't tell whether the old man was over his mad, so he said nothing while they filled their tanks with water from a cannery hose.

An hour later, when they were heading down the channel, he went to where Aleko stood by the wheel. "I make coffee?" he asked, knowing the Finn was always a sucker for a mug-up.

Aleko sighed, and looked at him with a shake of his bald head. "You get mad like that, Clint, I tell you some day you kill a man. But that iss over. Now we forget it, eh?"

"Fine with me," Clint said. But when he came back from the galley stove with the crockery mugs and the coffee pot, Aleko was still frowning into the night.

"Something go haywire?" Clint asked him.

"Ya. Kind of. Maybe we don't pay for the seiner this season after all. You turn in now, boy."

At daybreak, when Aleko rolled him out for his trick at the wheel, they were far along the sound, close to the open water. Fog hung like a curtain out there, and the troller was chugging into it . . .

The stuff was blinding him, clogging his throat so that he couldn't breathe. He pawed at it, fighting it.

He must have gone to sleep. He wanted to wake, but his body was sheathed in lead again, and he couldn't make it obey him. Inside him somewhere, a little fear was building as a fire grows from a flicker of crossed twigs. He was asleep and he was not asleep, because this was too dark and deep for sleep.

He was going down in the deep water, wavering down, sinking out of sight, and someone was screaming there under the water, screaming and screaming and screaming . . . He was under the water, but the fire was there too, and his head and his eyes were full of it . . .

HANDS REACHED FOR HIM AND HE snatched at them, they were drawing him up, and the heat and the smothering weight of water was lifting from him.

He woke and knew it had been himself screaming, and that he was safe now in the cool, hay-scented dark.

But the hands were real. They were firm on his shoulders, rough little hands that held him hard, all the world's comfort in them.

"It's all right," she was saying, close over him so that he could feel the stir of her breath against his face. "Clint, it's all right. You're safe. It's over."

His hands were wet but his throat was parched. "Sorry," he croaked. "Had a bad dream."

"Tell me," she said. Her voice was low, but there was controlled eagerness in it, and something else, something that might have been fear. "It wasn't a dream, Clint. You were back there again. Where you were last night. Tell me what happened."

"I can't. It's gone, Devvy. I can't remember." He'd never remember, not with his conscious mind—only asleep, in the dark where the fear could creep up on him, pounce on him, carry him burning down through the deep water. But he made himself try. It was like picking among the litter of a deserted house.

"There was another man on the *Maiija*," he said. "A Chinaman, at least I think he was Chinese. He had a green ring on his thumb."

"In Canada?" Devvy's low voice prodded him. "Was that in Vancouver, Clint?"

"No. On the high seas, away to hell out from Vancouver Island. It was night, and the fog was so thick you couldn't see the stem from the wheelhouse. Aleko kept me ringing our fog bell. Around midnight a ship's horn answered. Aleko took over; I think he gave them some kind of signal. After a while a boat came in. The Chinaman was in the stern sheets and two men were rowing. They had four gas cans on the bottom stretchers. They'd been opened, then soldered shut. The Chinaman handed them up to Aleko. He had to work hard to lift them. Then he came aboard and they went into the doghouse."

"What about the ship's boat?"

"It was gone when I turned to look. I didn't see the name on it, if it had a name. The Chinaman and Aleko acted as if they'd met before. He was a thin guy with a lump like a big mole behind his right ear. He had a green ring like I said. Next morning I asked Aleko what the deal was. He said I didn't have to know, that he hadn't taken me on to ask questions. He told me if I talked when I hit shore we'd both go to the pen or worse, but if I kept my mouth shut I'd have my own troller soon, just like he'd promised me. He'd said that about the troller before, but until then I thought he was kidding."

"Was that last night, Clint?"

"No. It couldn't have been. The *Maiija*'d never have worked down this far by morning."

"What about last night? Try hard, Clint. You're close to it."

But there was nothing more. Only the fear, small again now, far back and deep down.

"I guess I woke everyone up," he said.

"No. The children are asleep. They'd sleep through almost anything. Paddy stays in the barn. Aila came home drunk—she's probably passed out by now."

She took her hands away, and he sat up.

"Cigarette," Devvy said. "Tailor-made. Aila brought some home from town."

A match spat and spurted yellow light. He saw her by it, holding two cigarettes between the fingers of her left hand. She was wearing white pajamas open at the throat; they hung loose on her slim body and she should have looked sexless in them. But her eyes were luminous in the match glow, and her hair, light and soft around her shadowy face, was lovely.

He said, "Devvy," hardly knowing what he wanted of her. She'd be tough with him now, curt and short-spoken; she'd go away, and in the morning they'd fight again. Only that wasn't how he wanted it. Not now, not tonight, with the fear waiting.

"Here," she said. He saw the dull glow of the cigarette, and fumbled it out of her hand. She didn't go away, but stood by the bed, white and dim, with the open window and the flickering curtains behind her. He heard her breath go out in a soft sigh. "I don't know what I'm going to do with you," she said.

She sat on the edge of the bed. "I'd help you if I could, Clint."

It was as if she read the need in him, for she put her arms around him now, drawing him sideways and back until his head rested between her breasts. "Don't talk," she told him. "If you said anything it would be the wrong thing." Her voice, close over him, was low and dreaming. He could feel her even breathing, and the softness and warmth of her, where he had looked to find neither.

If he moved, shifted his face, it would be over. He lay still, watching her cigarette wane and glow above him.

"I'm glad you said that about my room," she told him. "People don't say things like that to me except Paddy, and I never can tell if he means them."

Her voice went on, close and quiet in the dim room. "I don't know what you are or what trouble you're in. I think it's bad, Clint. There was killing in it. But I'm not lonely now, and it's strange not to be. It's the first time I haven't been since Dad was drowned."

"I never had anyone to be lonely for," Clint said. "Not that I needed anyone."

"You can be tough tomorrow," Devvy said. "If you stay here you'll have to be. Not now, though."

He said, "Did you look at your present before you got home that night, Devvy?"

She was quiet for a moment, so tense and still that he thought he'd made her angry. Then she said, "So you remembered that too. I wish you hadn't. Clint, I meant what I told you that night. I didn't want you to come back, not ever."

"Did you look?"

"Yes. You don't know much about girls. Of course I looked."

"I wasn't sure you'd like it."

"I have it on now. Can't you feel it?"

He moved his face, and the totem's thin silver chain was under his cheek.

"I was sore at you," he said. "I figured, after, you'd just been handing me a line. Did you know your boy friend bushwhacked me when you left? He must have been tagging us."

"I heard there was a fight … Clint, don't call him that. I haven't any boy friend."

Maybe this was being in love. Only you don't fall for a girl with sunstreaks in her hair and with calluses on her hands, not a girl who carries a pack of fine cut in her hip pocket man-fashion, and who runs an island stump ranch as a man would run it.

He didn't know; and nothing learned from any girl he'd had to do with before could help him. They hadn't any of them been like Devvy. He didn't know, and his thoughts were running wild. All he was sure of was that he wanted to stay like this, her heart under his cheek,

65

her thin, warm arms around him. He had needed her and she had come to him, reaching down for him through the dark water. The fear would return but it was far away now, and there was only this wonder, this delight.

Devvy put her cigarette out, butting it in an ash tray on the bedside table, and he thought it would end then. But she didn't move, and she was quiet for so long, and her breathing was so even, that she could have been asleep.

He said her name, "Devvy?" and her voice came to him.

"Yes?"

"Nothing. Wondered if you were awake."

"I was thinking."

"About what?"

"You. Me. What's right and what's wrong."

"This?"

"I don't know." She was quiet again. Then, with her breath warm on his forehead, "I've had boys kiss me. You kissed me at Martinez. Joe Peddar pawed me around before I bit him. But I've never felt like this about a boy before. I don't know whether I like it."

"I do, Devvy."

"I guess I do too. I'm not a good liar, Clint. I wanted you to come back. I lay awake wanting it, wishing I'd treated you differently that night. If I hadn't been able to tow you clear this morning I'd have gone down the Boss-Foreman with you. I'd stay with you tonight if you asked me. It wouldn't matter to anyone but you and me."

Her heart was beating harder under his cheek. He felt a dark stirring of excitement that thrilled through him like a shiver, and his arm tightened around her. It was an excitement with a sickness in it, for he knew he was going to ask her, and he knew, beyond that, as if he could project himself ahead in time, that he'd regret the asking as long as he lived. And there was triumph in it too, and again he knew it for a triumph that would be bitter forever inside him.

"Do you want me to stay?" Her voice was so low he could hardly distinguish the words.

He whispered, lips moving against her skin, "Yes," and he felt the same sick excitement in her, and the yielding of her body to his arms.

He heard, too, reluctantly and with a savage disappointment, a shuffling rustle in the hall, and the creak-creak of a floor board. Someone stood in the door-way, formless and half-seen. A woman—Aila, and he could have got up from the bed and strangled her.

"Not 'ere you don't, miss!" Her voice was a knife with a turned edge, but under its stridency was a whine. "Not in my 'ouse with me and my children. You slut. You little baggage. I've known all along—you traipsing off to the woods by your lone. But you'll not bring your fancy-man under my root, do you 'ear? I'll not 'ave such goings-on."

She was drunk, she had a skinful, she swayed in the doorway, housecoat clutched around her with one hand while her tongue shrilled on with the maddening per-sistence of an alarm clock. He felt Devvy's arms harden, heard her suck in one deep and shaken breath. She got up and glided like a swift shadow to the door, and her hand smacked against Aila's face. He could hear her sobbing, and her voice broken and gusty with rage.

"You tramp. Oh, you tramp! It's my house, not yours. It'll never be yours, never ..."

Her hand cracked against the woman's face again, and Aila laughed in a high, drunken giggle.

He had to do something to stop them. Grab Devvy, take her away, break her out of this hysterical ugliness. He swung his legs over the edge of the bed, and he was halfway across the floor when a flat and sullen thud from somewhere in the night outside halted and turned him.

He stared into the dark. East in the direction of the water, the sky over the timber was blood-red. Bush fire, he thought for an instant; but the glow was too concentrated for that, and there had been the dull boom of the explosion. He knew what it was then, and whirled for the doorway.

"The troller." He had Devvy by the shoulder, shaking her, his fingers digging in. "She's caught fire!"

Her face lifted to him, a pale triangle, and he shook her again, savagely. "You hear me? I've got to get down there."

"She couldn't be on fire." She sounded dazed, as if he'd wakened her too suddenly for immediate comprehension. But she turned and stared through the window.

It was as if a spell had broken. "Wait for me," she told him. "You aren't to go alone."

He'd forgotten about Aila. She had slid to the floor and was whimpering there, under their feet. She was still whimpering as he blundered down the stairs. In one of the rooms at the end of the hall a child had wakened and wailed now in a thin frightened keening.

The night was black as the hubs of hell. He fell twice, hard, before his feet found the ruts of the lane. Then Devvy was beside him, a flashlight in one hand, her rifle in the other.

"This way," she panted. "It's quicker."

She turned east off the lane into wild pasture. Ahead, the woods stood black and solid, treetops a ragged fringe against the sky. They came to a snake fence. Clint snagged his pants scrambling over, and heard the cloth tear as he yanked free. More haywire—everything about this goddam place was haywire. Devvy took the lead, running recklessly, the circle of light glancing from the packed earth of the trail and from the shadowy hemlocks that pressed in on it. They ran for what seemed a long time through the woods. Then, somewhere ahead, the creek spoke with a subdued voice. They were close to the salt-chuck now—Clint could smell the tide flats, and the ragged lane of sky above the hemlock tops was rosy from the fire. The landing couldn't be far ahead.

Devvy switched off her flash. He halted, blind in the sudden blackness but knowing she was close in front of him on the trail.

Her hand groped back for him, and he whispered, "You hear it too?"

"No. There's nothing."

"Wait. It sounded like someone whistling."

He heard it again, level with them and to the left. Somewhere, not so long ago, he'd heard that same catchy tune. Listening to it now, he felt the hair prickle on the back of his neck.

The whistling pinched out abruptly. Straining against the dark, waiting for it to resume, he felt Devvy's fingers cold on his bare forearm. There was the hiss and sizzle of burning wood and frying paint. But he could catch no other sound except their own breathing and the heavy thud of his heart.

Devvy took her hand away and started to edge forward. He whispered, "No," and when she still moved from him, he grabbed for her wrist. She tried to wrench free and he locked his fingers, hauling her back.

"Damn you!" It was a furious whisper. "Let me go!"

"Stay here," he told her. It wasn't reason that imposed caution on him; caution had become a habit, instant and instinctive, developed in half a year of ducking cops, sharpened by the fear that he'd brought with him to this lost bay.

Mouth against Devvy's ear, he ordered her, "Cut it out! You stay till I call you."

She still fought him, breathing hard. He ground the slight bones of her wrist, knowing he was hurting her, till she gasped and stood quiet.

"Now stay here!" he breathed, and eased past her, feeling his way.

The night thinned ahead of him. Once his hand brushed madrona bark, smooth and cold. He knew approximately where he was now—upstream from the landing, close to the head of the long basin where the creek met tidewater.

Earth gave place to rock under his feet. He dropped to hands and knees and crept the rest of the way, cursing under breath at the squeak of a dry leaf. Water glinted below him. He took off his shoes, then slid quiet as an otter down smooth, beveled rock into the basin.

Deep water … his feet found no bottom, and for an instant panic clutched him. He'd never been afraid in the water before; he fought the panic away, treading water, keeping only his face clear.

Down the basin, at the landing, the troller hull squatted dark and very low. She was almost burned out, spring poles and rigging and upperworks clean gone. The glow above her was fading to plum-purple now, but small flames still writhed orange and metal-blue on the surface around her, where fuel from her exploded tanks had splattered.

The fire must have started hours ago. Either that, or it had bitten into the troller with all the intensity that spilled oil could give it.

The fresh-water flow of the creek was like a hand at Clint's back, easing him gently down the pool. He trod water outside the half-circle of burning fuel, sheltered by darkness, peering toward the landing. Once a fish, salmon or startled trout, flicked its cold length across his ankle, and he gulped back a yelp.

A man was moving on the landing, working there,

lowering a bucket and swinging it up full, tossing water on the steaming planks. He looked enormous in the light of the dying fire, and his body shone in patches through his ragged shirt as if oiled.

Clint listened; the man wasn't whistling.

Big, Clint thought, mad clear through now, mad and mean. Too big for me to take.

He stared at the man, hating him, his caution vexed and needled by the dourness that had been deepening in him since Aila's drunken shrilling at the house. He wanted to go in there anyway, grab the big guy by an ankle if he stepped close enough, take a chance on dumping him into the basin and settling with him there.

He let his legs pull him under. When he was sure he could manage it without splashing, he arched his back and began to stroke. Fifty feet. Twenty strokes ought to do it.

His luck was riding. He came up under the *Maiija's* canoe stern and rested in the milk-warm water, hanging straight down, oaring only hard enough to hold his position in the lazy current.

Out of the treacherous place where the fear stayed, it came to him suddenly now that he'd lurked like this before, under the troller's shadow. Only then she'd been in open water, in fog that blanketed sight and sound. Panic jabbed him again for an instant; then the sensation, the half-memory, passed as fog passes.

He ducked under, took two strokes, and let his face break the surface a foot from the edge of the landing.

The man was reaching down, almost directly above him, to fill his bucket. He grunted as if all the breath had been driven from his lungs. He had yellow hair, close cut. Even with his face a mask of slack surprise, he was good-looking in a heavy-featured kind of way.

Green fire winked from the index finger of his left hand.

It was the same man, the big blond who'd jumped him on the Martinez float. Clint stared up at him and Joe Peddar stared down, his lips drawing flat against his teeth, his surprise tautening into terror. He tried to speak, but all he managed was a thick gobbling.

As if the sound of his own voice had released him from a paralysis of fear, he straightened and backed away. His bucket clattered on the planks, the landing gave off a hollow, diminishing rattle under his feet. Clint heard him go crashing into the timber like some big clumsy animal bucking through brush with terror at its tail.

The crashing faded out. So much for that one. But there was still the other somewhere in the dark, the whistling man. Clint waited, listening, hearing nothing but the soft dying noises of the *Maiija's* hulk. She'd be sinking soon—if old Aleko hadn't built her well, that fuel explosion would have blasted her wide open. It wouldn't do to get caught under her when she dived.

Clint put his hands on the edge of the landing and hauled himself up. A shadow detached itself from the dark timber and Devvy came down to him, rifle slanted across her forearm.

"What did you do to him?" she asked. "He went past me like a bat out of hell."

"Look," Clint said crankily, "I told you to stay back there."

"You don't tell me what to do," she said. "Nobody does." She laughed then, sudden and low. "He couldn't have been scareder if he'd seen a ghost. I've never seen Joe scared before. He'll run all the way to The Retreat."

Clint said, "Maybe that was it."

"What?"

"Maybe he thought he was seeing a ghost. I saw something too. You know that ring I told you about? Well, it was on his finger." Clint studied the troller's gutted hull

72

glumly. "If I'd had the gun I'd have shot him. He burned my boat."

"She wasn't your boat," Devvy told him, "and you don't know he burned it."

"He sure as hell did. I came up right under him. He stunk of oil." He shot her a frowning glance and said, "I notice he didn't want your landing to burn, though."

"Just what do you mean by that?"

"I'm not sure myself, yet. That mick hired man of yours was hanging around too. It was him I heard whistling in the woods."

"You're crazy! But even if Paddy Burke was around here, why would he want the troller to burn?"

She must have heard. He'd recognize that tune anywhere, the Bat d'Af marching song the broad little Irishman had been singing in the hayfield. He shook his wet hair back, feeling his skinned elbows and knees now, and the chill of the night against his chest.

"He cleared out of the hayfield pretty fast this afternoon. He wasn't anywhere in sight when I looked around. I figure he hightailed it down here as fast as he could travel."

"To start a fire?"

"To arrange for one, maybe. To talk to your friend Peddar."

Devvy had pulled on her blue denims and a Siwash sweater over her pajamas. There was a dangerous stillness about her as she fronted him.

"A lot of things could have happened. You were smoking when you went back on board. You could have dropped a live butt in some engine waste. Why don't you go ahead and say I had something to do with this, Clint?"

"I don't think you had. But I'm pretty sure your friends did."

She said, "You'd better get something straight. I've gone to dances with Joe Peddar. I even went steady with him for a while. But he's not my friend now. He never really has been. I'm afraid of him."

"Well I'm not," Clint said sullenly. "And I'm not through with him for this, either."

"No," Devvy said, something odd in her low voice. "We're not through with him. I wish we were."

The *Maiija* gave a bubbling gurgle. Her bowline snapped with a tiny pop, and she lifted her stem and began to sink very quietly by the nose. She bubbled for a moment like a person drowning, then with a tired long sigh of quenching wood and cooling metal, she snapped her sternline and went down.

Devvy said, "That's that. We haven't anything to show the police now. Maybe it's just as well."

They stood together in the late night, close but not touching. Through the hush the mutter of the Boss-Foreman came to them very clearly. After a while Devvy turned, facing the bay, and he knew she was listening.

He asked, "Is Peddar heading back?"

"No. Someone's coming up the channel in a rowboat."

"Who?"

"How should I know?" Her voice was impatient. "Someone from The Retreat, I suppose. Lum Kee, the cook, or maybe Doctor Morse."

She took the flashlight from her hip pocket and handed it to him. "Here, hold this," she said. He heard the hammer of the little rifle click back under her thumb.

IT WAS AN EERIE BUSINESS, WAITING here in the heel of the night, listening to the gentle creak of rowlocks somewhere in the channel below. The boat was making slow way, poking around the kinks and twists of the narrow gut between the saltgrass flats.

74

After a long five minutes, Clint heard a grating at the tail of the basin.

Devvy said, "Put the light on them."

The flash sent a strong white beam skipping along the water. It picked up a flatbottomed skiff. The man at the oars swiveled his head. His mouth opened and he blinked at them, eyes shiny black in the light. It was hard to be sure at this distance, but Clint thought he was Chinese.

He centered the beam on the man in the stern. Spectacles flashed; he saw a bearded face above a parson's round collar.

"It's all right," Devvy said to him. "Just Lum Kee and Doctor Morse."

"Hullo the landing!" The voice was mellow and deep. "Devvy. Is that you?"

"Yes. Come on in." She told Clint, "Take the light off him. Can't you see you're blinding him with it?"

"Hell," Clint muttered. "I ever do anything right?" He thumbed the switch, and heard Devvy click her tongue in irritation at him.

Glad of the dark, tense and wary, he waited beside her. He'd heard that voice just once, but he'd know it anywhere. It had stopped Joe Peddar in his tracks, on the Martinez float that Saturday night—it belonged on the edge of the fog, close to the dreadful thing in the fog that reached for him in his sleep so that he wakened screaming.

The skiff poked along the basin, a moving shadow, the current pat-patting gently under its nose. The Chinaman reached up with the painter and Clint trailed the skiff past where the troller had lain to make fast alongside Devvy's outboard rig.

Lum Kee did not get out, but sat hunched forward over his knees. The man with the parson's collar clambered spryly past him and stepped to the landing.

He said, "My dear, I'm relieved to see you safe. For

a while we were sure it was the house … Is that Joe, beside you there?"

"Joe left some time ago," Devvy said. "I thought you'd have seen him."

"Why, no. I'd expected to find him here." Spectacles gave off a phantom gleam as he peered at Clint. He said, out of a flat silence, "Well bless my soul!"

Devvy said, "You sound surprised, Doctor Morse. Have you met before?"

"Yes, you might say so, Devvy. In a sort of a way." He was still peering owlishly, head thrust forward. "And not under the most pleasant of circumstances, I'm afraid."

"You've got me," Clint said. And to Devvy, "Maybe he's right. Far as I know, though, I've never run into any preachers."

Devvy said, "His name's Clint Farrell. He's working on my place for a while. He got banged up in some kind of fishing accident and can't remember anything." She added casually, "It was his troller that burned."

"His boat?"

"His partner's. He was fishing on shares."

"Too bad, my boy. She's gone past salvage, I suppose?"

"I don't know," Clint said. "We might be able to raise what's left of her. But I don't think it's worth while."

"How did the fire start?" the kind voice asked, startlingly deep for such a sparrow of a man. Clint felt Devvy's warning nudge, but he was too mad to care.

"It didn't start. It was started. I saw the dude that did it, and …"

"He means Joe Peddar," Devvy said, her voice cutting sharply across his words. "Joe was here on the landing when we came down."

"Joe?" Doctor Morse chuckled in the gloom. "No, Devvy. Of course not! Joe is a handful at times, but

76

believe me, he isn't vicious. I sent him down through the woods as soon as we spotted the glare in the sky."

His voice was mildly reproachful. "Joe came to help, if he could."

"Don't send him again," Devvy said. "We don't want his kind of help, Doctor Morse."

"As you say." The little man sighed, amusement and exasperation mixed. "Devvy, you're a queer, grim child and you worry me. You worry me a great deal! You ought to be in school, meeting other girls, doing the things a girl should do. You're a good neighbor, but I must confess, Devvy, I'll be heartily glad for your sake when you get rid of the farm."

He added gravely, "Your mother is right about that—at least."

"Not my mother," Devvy said. "And she isn't right. I'll never sell my farm. Why should I? It's good bottom land. I'll have most of it in tree-fruit some day. And I can get along without other girls. I'd a lot sooner have it that way."

"You may think so. But you're young, my dear, young … The spectacles flashed, and Clint knew the little, bearded man was studying him again in the dark. "It distresses me to realize how very much you're missing. It's neither right nor healthy."

"Don't worry about me," Devvy said. "You could worry more about Lum Kee, Doctor Morse. He's too old to be out this late."

"I'm sorry! Really I am. But it wasn't my idea. He worries about you too, you see. He insisted on coming, and since I'm helpless in this—this infernal channel of yours, I let him take the oars."

He sighed again, and said, "Well, we'd best be pushing along now. Devvy, be a good girl and don't give us another scare until we've recovered from this one." He said to Clint, "Good night, young man. I'm sincerely

77

sorry about the boat, but I'm certain you've jumped to a wrong conclusion. It isn't wise to make such charges in hot blood."

Clint didn't answer. He stood beside Devvy while Doctor Morse stepped down to the skiff. The missionary addressed Lum Kee in a soft singsong, and the Chinaman changed places with him. squatting in the stern sheets while Doctor Morse settled to the oars.

The spectacles glimmered again. "Mr. Farrell, I'm rather concerned about you. If your condition is as you say, you're probably suffering from amnesia, traumatic amnesia. I'm a doctor of medicine as well as of divinity. Will you call on me tomorrow? There's a very good chance I can help you."

"Sure," Clint said. "I'll be around. There's something you might be able to straighten me out on right now "

"Tomorrow," Devvy said. She flipped the painter inboard and shoved the skiff away from the landing with her foot. "I'm dead for sleep. Good night, Doctor Morse … 'Night, Kee."

Distance absorbed the creak and splash of the oars. Clint more than half expected Devvy to be mad at him— she seemed to be mad at him most of the time—but he was still not prepared for her cold fury as she turned on him.

"You and your big mouth! You were all set to tell him about the ring, weren't you?"

"Yes, and I'll tell him next chance I have. I want to know where Peddar got it." He scowled down at her, feeling his weariness, and the chill of the coming dawn. "Peddar's done worse things than burn a fishboat, and if you think I'll let him get away with any of it, you're crazy."

"It's you that's crazy." Her voice was quivering. "I don't care about you. But you can get other people into trouble. That wouldn't matter, though, would it?"

He said, meeting her anger with his own, "Another thing. Your neighbor with the whiskers was at Martinez Cove that night too. But he was forty feet away from me, and the only light was up by the freight shed. How do you explain him recognizing me right off tonight?"

"I don't know." Devvy didn't sound mad any more, just worried and tired. "I'm sure Joe wasn't wearing a ring when he boarded us this morning, though. You could be mistaken. It could have been a shadow on his hand."

"It wasn't any shadow."

"You said you saw a Chinaman wearing it. Would you know him if you met him again?"

"It wasn't Lum Kee, if that's what you're getting at. The other one was taller. Anyhow, I don't figure on seeing him again."

"You think he's dead too?"

"I'm sure of it."

She said, "Clint, did you kill Aleko?"

Touched by a cold that didn't come from his wet clothes, Clint said, "I don't think so. But I can't be certain. I was pretty sore at him after we'd taken the Chinaman and those cans on the *Maiija*. When I get mad I kind of let go in all directions. I didn't used to be like that."

Devvy said, "I shouldn't have asked you. You haven't killed anyone." She swung away from him abruptly. "Come on. There's nothing to hang around here for now. It's almost daylight."

He was too confused to think straight. There was only one certainty—whatever his trouble might be, it was deadly, and if he stayed around here, she'd be sucked into it along with him. A few hours ago it wouldn't have mattered, she could have taken her chances and welcome. Tonight had changed all that. Caught in this dark whirl, there was only one thing he could see to do. Lam out as he'd done before. Make sure, whatever else happened, that Devvy stayed in the clear.

He poked off up the basin trail to the rock bluff where he'd left his shoes. Devvy didn't follow him, but waited at the top of the landing. When he whistled to her she called, "Not that way. We'll go by the road."

He tied his shoes, breaking a lace and swearing over it in the early light.

"You took your time," Devvy told him when he jogged back to her.

No use talking when this mood was on her; he'd learned that much about her. Anyway, he didn't want to talk. He needed to think, and it looked as if Devvy felt the same way, because she didn't speak to him again till they were past the hayfield gate. She stopped then; and he halted too. Sunup was still an hour off anyhow, but the fir snags in the wild pasture back of the farmhouse stood out black against a graying sky, and a cool little wind ran over the hay to finger their faces.

Devvy said, not looking at him, "That was my broken arm you twisted. You hurt me. It still hurts."

"I'm sorry," he said. Then, gruffly, "No, I'm not! You had it coming to you. There's times when you can't be boss."

"Was that why you hurt me?"

"No." She wasn't going to stampede him this time, as she'd done before, in the afternoon, when he'd tried to be nice to her. He said carefully, thinking beyond his words, "You could have got hurt a lot worse down there. Something's wrong with that Peddar's head."

"Don't be too sure. He's smarter than you, Clint."

"All right—argue. You asked me, I've told you what I think. Let's not kick it around."

"Plenty of girls like Joe. He's nicer natured than you, except when he's mad or jealous. And he's better looking."

"Not for long, he won't be. Not when I'm finished with him."

80

"Don't, Clint. I'm thinking. I'm trying to figure things out."

She turned toward him, hands shoved into her pockets, the two of them alone in the gray light, on the lane that threaded the hayfield. The collar of her heavy pullover was turned up, but her throat lifted out of it, slender and sweetly round. Her grave, small face was raised, and her eyes were steady on him, the considering frown between them.

"What, for God's sake?" he asked. "What is there to figure?"

"About us." Her eyes didn't waver; but he knew if he reached out and touched her cheek it would be hot from the quick rise of blood. "About what happened last night in my room. About what's been happening to me ever since you put in at Martinez. I wanted you to come back, Clint."

She said, against his hard stare, "Clint, I want to know what hit us."

"Why don't you ask Joe Peddar? He's so bright, he could tell you."

"You're acting like a child, Clint. Like Aila's little boy in a temper. Help me get it straight … please."

"There's nothing to get straight. I was fixing to make a pass at you. Then she started sounding off at us and spoiled things."

"It wasn't like that."

"Wasn't it? What else were you expecting?"

That hurt her. He could see it in the quick narrowing of her eyes. But he'd go on with it even if it meant cutting his own throat. She had come to him, saved him, reached her hands down to him in the deep water. She had given him something wonderful, a thing he'd never had, or ever thought to have, before. He had to break her away from him, into the clear.

Deliberately, making himself meet her steady gaze,

he said, "You figure on me sticking around here and marrying you or something like that. Well listen. You did haul me out of a jackpot, so the least I can do is hand it to you straight. I don't want to get tied up with any girl. You know what I was after last night. If I got it, how long do you think I'd stay in this hole?"

Still she didn't answer. He was ready and braced for anger, but she just stood looking up at him with her small frown. The dawn wind stirred her hair like a light hand going over, and the hunger for her was a physical ache, hollowing him under the ribs, tightening his throat.

"So there it is," he told her. "I'm not the fireside type. Now, I'll be on my way."

"Where?"

That stopped him. He glowered at her, his will against hers, wishing she'd flare up, make it easier for him. Just for that moment he was sure, quite sure, that he hated her.

She said coldly, "You won't be in my room again. There won't be any passes. You can stay in the barn with Paddy. But you aren't going away. There's something I've got to find out first. Maybe you can tell me, when you remember."

"You can't keep me here."

"No? But I can have the police pick you up. I can tell them you quarreled with your fishing partner and came in alone, with your boat a mess of blood. I think they might take you back to Canada and hang you." With a small, cool smile, she told him, "You can forget about last night, Clint. It didn't mean anything."

"Not a damned thing," Clint said.

He'd fallen for her, for a stump-ranch girl with rough little hands and lovely sunstreaked hair and strange eyes with flecks of gold in their depths. But all he could give her was a killing trouble. He had lied to her and he'd keep on lying even though it twisted the heart out of him, until he could get away from here.

There'd been something wrong with him for months, a sullen tiredness that never quite lifted, that could boil without warning into a rage that scared him when he came out of it. He could have dreamed up the ring too, his sick brain making excuses for him, seizing on innocent people and pointing a finger at them. He'd pinched a ring like that himself once, in Portland as a kid. There were lots of them around, flashy rings that anyone could get for ten bucks across a Chinatown counter.

He could even have dreamed up the cans, and the Chinaman. As far as he or anyone else could say for sure, there'd been only the two of them on the troller, himself and Aleko. He'd come back. Aleko had stayed out there in the deep water.

Devvy brought out her fine cut. But this time she didn't pass the pack to him. She rolled a cigarette for herself with steady fingers, licked it shut, snicked a match on her belt buckle and lit up. Trudging along the lane toward the farmhouse, she kept a full pace ahead of him. But he glimpsed her face as she slipped through the upper gate. He'd seen a fighter look like that when he'd taken the heel of a glove in a dirty clinch. He realized she was crying.

There was nothing he could do about that—not without undoing the good and bitter thing which to his own vast surprise he'd succeeded in accomplishing. He closed the gate. Devvy didn't speak to him or look at him, but walked on toward the house, her back straight, the rifle under her arm.

Clint mooched down to the dilapidated cedar-shake barn above the creek branch. There he found Paddy Burke, cheek pressed to a Jersey's flank, humming between his teeth while he squirted milk into a pail.

Paddy swiveled his head and gave Clint his bright black disconcerting stare. He said, "You made a night of it, I observe."

"Kind of. Speaking of last night, where were you?"

"Why, I was walking the woods, Clinton," the hired man said. "I'm a great one for night-walking."

"What kind of answer is that?"

Paddy resumed his humming, his blunt fingers stripping the last of the milk. "You'll weasel the truth out of me. If I reveal it to you, you'll not peach on me?"

"I know you were down by the landing. I heard you whistling."

"To keep my courage up, just. I was breaking the law of the land. I was pit-lamping, Clinton." Paddy ducked the Jersey's swishing tail. "Steady, ye scut. … We're into a meat shortage here, d'you see. It's been chicken and eggs, eggs and chicken, and I am a hearty man. Without meat I become a shadow of myself. So thinking that wild beef would be better than no beef at all, I scuttled my conscience. I took Callahan's rifle and a light to flash a buck's eyes by, and went ahunting."

"I didn't hear any shots."

"Will you believe me, Clinton, there was not a deer to be found! With beef in the larder they're into her orchard saucy as billy-be-damned. But take up a gun, and the creatures are off to the other side of the island."

"Did you expect to flash a buck down by my boat?"

"I did not know what I might flash," Paddy said. "I was prepared for anything, you might say. You returned alone, Clinton?"

"Devvy's up at the house." Clint yearned to hit him for a smoke, but there was something in the heavy-set little Irishman's look that discouraged him. "I'll be bunking in the barn after this."

"Will you indeed?" Paddy turned the Jersey loose with a slap on her flank. "You are not a house guest any longer, then?"

"Are you ribbing me or what?"

"I am not. I'm curious, just, as to your status here, Clinton."

"Stop calling me Clinton."

"That's your name. I have no special liking for you, but I will not help a man miscall himself. The science of numerology …"

"Hell with numerology. Lay off me."

The black eyes continued to probe his face. "Here speaks the voice of ignorance," Paddy said. He got off his low stool and stood with the milk bucket aswing in his fist. "There's the look of the tough monkey about your mug," he said reflectively, "but at the same time it must be conceded she's worked a change in you, Clinton. Either that or you're more of a man than a first glance showed. What was between you and Devvy last night?"

"That's our affair."

Paddy still considered him. "So?"

"She pinned my ears back, if you have to know. What's it to you, anyway?"

"I'll be blunt. I'm old enough to be Devvy's father and young enough to be her husband. It is not a comfortable position as you'll understand. I have a fondness for the girl. I would not like to see her hurt."

"She won't be," Clint said. "Not by me. I've taken care of that."

"She had better not be." Under Paddy's tough humor—not really humor at all, Clint realized—was a grimness. It showed more strongly now as he stared, his hard jaws blue for want of shaving, his black eyes a little narrowed. "While you're amongst us, Clinton, no more tomcatting. Let Devvy alone. She has enough and to spare on her shoulders without another young sprig o' sin randying after her."

"You mean Joe Peddar?"

"I mean both of you."

"What's the matter with that guy?"

"Nothing that killing won't cure."

"Look," Clint said, "who are you? What are you,

anyhow? You knew my boat was on fire last night. Why didn't you come down?"

"What am I, Clinton?" The black eyes twinkled at him. "I'm a rambling man, a man born to fine things, but with an affinity for the bottle. You find 'em among these heathen islands. As for why I did not come down to you, there are times when it's as well to have a rear guard, one to see and not to be seen, with a rifle upon his knee."

"She told me you were a friend of her father's overseas."

"A black lie. I never set eyes on that man. It was done so she would let me stay."

Damn it, Clint thought, he's tougher than me, tougher than anyone I ever ran into. But I could like the little guy.

"Don't you know anything about her father?" he asked.

"What I've heard in the town and what she's told me." Paddy reached for his other bucket. "Callahan was born to trouble like yourself, Clinton. One of those who misdirect their lives past straightening. Remittance men, they call them in Canada. He came here from the Old Country with the short end of an inheritance to be a gentleman farmer."

He looked around at the tumble-down barn. "He was a gentleman but no farmer. You see what he made of it. He would swim the Boss-Foreman on a bet, but he would not turn his hand to clearing his own stumps. If he had money for a tractor he would then decide that the age of the horse was returning, and buy a horse. He would go to buy a work horse and end up with a blood beast, one that could clip off a fast quarter. And he would still have his stumps, but no tractor."

"A hot sport," Clint said.

"Ignorance again," Paddy told him. "Call him one of the fools o' God and you're nearer the mark. He tried his hand at rumrunning after Devvy lost her mother.

The law took him and his boat together, and put him away for a year."

"What happened to Devvy?"

"Mike Peddar, Joe's uncle, had been Callahan's partner in the venture. The Peddars took her in. She was a baby, but she has not forgotten that year. The rest was happy enough till himself went flitting off to Canada a month after they were into the war, and left her to the Peddars again, and his farm to the thistles."

"But he came back."

"With a lieutenant commander's stripes on his sleeve and a DSO, and another mistake for his collection." Paddy tipped his chin. "Her up at the house. His worst mistake of the lot."

"I know what you mean," Clint said.

"You don't, Clinton, you do not know the half of what I mean." Paddy swayed the buckets in his fists, the humor that was not humor strong in his eyes. "His luck was in only twice, so far as I can see. Once was when he brought Devvy's mother out of a nest of wild Finnish folk upcoast, and again when he got Devvy. The girl was too good for him, Clinton, and she's too good for the likes of you."

"I don't need you to tell me that," Clint said. "I meant it—I'm not staying here, Paddy. No longer than I have to."

"And how long will that be?"

Clint shrugged. "Ask her. She's the boss." A bell began to dong up at the house, and he said, "That for breakfast?"

"It is. It will be eggs again." Paddy started for the barn door with his buckets. Over his shoulder he said, "I'll have a fatherly eye on you while you're with us, Clinton. Remember it."

"And on Devvy?"

"I'll have an eye on Devvy."

❖

A FIRE CRACKLED IN THE RANGE, but its warmth wasn't enough to drive the chill of early morning from the stone-floored kitchen. Devvy stood over the stove, still muffled in her Indian sweater. She had tied her hair in the blue bandanna, and the kerchief ends stuck up like horns on top of her head. She didn't turn, and when Paddy gave her a hearty "God save all here!" she did not answer him.

Clint squeezed behind the table. The two children across from him, already eating, would be Aila's. The girl, seven or thereabouts, was redhaired, a coltish, lathy kid with green eyes too large for her thin and sulky face. But in spite of his dark hair, there was something of Devvy in the boy. He had her eyes, well-spaced, with dark long lashes, and Devvy's stubborn mouth. Three years old, maybe four.

Clint gave the pair a tentative grin. The girl scowled at him. The boy downed another spoonful of soft-boiled egg, eying him critically, then stuck out his tongue.

"It is the little man's way of giving you good morning," Paddy Burke said.

"Brian, you stop that!" Devvy plunked the coffee percolator on the worn oilcloth. "It's your fault, Paddy," she snapped. "I wish you wouldn't encourage him."

Paddy sighed. He said, "Would you deny 'em the pleasures of childhood, Devvy?" and applied himself to his plate.

Both children were in overalls. They had a scrubbed look, and their hair shone from brushing. That would be Devvy's doing—there was no sign of Aila, and Clint suspected she was sleeping off her jag in her flossy, frowzy room upstairs.

Devvy might have been putting food down for a dog, the way she clattered a plate in front of him.

88

"Thanks!" he said, his teeth in the word. His eggs had a charcoal fringe; he wondered whether she'd done that on purpose.

She didn't speak till they were through eating. Then she said to Paddy, "You'll have to go on with the haying alone today. I've another job for him."

"I will make shift," Paddy said. "I doubt he'd be much use with a fork anyway. He lacks the back for it."

Clint tried to give him a dirty look, but it came out a grin. He'd never liked to have anyone rib him before, but with Paddy it was somehow different.

He said cautiously, "What's this other job?"

"We're going after salmon," Devvy said, still to Paddy. "There's no money left, and we need things."

"Aila brought nothing back from Halem?" Paddy asked.

"Herself," Devvy said. "And a hang ... headache."

The boy, Brian, said, "Money upstairs." Clint saw Paddy's lips tighten. Devvy flushed, but she said kindly, "If you're finished, Brian and Elsie, you can go outside. You can hunt for eggs."

"He takes all the brown ones," the girl said in a small, complaining voice.

Devvy told her, "That's because he looks harder, dear. Run now!"

She said to Clint, "Ready?"

"Sure. If you call that work."

Paddy lifted his head and gave Clint a look that would have been pitying if it were not for the black mirth in his eyes. "As a trollerman," he said, "you would of course know all about fishing. I'll wish you luck, my son."

Clint had been hoping he'd roll a cigarette, but instead Paddy brought out an ancient cherrywood pipe, tamped coarse-cut tobacco into it with his thumb, lit up, and tramped out of the kitchen humming his song of the Bat d'Af off-key between his teeth.

Damned if I'll ask her for a smoke, Clint thought. I can't do anything or say anything to change things now.

But Devvy was already clearing the table. She stacked the dishes, then started for the door.

"Come on," she said over her shoulder, as if she were calling a dog.

He tagged after her through her garden and into the cedar-shake woodshed behind. She took a handline on a wooden winder from a peg on the wall. The line was thick as seine cord and the sinker would weigh at least three pounds. It was knotted to a piano-wire leader; swiveled to the leader was a narrow brass wobbler with an oversize Siwash hook. Chinook rigging, the kind of tackle they used in rowboat fishing for the big boys.

Devvy lifted a short-handled gaff hook from another peg. "Carry these," she ordered, and brushed past him out of the woodshed.

They climbed the snake fence and he followed her into the narrow trail down which they'd raced the night before. The pullover was too big for her, she'd turned up the sleeves, and the waistband sat low on her hips. She walked fast, more like a slim boy than a girl, balancing her rifle in one hand.

The tide which had flooded into the basin last night, carrying a scurf of drift litter and kelp almost to the feet of the red madronas, was far out now. Below the channel and saltgrass flats, the bay lay like mother-of-pearl under a pale sky. Nothing remained of the troller except the frayed ends of bow- and sternlines. Devvy shook them loose from the landing cleats and tossed them into the basin before she stepped down to her dinghy. She sat in the stern, Clint on the middle thwart. The outboard caught at the first spin, and Devvy sheared them away from the landing. They sat with knees almost touching, staring past each other, the motor unreeling its exhaust smoke and din behind them. This, Clint thought grimly as he shifted his feet on the bottom boards, was going to be no pleasure jaunt. Too bad—it could have been a lot of fun, taking her fishing.

Devvy told him sharply, "Sit still. You aren't in an offshore Diesel!"

She wasn't heading directly down the bay, but was swinging over toward the sawmill dock. The dock was almost falling apart, Clint saw when they drew close—half of its piles were rotted clean away, and the rest wore pantalettes of barnacles. They sputtered close past the end of the dock. Beyond was a cove with weather-beaten swifters and dolphins marking where the mill's log booms had once been, and at the head of the cove, a float and boathouse.

Alongside the float, tied bow and stern, lay a long gray powerboat with a cruiser hull. One glance told Clint it was the fast job he had seen that night across the channel at Martinez. By daylight, her lines yanked a startled whistle from between his teeth. She fairly shouted of speed. Her cabin raked sharply aft, humping into an abortive wheelhouse, and her bow had an exceptionally wide flare.

At least fifty feet from stem to transom, he estimated … nearer sixty.

Devvy was watching him, her face expressionless. She said, "Have you seen her before?"

"At Martinez. She came in after you left. Aleko was on her. Aleko and the parson."

"Not since then?"

"No. I don't know …"

He ducked his head, staring at his hands spread stiff-fingered on his knees. He could feel the sweat trickling down his sides under his shirt. If he looked up he'd see the name on her bows. She'd be the *Helene*.

He looked up, and she was.

That other time, when the fear woke and churned

inside him, he'd been asleep. And when his memory sidled along the edge of that pit of night and fire, he'd had Devvy to help him. It was different now. This time he was broad awake and on his own, alone with it.

"Take us out," he said.

"No. We're going in."

Devvy twisted the fluted rubber throttle grip and the outboard popped faster, shoving the dinghy into the cove. He tried to keep his face from betraying him, but she knew, damn her—she knew what was happening inside him.

"Who owns her?" he asked, forcing his voice to stay casual.

"Mike Peddar. Joe's uncle. He used to be a rum-runner."

"What's he run now?"

"Tourists. When he's not carpentering for Doctor Morse he takes fishing parties into the Boss-Foreman from the north end, around Martinez Island."

"She doesn't look like any tourist boat."

"Doesn't she?"

"No. Half of her must be power plant."

"Where Mike goes he needs power."

Her tone made it plain she didn't want to talk to him.

A man squatted cross-legged, whittling, in the sun on the cruiser's foredeck. His tan was as dark as Devvy's, and his yellow hair shone like brass. When they were close alongside he glanced down at them, and got off the deck in an easy lift.

He called in his heavy, lazy voice, "Hi, Devvy."

Devvy cut the motor. "Hello, Joe," she said.

It was the first time, Clint thought, sizing him up sourly, that he'd seen Joe Peddar by daylight. He looked to be twenty-two or twenty-three; he was stacked like an All-American. The weakness of him, the viciousness, lay in his mouth and chin. His jaw was too heavy and long, his lips straight and thin.

But good-looking, the kind girls went for.

You couldn't always tell about those showy-built ones. Sometimes they were pushovers, all muscle and no brains or guts. But it was never a safe bet to dope them that way, and he knew if Peddar had nailed him on the Martinez float with that first swing, or sucked him into a clinch, he'd have been cooked.

He watched Peddar peel off another leisurely shaving from the cedar billet in his hand. He might have the punch to put the guy away, but he doubted it. Thing to do would be to keep in the clear, cut him up and wear him down, never let those long heavily muscled arms get a grip on him …

Devvy said, "Is Lum Kee around, Joe?"

"What you want with him, Devvy?" He had given Clint one cool, measuring look; now he ignored him.

"Never mind. Where is he?"

"Come aboard and I'll tell you."

"I'll stay here, thanks."

"Okay," Peddar said. The block in his hand was a half-shaped hull. Another delicate shaving curled away from the slip knife's edge. "Have it your way, honey. Your Chink's up in his kitchen, I guess."

"Is he all right after last night?"

"Sure. Why shouldn't he be?"

"He's too old for rowing, and you know his heart's bad. Doctor Morse shouldn't let him."

Peddar chuckled. "Doc takes good care of him. You ought to come here oftener. You'd find out."

The dinghy drifted closer to the cruiser's side, and Devvy fended it off with her hand. Clint looked up into Peddar's face, trying to figure him; but the cold, pale eyes revealed nothing. He could feel the big guy hating him, though—it was tangible as the knife in Peddar's hand.

Devvy said, "I'm going fishing. Tell Lum Kee I'll try to get him a red cod, will you?"

"I'll tell him."

"Is there a dance at Martinez Saturday night, Joe?"

"Yeah." Peddar glanced down at her; just for an instant there'd been surprise in his eyes. "Leave your gun at home and I'll take you, sweetheart."

"I'll let you know."

Peddar flicked the knife blade into the slender bone handle. He looked directly at Clint. "I thought maybe you were dated. How about him?"

"He works for me. That's all."

She started the motor. Joe Peddar watched them out of the cove, standing tall and brown on the *Helene*'s foredeck. Then he dropped to the float and sauntered ashore, toward the huddle of bungalows and mill boardinghouses on the hillside above.

Devvy said, "He wasn't wearing any ring."

"He could have taken it off, couldn't he?" Clint said. "Now why the hell did you do that?"

"Do what?" There was a curious smile around her mouth, but she looked at him without warmth.

"Make a date with him." He was sure again that he hated her, sitting there watching him with her small cool smile.

"Why not?"

"For God's sake, he's a wolf, you told me yourself ..."

"Suppose he is? It's time I started going to dances again. I can see now what Doctor Morse meant. I'd got so that anyone who drifted in here looked good to me."

After all, it was what he'd set out to do. He said, "Go ahead. Get into a jam. It's no skin off my nose."

Peddar hadn't been wearing the ring, but he was certain now that it was no sick-headed dream. Seeing the *Helene* had convinced him of that. The ring had been an oblong of green stone, cheap jade most likely,

94

with milky veinings running through it. Half an inch wide and nearly an inch long; he remembered it well now. Too well.

When he'd seen it the one other time, they'd been on the *Maija*, drinking in the doghouse, he and Aleko and the Chinaman who'd come in from the steamer in the fog.

He glanced at Devvy, but she was gazing past him as if he weren't there.

THE TIDE, CLINT JUDGED, must be on or close to low-water slack, for the voice of the Boss-Foreman was only a drowsy murmur beyond the mouth of the bay. One more rock point and they'd be into Martinez Channel.

Here, with the sawmill astern, he could get a better idea of the layout. He remembered the roll of charts in the troller's wheelhouse and tried to fit into them what he saw.

They'd shown the Boss-Foreman, three miles long, running between Cultus and Martinez Islands. It was nowhere more than half a mile wide. A reef, covered at high tide, sat plunk in the middle of its south approach. There was another, dirtier reef, he recalled, something less than halfway through the pass. The island they'd left was Cultus, and this would be Cultus Bay. On the far side of the Boss-Foreman was Martinez Island, then Redoubt Pass, the steamer and tugboat route between Martinez and Fox Islands. The three islands lay in the mouth of the Straits like a triple-split cork in the neck of a bottle. Through their passes, the tides of the North Pacific ripped with a twenty-foot rise and fall.

Redoubt had no reefs and no bends. It was much the longer route, but Aleko had told him that nobody, not even the trollermen, tried to run the Boss-Foreman.

He hadn't been thinking about Aleko, but he could see him quite well now, tracing the dog-leg course of that pass with a brown hook-scarred finger on his chart.

"There iss here the reef they call Paul Bunyan's Chair," the old man had told him, "and south here the damnedest whirl you ever see. Spring tide runs twenty-three knots in the surges."

But even with what Aleko had told him, and the pilot book's black-lettered warning, Clint was not prepared for what he saw when the dinghy poked around the north headland of Cultus Bay.

Inside the bay, which was no more than a deep and narrow bight of Martinez Channel, the voice of the tidal pass had been muted, blanketed by the high rocky succession of points. Here, outside, it jarred against the ears in a steady concussion. Not loud—more like the premonitory rumbling of a bull in a field. It was the voice of water cramped by rock, deviled and compressed into this slot between the islands by the North Pacific tide.

Almost straight out from the headland, strange in a glassy calm, the channel lifted and curled in three lines of breakers. The breakers never shifted position. They growled in a crescent half a mile from horn to horn, eternally toppling and crumbling. Beyond them, south in the direction of open water, the channel widened. To the north, on into the Boss-Foreman, the water ran slick and smooth, worried here and there by minor boils and surges. Somewhere yonder the pass gathered its main voice, the rumbling, heavy undertone that shook the air. A high bluff thrust out from the east shore of Cultus Island down there, diverting the flow as a wing-dam would, thrusting the salt-water river sharply off course toward the bald cliffs of Martinez. Spray hung in a rainbow haze over the point, clamping a limit on vision.

Clint swallowed hard to clear his ears of the concussion. They'd run dirty enough passes, he and

96

Aleko in the *Maiija*, but none of them had been a patch on this widow-making brute.

He glanced at Devvy. She was frowning again, staring beyond him, one hand on the throttle and the other tense against the gunwale. The outboard was working harder now, wheezing as it fought the current that gripped them beyond the sheltering tip of the headland. Clint watched her, trying to read her intention from her face.

She swung the dinghy north, directly into the pass. What her landmarks were he had no idea; but when they'd run something less than two hundred yards, she began to quarter out from Cultus on a long diagonal. She seemed to be following some obscure slant of tide, an offshoot current of the main stream that ran almost opposite to the southward set. For the first time, he noticed that Devvy wore a watch today, a man's rig with a military face-guard and a broad tooled-leather strap on her right wrist.

She'd jockeyed them midway between the islands, and the dinghy hung almost motionless, stern pointed at the inside line of fixed breakers. Between the boat and the reef responsible for those breakers, the green glass-smooth surface shattered over a twenty-foot area as if from successive charges of buckshot. Little silvery fish flipped and skittered in a panic swarm, shooting into the sunlight. A gull wheeled and dipped to the water with a high and lonely cry.

Clint knew well enough what those signs spelled. Big fish, salmon, were working below, slashing into the bait schools and driving them helter-skelter to the surface. Devvy was looking fixedly over her shoulder; he wondered, unease building in him, just how far in she intended to take them.

He began to understand, now, the meaning of Paddy Burke's odd smile at breakfast.

Her hand moved on the throttle. Choked to half speed, bow into the current, the dinghy held her own. Devvy glanced at her wrist watch. "We've got forty minutes," she said. "Twelve of slack, twenty-eight on the rise. Get the line over."

Clint reached for the winder, glad of something to do at last. He freed the big blued-steel hook and buffed the six-inch spoon against his thigh.

"Don't fool around," Devvy told him. "Get it working."

He flipped the spoon overside. There was a kink in the piano-wire leader—Devvy snatched for the leader and straightened the kink with her fingers. The spoon wobbled astern, riding the surface.

"Hurry," Devvy said; and he let line spin off the winder, cord thick as a lead pencil, green once but salt-bleached now till it was nearly white. The heavy sinker plopped in and the spoon dived under. It wavered out of sight, throwing random flashes like a crippled herring.

Devvy said, "There's a marker at sixty feet. Hold it at that."

The sinker dragged hard against Clint's wrist. He saw the red string marker flash over the side, and snubbed the line around his hand, letting the winder clatter to the bottom boards. Down under, he could feel the spoon throbbing like a live thing.

Again, closer this time, a shower of candlefish shattered the surface. While they were still skipping in air, a great bronze-and-silver fish lunged half out of water in gape-jawed pursuit. Chinook. The size of him made Clint gasp.

"Watch it," Devvy told him sharply. She looked at her wrist again. Her head was still bent when the line slashed taut with a violence that all but threw Clint off the thwart.

"Got 'im!"

He stood up, balancing with his feet braced against the uneasy quivering of the dinghy in the tideway, and began to haul.

"You fool, keep down," Devvy snapped at him. "Bring him in—we haven't time for games."

He snapped back at her, "Quit riding me!" The line came in so easily that it was hard to believe there was a hooked salmon below. But he'd landed enough chinooks from the troller to know how they acted. The sinker lifted clear; and on the instant, four fathoms out, the fish crashed the surface in a swashing, straining plunge.

"Keep him coming," Devvy said in her edged voice. "Don't let him run."

The chinook hung down now with a weight and power that set the line humming. He shook his head as a bull fights a nose ring. Once he burned a dozen feet of line across Clint's palms in a rush that he couldn't check. He hauled again, panting; it hadn't been like this on the *Maiija*, where you threw a gurdy into gear and walked your fish home by horsepower! This was a rawer, tougher game—he could see where Devvy got at least some of her calluses!

Another fathom and the brass swivel between line and leader shone in the sun. He peered overside, and he could glimpse his fish now, and the size of it frightened him. It looked half the length of the dinghy, finning four feet down with the spoon hooked into its jaw corner.

Devvy reached under the stern seat for a foot-long section of iron pipe. She jammed it through her belt, then picked up the gaff with its heavy, wide hook. Clint lifted the chinook a yard higher, sensed a rush coming and heaved once more. The dorsal fin, then the broad back broke water, and Devvy, in a single smooth motion, clipped her gaff home under a gill plate.

For a moment Clint thought the dinghy would swamp or capsize. Spray flew into his eyes, half blinding him. He heard a rapid dull thudding. Devvy had the chinook's fierce hook-nosed head clear. She was holding him with the gaff short-gripped, and with the other hand she swung her club.

"Keep us trimmed," she ordered. Clint leaned to the other side while she got both hands on the gaff and slithered the long, wide, deep-bodied fish over the gunwale. It flopped once with quivering tail on the bottom boards, silver and bronze, shaped like a stream trout and peppered lavishly on its green back with black spots.

"Fifty pounds easy," Clint breathed in awe.

"Maybe thirty-five." Devvy was staring at the crescent of fixed breakers again. They were toppling the other way now, north toward the Boss-Foreman.

She twisted the throttle and the outboard sang louder. "We've got twenty-five minutes. Get the spoon over. Hurry!"

They waited longer for a strike this time, but when it came, it dragged Clint's hand and wrist under water.

Devvy said, "Let me," and grabbed for the line. Kneeling, facing astern, she yanked the fish up in quick, vicious snatches. She'd shed her sweater, and her short-sleeved white shirt stretched flat across her back and shoulders as she pulled. The line fell in precise coils between her knees. She held the fish hard, battling it in, snubbing its wicked bucks and surges after the sinker lifted clear.

Clint reached for the gaff, but she shook her head. "I can do better alone."

She brought the swivel out in a high lift, dipped with the gaff, and whipped the club from her belt.

Heavier this time, Clint saw. Forty-five pounds anyhow, and she'd killed it in minutes less than he had taken for his smaller one.

They lost the next chinook on the strike. Clint tried to steal a look at Devvy's watch, but perhaps deliberately, she turned her wrist over. The bull muttering deepened second by second; the dinghy had swung now till she was bow-on to the breakers. They'd swapped ends, the rise must be well under way. The outboard was popping full throttle, and the stern swung uneasily as the boat fought to go down with the current.

Candlefish and herring were hop-skipping everywhere Clint looked, and the big bright salmon were slashing at them like wolves in a mob of sheep. There was a wildness here, a savagery such as he had never known on land. The scattering swarms of bait, the high triumphant crying of the gulls, the mounting roar of the pass were all parts of that wildness, elements of a tension which was racing toward a climax.

Deep below, the spoon throbbed like a heart, pulsing in the current. Clint shot a frown at Devvy. She was staring at her wrist. Her other hand, balled into a fist, beat softly on the gunwale.

"How about it?" he asked her. "Shouldn't we clear out?"

"I'll tell you when."

Hard on her words, a fish hit. He felt smaller than the others—Clint ripped him in with yard-long snatches. He shone like solid silver as Devvy clipped the gaff into him, slugged him and slid him in on top of the other two chinooks.

She swung the tiller. Tide shoved them broadside with a solid impact, battering the dinghy and tilting her. The shoreline of Cultus Island was dancing past. Little boils and water blisters were opening all around them with the sucking pop of a cork coming out of a bottle.

"Get the oars over," Devvy said. "The motor can't do it alone."

Clint rattled the short cedar oars into the rowlocks. The current set malicious fingers around the oar blades, fighting to tug them deep. The Boss-Foreman was sounding off now with a full-throated bellow that shook earth and sky.

Rowing his guts out, Clint swiveled for a glance down-channel. He saw a derelict boom stick lift its nose into the spray haze down by the wing-dam point. It climbed high and higher against the sky till it reared perpendicular from the narrows, then sank as if a giant fist had locked on it and was dragging it under. The sight dried his throat. If the outboard conked here, they'd go the way of the boom stick.

Damn her anyway, he thought, running us into a jackpot like this.

"Scared?" Her voice was high and wild as a sea gull crying. She was grinning, the gold lights alive in her eyes.

"Hell ... no!" He clenched his teeth and gave the oars all he had. The current veered them inshore, then, so suddenly that he almost sprawled backwards, released them. It was as if the Boss-Foreman had tossed them scornfully out of its gut. The dinghy cut easily through aimless eddies into a cove below the bluffs of Cultus Island.

Clint shipped the oars and leaned over his knees, breathing hard with mouth open. His hands and wrists were numb, the muscles in his calves burned from the strain of that haul.

Out where they rode ten minutes ago, behind the black low reefs of the breaker crescent, the water rose in a mushroom-shaped hump. The hump shattered swift as a bubble breaks, and in its place was a white and green boil wider across than their cove.

"You always cut it that fine?" Clint asked her.

"Finer sometimes," Devvy said. "When I'm with Joe."

They ducked from point to point, following the inshore reverse run of tide, until they were around the home point and bouncing through the white-and-blue morning chop of Cultus Bay.

Midway across the mouth of the bay, a green troller plodded with spring poles lowered. Devvy gunned the motor and headed them over.

The trollerman lounging by the wheel lifted a hand in casual greeting. When they ran in between his lines, Clint saw that he had a Swede's blue eyes and fair hair, and a square face scorched from chin to forehead by sunburn.

"Devvy," the fisherman called down, "you sure get your groceries the hard way. I been sweating for you."

"Easy if you know how, Gunnar." Devvy slipped the blue bandanna from her head, and the wind whipped her hair past her cheeks. "Dad used to call that hole his icebox. How you doing?"

"Few silvers. Fishing's rotten, kid. Not enough to pay for my gas." He leaned over to peer into the dinghy. "*Tousan' yevela!* Say, you done all right!"

"Buy 'em?"

"Sure. T'irty cents on the market. I'll give you twenty a pound."

"Two bits."

"Twenty-two."

"You're a robber. I'll take it." She nodded to Clint, and he heaved the three chinooks up to the troller's shallow cockpit.

"Hundred pounds," Gunnar said. "Take my word for it?"

"I'll have to."

Chuckling, the fisherman pulled a wallet from his hip pocket. He skinned out a ten and a batch of ones. Devvy took them, not bothering to count them, and shoved them into her jeans.

She said, "What's new on Martinez, Gunnar?"

"Oh, nothing much. Little excitement yesterday. One of the handliners brought in a floater. Big old bald-headed fella wit' a mustache, Finn or Swede-Finn, I'd say."

Gunnar replaced his wallet. "You hear Mis' Anderson's got another baby? A girl again. They run to girls."

Clint said, fighting to keep his voice easy, "That guy they fished out. Had he been in long?"

"Not more'n a day or so. Them big ones come up fast." The blue eyes that looked down at him were curious-friendly. "We called the cops over from the mainland. They took him away."

Gunnar said to Devvy, "Who's your friend?"

"New hired man," Devvy said. "His name's Clint Farrell."

"Huh?" The glance became a stare. "Are you from the other side, Mister?"

"No."

"Yust wondered, that's all."

"Why?" Devvy's voice was calm, but her knee brushed Clint's, and he could feel it shaking. "What makes you ask, Gunnar?"

"Nothing." The trollerman shifted awkwardly. "Just somet'ing we heard on the radio from Seattle. The British Columbia cops are looking for a kid wit' some name like that."

"What for?" Devvy asked.

"Murder. Look, you know what I'm like wit' names, Devvy. Anyhow, my damn radio, it's hard to get anything straight on it... Buy me a new one when the fish start booming. No offense, Mister."

He touched the wheel to straighten the troller on her course, then said to Devvy. "Dance at the Cove Sat'day. Guess you wouldn't be interested, no?"

"Might be," Devvy said, "if I can get a new dress in time." Her smile, Clint thought, was a lot too sweet. "I'll leave word in town, eh?"

"Do that. I'd like fine to take you. How's it wit' that Peddar dude these days, kid? He leaving you alone?"

"I keep out of his way."

"He pesters you, tell me … And for God's sake, keep out of them narrows. You get caught in a boil or your engine quits, you'll find yourself roostin' on Paul Bunyan's Chair quick as that."

"Not me," Devvy told him with a certain pertness. "I'm careful, Gunnar. G'by."

"Come to that dance, Devvy." The trollerman showed horsy white teeth in a grin. "You'll make them Martinez girls look like a bunch of crows."

They putted on into the bay, leaving Gunnar to plod with his ten-line spread after salmon.

Clint said bitterly, "Thanks! I'll remember that when they're measuring me for a collar."

"What do you mean?"

"You know what I mean. You had to tell him my name."

"I had a good enough reason."

"What do you do now? Keep me around till the cops come for me?"

"I'll keep you around."

"You really do think I knocked off Aleko, eh?"

"You don't know you didn't. Neither do I." Her voice was so low he could hardly catch the words under the outboard's din. "Clint, I don't know what to think. I was wrong about you once. I could be on this."

"But you still want to keep me here."

"I have to. I'd sooner not, but you've got to stay. Believe me, I'll be glad to see you go."

Her voice wasn't impersonal now, as it had been all morning. She gave him a quick, direct look, searching his face, studying him with her small, weighing frown. "When you do go, you'd better head for the cities. You don't belong down here."

"You're telling me!" He wanted to hurt her, take his anger and bewilderment and the cold underlying fear out on her. "You know, you get around right smart for a country mouse. Joe Peddar, this Swenska boy, Paddy Burke, me—any more?"

"Plenty."

"You should have fun at your dance. Gunnar looked like a good joe. Maybe he'll get beat up. You'd like that."

"Who I go with is my business. But you're right. I'll have fun."

The skin was golden in the V of her open-throated white shirt. His lips had rested there, in the cool dark last night, and whatever else he forgot, he'd remember that always. He'd remember her sullen face with the high cheekbones, and her eyes, and her light hair pushed back from her temples by a morning breeze. The part of him that wasn't tough and wary and chip-on-shoulder would always be hungry for her, crying for her.

There was no glint of silver at her neck. She'd taken off the little silver totem.

THEY WERE PAST THE HAYFIELD and well in sight of the farmhouse when someone whistled behind them. Clint I turned and saw Paddy Burke pushing out of thick spirea brush at the edge of the woods.

The hired man called to him, "You enjoyed your fishing?" and Clint answered him with a glare.

Devvy said, "Has Lum Kee come yet?"

"He has been and gone. A man of parts, that one. We discoursed for an hour up yonder."

"I wish he'd stop coming here. Doctor Morse hasn't said anything, but I don't think he likes it."

"Indeed?" Paddy lit his pipe, studying her over the match. "You'll be going to town, I suppose."

"Yes. Unless you want chicken again tonight."

"And taking Clinton?"

"He's to finish the day with you."

"Take him. There's little help he can give me here yet, Devvy."

"He can come if he wants," Devvy said carelessly. She asked, "Anything new at the mill?"

"The parson has guests from the mainland expected on tomorrow's steamer, Lum Kee tells me. Mike Peddar has fought with his wife again and taken up residence at The Retreat. But here's my choicest morsel. You have a ghostly caller. Himself drove in from the highway not ten minutes past."

"Doctor Morse? What brings him around, Paddy?"

"Perhaps he hopes to catch Aila in a mood of Christian repentance. Well, I'll be off to my dog's work now."

"Push it all you can," Devvy said. "The moon's changing. We don't want the hay rained on, Paddy."

"I will do my best," Paddy said, and headed back, with his hat tipped over his eyes and his short-man's swagger, toward the hayfield.

They found Doctor Morse ankle-deep in the farm-house lawn, a small black figure with his shadow short behind him on the sunburned grass. He stood with feet apart and hands thrust into the pockets of his clerical jacket, his beard cocked upward as he eyed Devvy's tall hollyhocks.

As they came up the flagged walk, he turned and moved briskly to meet them. On his mild face, behind his steel-rimmed spectacles, distress was obvious.

He gave Clint a stiff little nod. "Devvy," he said, "forgive me, but I've had very disturbing news this morning. It concerns this lad here. I hope it may not too deeply concern you."

They waited. The parson said, "Did Mr. Farrell inform you he was not fishing alone? That he was in the position of deckhand for a Captain Johannsen?"

"He didn't mention it," Devvy lied calmly. She looked

at Clint. "What about that? Does it mean anything to you?"

She was stalling. She was warning him, giving him a chance. "It's like I told you yesterday," he said. "I don't remember."

Doctor Morse said, "You don't recall putting in at Martinez Cove for fresh water on the second Saturday of this month?"

"Nope."

The brown eyes behind the thick lenses blinked twice, rapidly, then steadied on his face. "You say you were injured in a fishing accident, Mr. Farrell."

"I got a bang on the head somewhere. I figured it was while we were trolling."

"We?"

Mistake. He'd fluffed that one. "Well, a big boat like that, it takes more than one man to fish her. I wouldn't have been by myself."

"You were not, my boy," Doctor Morse said. "As a matter of fact, you were with Captain Johannsen." He paused for a long moment, then said soberly, "Captain Johannsen's body was recovered off Fox Island late yesterday, Mr. Farrell. The announcement came over the radio this morning. He had ... well, met with foul play. I'll be quite blunt. They say he had been shot."

"I don't know anything about that. God damn it, you think I go around shooting people? I never even heard of the guy ..."

"Violent language won't help," Doctor Morse said in gentle reproof. Then to Devvy, "My dear, I don't wish to alarm you, but this is an ugly business, and there are certain facts you should know. This boy, and Captain Johannsen did put in at Martinez. You see, the captain is, or rather was, an acquaintance of mine. We met while I was engaged in mission work north on the British Columbia coast, and finding himself in these waters, he paid me a very welcome call. He was a rough man, but good-hearted, perhaps over-eager to show kindness to those in trouble. From him, I gathered that your … your friend here had been in difficulties with the police."

He paused again, and when he resumed, his agitation was even more plain. "Due to the state of the tide, I thought best to have Mike Peddar return Captain Johannsen to Martinez in the *Helene*. Joe was already at Martinez, attending a dance. We arrived in time to … to part Joe and this boy. They were fighting, I'm afraid over you, Devvy, although I'm sure you had no intention of provoking an incident. As I say, we separated them, that is, Captain Johannsen did. Mr. Farrell was then heard by myself and others to threaten his life."

"I *what?*"

"Your exact words were, 'I'll murder you.' They were accompanied by a push or blow. You were violently angry."

"Listen," Clint said; and there was no need of pretending to be mad now. "Holy Joe or not, you can't hand me that stuff! If all this happened, why didn't you bring it up last night? You didn't say anything about any Captain Johannsen then!"

"I presumed, naturally, that he was safe ashore." Doctor Morse stood stiffly, peering at them. His voice was sharper. "I did not know—I had no possible way of knowing—that Captain Johannsen was at that moment the prey of dogfish in Redoubt Pass, Mr. Farrell."

"All right, come out with it. You're saying I murdered this guy."

"My boy, I've already warned you of the danger of jumping to hasty conclusions. But this is no time to mince words." Doctor Morse said to Devvy, "We must look on him as a potential murderer at least. As such, I feel very strongly that the place for him is not here."

Clint said sullenly, "I'm not looking up any cops,

if that's what you're driving at. Not till I get it straight what happened to me out there."

"Last night, Mr. Farrell, I offered to help you. In spite of the ... the altered circumstances, my offer remains open. If you're sincere, if you actually are in an amnesiac condition, turning you over to the police at present would be an act of folly. What I do propose is that you place yourself in my custody, as it were."

He spoke kindly, persuasively. "Devvy, I'm sure you'll see the wisdom of that course, even if Mr. Farrell doesn't."

"I'm staying here," Clint said. "That's unless she wants to kick me out. When I remember I'll hunt up the cops myself."

Devvy said, "You'd better leave it at that, Doctor Morse. He can't get off the island, and you don't have to worry about me. I can take care of myself."

"I don't like it," the parson said. "You already have that Burke fellow hanging about your place. Really, now."

"That's the way it's going to be," Devvy said.

"You won't change your mind?"

"No."

Doctor Morse pulled a white handkerchief from his jacket sleeve and wiped his forehead. He had the look of a fussy little man completely baffled. "Fantastic," he muttered. "Quite fantastic!"

He turned, and scuttled rather than walked toward the station wagon parked in the lane.

They watched him go. Presently Devvy asked, "Did you say that, Clint? About murdering Aleko?"

Clint said, "I may have. I'm pretty sure I did. I was mad enough to slug him. Peddar was trying to get at me with a knife, and Aleko kept grabbing my arms. Sure I said I'd murder him! I could just as easy have said I'd kick him in the teeth. It was only mad talk. Nobody but a little dope like that one would take it seriously."

"The police would," Devvy said. "I think a jury would too." She was quiet, poking at a dandelion with her sandal toe, frowning down. "Doctor Morse isn't a little dope. He's kind, he's been good to me in lots of ways. Maybe I should have let him do what he wanted."

"It'd be a lot simpler if you'd just let me head out of here."

"No. Come on. We'd better eat if we're going to town."

PADDY HAD WASHED HIS LUNCH dishes and set them on the drainboard, but the breakfast accumulation was still piled in the sink. The children were playing upstairs—Clint heard their light voices, and the little boy's squealing laugh. Then a heavy stirring, and Aila calling to him, "'Ush up, you little devil."

"She's awake at least," Devvy said, tugging at a cupboard door. "She'll be down soon … swishing her train." The door banged open, and she added viciously, "If she thinks *I'll* do her washing up!"

"Doesn't she like her kids?"

"She's all right with Elsie when she's sober. She hates Brian."

"Why?"

"Because he was my father's," Devvy said. She was cracking eggs into the big black frying pan.

Clint said, "Look, not again!"

"You don't have to eat them." Her voice and her glance were entirely hostile. "Do you think I go into the Boss-Foreman for fun? We haven't anything else. Eat eggs or go hungry."

"You could cook them some other way, couldn't you? Boil 'em or scramble 'em or something?" He watched her, wanting perversely to rile her further. "If you don't know how, I'll show you."

That swung her around. "You can't show me any-thing. You're more helpless than anyone I ever saw. And you were scared this morning. You were scared stiff."

"Oh, was I?" He glowered back at her, and from the stairs a soft voice said, "Scared of what, my dear?"

Devvy snapped, "You mind your own business," and whipped back to the stove. Clint gave the woman a sur-prised, careful look.

He'd expected someone completely sluttish, a bag to go with the voice that had yammered at them in the half-light upstairs. But Aila, standing with one white hand on the banister, was very close to beauty. She was wearing bright red lipstick, but her full oval face was creamy white. Her smooth black hair was pulled to the nape of her neck and tied with a blue ribbon, and the checked housedress couldn't hide the shapeliness of her body. Her legs were smooth in Nylons, and she wore wedge-heeled sandals with braided black-and-white crossties that emphasized her high arches.

She came gracefully down into the kitchen and stood in the doorway, smiling at Clint like a sleek, complacent cat. Her blue eyes were long under the thin line of plucked eyebrows; Paddy, he remembered, had said something about Aila's eyes and Mary Queen of Scots'.

She said to him, "I wasn't myself last night. You'll forgive me—it's just that I'm still not used to having strange men around my house, and Devvy gave me no warning." He'd have sworn this wasn't the same woman. That other Aila's voice had been a strident whine. This one spoke with only the faintest of accents, and graciously as if he were a welcome guest. He studied her, saying nothing; in this brighter light he could see faint bitter lines on either side of the too-red full-lipped mouth.

Devvy brought the skillet to the table. She was white around the roots of her nose, and he knew she was fighting her temper, hanging onto herself grimly.

"Don't bother about me," Aila said. "I'll have my lunch later."

"I'm not bothering about you," Devvy told her curtly. "I'll expect those dishes, and these, washed before we get back."

"Oh. You're going to town?"

"I am."

"Like that?" There was a hint of laughter in the soft voice.

Needling her, Clint thought. Prodding her for a blow-up.

But it wasn't his show. He put his head down and ate fast, knowing that Aila watched him, lounging in the doorway. He heard the click of a lighter and smelled cigarette smoke. Turkish. You'd know she'd smoke those things.

The air in the kitchen was loaded. He was sorry for Devvy of a sudden, and he yearned to get up and go to her, take her out of this unequal battle.

He said, "Finished, Devvy?" and she gave him a quick nod.

She pushed her chair back and rolled down the legs of her jeans. "If you're ready," she said, and got up and crossed the kitchen. Her rifle stood in the door corner; she picked it up, and took a packsack from a wall hook behind the door.

"You know, Devvy"—and this time there was a suggestion of last night's whine under Aila's sleek-cat purr—"with decent clothes, and a haircut, of course, he'd be quite handsome. Really he would!" She laughed softly, and again it was a lazy purring sound. "You've treated poor Joe so horribly that I'd almost decided you were bound and determined to die an old maid. I'm glad you've found a boy you like at last."

Devvy said, "Clint, come on."

"Who knows?" Aila said lightly. "He might even

make a woman out of you, my sweet. If you give him a chance ... and buy yourself some proper clothes. Do you need money, Devvy? All you need do is ask me. If you'd only look on me as your mother ..."

"My mother wouldn't have stayed in the same room with you," Devvy flared at her. "And I won't either." She stepped swiftly past Clint; the knuckles of the hand that gripped the rifle were white.

At the bend in the lane beyond the farmhouse, Clint looked back. Aila lifted a hand in a gesture which even at this distance had something hateful and mocking about it.

He glanced sideways at Devvy. Her eyes had darkened almost to black, and her jaw was still set. Snap her out of it, give her something else to be mad at ...

"You ever wear skirts?" he asked. "Don't you get tired, going around playing tough like a tomboy all the time?"

"You shut up!" That had done it—she was sore at *him* now. Her chin was quivering, and she looked at him as if she'd gladly shoot him. "I don't want you to talk to me."

"Hell, I only asked. I thought maybe those were all the clothes you've got."

"Well, they aren't. When I work like a man I dress like one. Shut up!"

She wouldn't look at him, but walked on, straight and angry; and he knew, with his own pity and anger a hard lump in his throat, that she was lying.

A mile or so west of the farm, fir-log pillars lifted on either side of the lane ahead. Devvy waded through bracken to where an old survey post poked its tip above the young green. When she came back, she didn't have the rifle.

"Why?" Clint asked her.

"I don't carry guns into town. I'm not quite that

much of a tomboy." She settled her packsack with a vicious tug. "Look, Clint, I told you not to talk to me."

The lane passed between the log pillars—another of Callahan's ideas, Clint supposed—and opened into a graveled highway which ran south-to-north along the island. Most of the land was in open timber, but when they rounded the second curve, Clint saw a square, ugly box of a frame house with a peeling barn too close behind it. In black letters on the mailbox out front, he read, "Michael Peddar."

Devvy lengthened her stride; this would be the house where she'd lived while her father was overseas or in jail. He had a feeling that she longed to run past the gray house, that she didn't even want to look at it.

An odd, grim girl, Doctor Morse had called her. She was all of that. The guy she married would probably spend his lifetime trying to straighten the kinks out of her.

They'd been walking half an hour when a logging truck passed them and slowed. The driver leaned out of his cab and gave Devvy a gold-toothed grin under a rain-test hat once red but weathered now to pink. They ran for the truck. Devvy swung up to the cab and Clint jammed in beside her. He could feel her body tensing away from him, and he stared dourly through the windshield, watching the road unreel ahead. Trouble with her, she was too much like him, she'd been pushed around a lot. He might have made that up to her, made her forget plenty of things if the breaks had been different. No use kidding himself. It would have been good to stay here with her.

Presently he glimpsed blue water ahead, and saw the roofs of a town below. The driver slowed, flashing his gold dogteeth at Devvy.

She said, "Much obliged, 'Ric," and the driver said, "I'll be heading back for the claim around five. I'll watch for you, Devvy."

They scrambled out. The truck skinner turned into a side road, dust boiling behind his trailer.

"What's this place?" Clint asked.

"Halem," Devvy said. "Come on. We haven't much time if we want that lift."

There was more to the town than he'd expected. Its main street sprawled along the water front. He saw a steamer dock with a red-painted freight shed, trollers and small craft tied to the floats like ponies at a hitching rail, and a larger boat that looked like a Diesel ferry, moored alongside the dock.

At the head of the dock was a general store, a two-story frame building with a wide veranda, its white paint blistered by sunlight.

"You needn't come in," Devvy said. "Wait for me here."

"Mind if I look at the town?"

"If you can keep out of trouble for half an hour, go ahead."

He walked on along the street, scuffing dust with his broken shoes. There were half a dozen other stores, a garage with bright yellow pumps, and a bank on the corner across from it. Farther on, where the town began to peter out, was what looked like a hotel. The street was almost empty; the town seemed asleep and dreaming comfortably under the June sun.

Tide must be bucking hard through the Boss-Foreman. Even in Halem, miles away from the pass, you could hear its voice faintly in a steady snore. It came to Clint that since he'd landed on the island he'd never been entirely clear of that sound, day or night. It was the violent undertone to existence here, this mutter of tidewater gone crazy in the narrows.

Well, he'd be away from it soon. The ferry captain might let him work his passage across to the mainland. If he wouldn't, he'd find some other way to pull his freight.

Without expectation, he started to explore his pockets. He found a khaki handkerchief, never used, the store creases still in it. Nothing on his other hip or in his side pockets. But his fingers, poking under his belt into his watch pocket, touched a still-damp wad.

He worked it free, mildly interested but not letting his hopes rise.

Money, all right!

Carefully he opened the wad, smoothing the bills on his palm. King George the Sixth gazed up at him solemnly. Canadian bills. Four twenties, three tens and a five. He wondered if they'd accept Canadian money here.

It was his cut from the last three weeks of their fishing. He'd been a good old guy in his way. Aleko hadn't tried to clip him.

He stood in the shadow of a drugstore awning, shoulders leaned against a doorpost. The line of red in the thermometer on the opposite post registered eighty-four degrees; hot for June. Loafing there, thinking, he saw Devvy come out of the general store. Packsack sagging heavy on her shoulder, she crossed to the barber shop on the other side and went in. That should keep her out of circulation for twenty minutes anyway—he wondered if his needling about tomboys had anything to do with it, or whether she was just getting slicked up for the Saturday night dance.

He took his shoulders away from the post and went into the drugstore. There was a kid behind the counter—probably helped his old man run the place in the summer holidays. Clint asked him what time the ferry pulled out, and the boy gave him a chipper "Four o'clock, Mac."

A pleasant town. Nobody seemed to be worrying about a murderer on the loose. It was not quite twenty to four now, he saw by the clock on the end wall. Time enough.

He walked back to the big store above the dock. Its windows were cluttered with work clothes, mostly men's, but in a place like this they'd carry everything from needles to horse collars. He went in; he had the store to himself except for an old lady behind the far counter by the cash register. He felt shy now, and a little sheepish. He'd never done anything like this before.

Impatient with himself, he crossed between the high-piled counters. He said, "I want to buy some clothes for a girl. I'm not sure of her sizes, so maybe you'd help me." The storekeeper glanced at him sharply through rimless glasses. She was white-haired and she had a bony long face; she reminded him of a mathematics teacher he'd liked in first-year high, back home in Portland.

"I'll try to," she said. "If she's an island girl, I expect I'll know. What had she in mind?"

"Can't say, quite." He could feel his ears reddening. "Some kind of dress-up rig, I think. Something she could wear dancing."

"That doesn't give me very much to go on."

His courage was oozing fast. He said rather desperately, "Look, it's for Devvy Callahan. You know her, I guess."

"I should," the old lady told him dryly. "She's been buying here since she was no higher than this counter."

"Well, it's for her." He laid the four Canadian twenties on the counter. "I'd like to get her all I can for this. It'd be a big favor if you'd look after it. I don't know much about girls' clothes."

The sharp gray eyes were sifting him with a squirrel's curiosity. He could tell she was puzzled.

"I'm not sure I should do this, young man. It's—I've never been asked anything like this before. And I doubt if Devvy will like it. She's a very independent girl."

"Don't tell her," Clint said. "Just send the stuff out before Saturday, will you?" He said earnestly, "It's okay. There's no angle."

She studied him for a moment, and what she saw must have satisfied her.

"Very well." She turned briskly to her shelves. "It isn't my business, and it's time someone did something about Devvy Callahan, heaven knows. She's had nothing new this year. And a young girl should have a party dress."

"Thanks," Clint said. He added awkwardly, "I won't be around. Could I write her a note to go with it?"

He liked the old lady; she was opening boxes down at the far corner, carefully not watching him. He scowled over the writing tablet, chewing the pencil she'd given him. He knew what he wanted to tell Devvy—but how the hell to get it into words on paper? The wall clock said three fifty. He hadn't much time.

He wrote, "Like I told you, I'm trouble. That's why I'm pulling out. If I stick around you'll get hurt, Devvy, and I don't want that to happen. Here is something to wear to the dance Saturday night with Gunnar and make the Martinez girls look like crows." It wasn't all he wanted to say, not what he'd tell her if he could, but maybe she'd get the general idea.

"Last night meant a lot," he wrote. "I lied to you about that. Take care of yourself."

For a moment he studied the sheet, frowning with the pencil between his teeth. Then, slowly, he tore it up. He wadded the scraps in his hand, and went over to the upright heater, opened the firebox door and dropped them in. Better break clean.

The storekeeper was holding up a pleated tan skirt, inspecting it critically. She looked across as he latched the stove door, and he said, "There won't be any note," and headed for the street.

He'd get to the mainland okay. But the mainland cops would be watching for him, really after him this time; they'd grab him off for certain. Even if he remembered, even if he hadn't knocked off Aleko, he couldn't prove a thing. He'd be out of circulation for a long time—if he was lucky. Too long. It would be better for Devvy if she'd never towed the *Maiija* away from the Boss-Foreman's mouth. Sawing off like this was the next best thing.

She could think what she liked about the clothes. Chances were she'd be mad as blazes. But he hoped she'd keep them and wear them, if only to spite Aila.

On the hot street again, he saw that Devvy was still in the barber's chair with a striped cloth spread over her knees and tucked under her chin. Sitting like that, hair combed down, she looked like a sulky kid. He watched her for a minute, trying to memorize her face. Then the ferry whistle tooted below at the dock, and he turned sharp away.

He'd been with her less than two days, and he'd known her forever. She might go to the dance at Martinez with Joe Peddar, but he didn't think so, maybe because he didn't want to think so. He hoped if she went it would be with the sunburned trollerman with the fair hair and the sea-faded eyes. She could do worse than marry a guy like Gunnar. If she did, he'd be lucky; she'd ride a man hard, she'd be no meek wife to be shoved around. But she'd be worth it, Lord God, she'd be worth it!

He headed along the dock determinedly, not looking back. The ferry whistle cut loose with an impatient toot, and he stretched his pace to a trot.

A tall man stepped out of the freight shed and blocked his way.

Clint told him curtly, "Shove over," but the man didn't move. He looked to be in his middle thirties; his heavy face was somehow familiar. He wore suspenders over a blue cotton shirt. Clipped to the left strap was a badge.

"Easy, kid," he said. "You're not going anywhere."

Clint said, "You can't keep me. I haven't done anything."

"No? Maybe not. But stick around, son. There's some talk about a kid came in on a gas boat. Needs investigating. Boat may have been stolen."

"You mail-order cop," Clint snapped at him. "There's no law says you can hand me that!"

"There's a law says I can jug you on a holding charge, son. I don't want the bother, so don't get fresh with me. Understand?"

He could do it, too, the bum, the tanktown flatfoot! Clint bit back his rage, caution wide awake now and whispering to him again.

Careful, he told himself. The cop, town constable or sheriff's deputy or whatever he was, had been waiting for him down here like a cat at a mousehole. He hadn't asked him his name, which meant he already knew it. And he hadn't said anything about a Canadian warrant, and he'd know about that too. Then why hadn't he pinched him?

By the look of him, he belonged to the Peddar tribe. All Clint could be sure of was that it added up to more trouble. Anyway, there was no percentage in arguing it further. The ferry had hauled out, green water showed between her side and the dock now.

"Okay," he said. "Is there any law says I can't go up for a beer?"

"How old are you?"

"Twenty-two," Clint said.

"You're a liar," the constable told him. "All right— go ahead. But remember, don't try to get off the island."

So HE WAS STUCK HERE, caught like a salmon in a gill net. Even in reform school he'd never known quite this sensation of being helplessly box trapped. Devvy couldn't have kept him on the island. With warrants out for him anyway, nothing she could have said or done would have made much difference.

Unless, of course, she'd tipped off this country cop with the Peddar face. That possibility he shoved aside at once. She hadn't had a chance, for one thing. For another, he couldn't imagine her doing it. She knew more about this whole ugly and obscure business than she'd let on to him, but she wasn't part of it, he was sure of that.

Caught on the edge, perhaps; but he was at the center, trapped like the boom stick in the Boss-Foreman whirlpool. He guessed now that the Chinaman off the steamer had gone the same way as Aleko; and ever since he'd seen the green ring on Joe Peddar's finger, he'd had his own idea about that part of the affair.

It was just an idea, though. The whole thing continued to baffle him, and the knowledge that the solution lay with him, buried inside him, was no help. It was like fighting the tide of the pass. There must be a course somewhere among the treacherous boils and surges, but this far it had eluded him.

There was Paddy Burke too, the night-walking man, and there was Aila. Somewhere and somehow, those two meshed into the pattern.

Head down, he trudged along the landing. He felt foolish now as well as mad and bewildered. But it was a big island, the cop couldn't be everywhere. Hell, there was one way he could get off if others failed.

No sign of Devvy yet. The barber must be giving her the works. He walked on up the street toward the hotel.

Even this early in the summer, its front lawn was baked brown. A sign dangling by chains from a gallows rig beside the graveled court read, "The Plaza." Underneath in smaller letters it said, "Dinners and light lunches. Beer. C. Jukes, Proprietor."

Nothing to do now but wait for Devvy, and he might as well finish his thinking away from the heat. A beer would go good.

The tavern had the same beat-up look as the rest of the hotel, but it was dim and cool, and the scuffed red-leather chairs looked comfortable, right for loafing on a day like this. The vague old man didn't look twice at the Canadian five spot, but gave him cigarettes and change, and lifted a bottle out of the icebox.

He asked, "New here, son?"

"Working down the line." He never liked being called "son." The word stood for a relationship he'd a lot sooner forget. But there was something he might as well make sure of. He said, "I was talking with the town cop. Didn't get his name. Would it be Peddar?"

"No. Johnny Beamish. He's a Peddar, though, on his ma's side." The old man leaned his elbows on his bar and settled down to talk. Weekday afternoons, he wouldn't get many customers. "Used to be a pretty good fella, Johnny."

"What happened to him?"

"Got tangled up with a loose woman. Watch out for that, son. Raises hell with a man quicker'n anything else."

"Island girl?"

"Foreigner, and no girl. Don't ask me her name 'cause I won't tell you. I don't trade in gossip."

Hell you don't, Clint thought. He said, "Seems to me I heard about that. Some widow from up-island?"

The old man said, "Widows is the worst," and Clint knew that hunch at least had been right.

"Those Peddars," he said, pouring beer into his glass. "How many of them are there in these parts?"

"Son," the hotelman told him, "there was fourteen hund'erd people on the island last census. I'd say a third of 'em are hooked up with the Peddars by marriage or one way or another."

"Enough to run the show, eh?"

The old man's Adam's apple climbed his withered throat. He muttered with a bare moving of his lips, "Speak of the devil."

Clint turned, bottle in one hand, glass in the other. The screen door latch clicked, and Joe Peddar stood, watching them with his lazy grin.

Joe said, "Break out another, Charley."

Clint walked over to a corner table by the fly-specked front window. This wasn't the time for a showdown, his caution warned him, nor the place.

He lit a cigarette. Joe got his beer and brought it across. For a man who'd weigh close to two hundred, he moved lightly, even if he did toe in like a Siwash. He had shaved since morning. In tan sport shirt and green slacks he looked less like a yokel, a Snerd Corners tough boy. No use writing him off as just a backwoods slugger; if he was right about the ring, Joe Peddar was a tougher proposition than that.

Joe hooked another chair over with his foot. He sat down, and took a leisurely pull at his beer. He said, "Thought maybe I'd find you here."

"You were looking for me?"

"Kind of. I'm curious. I'm wondering what goes on at Callahans' to keep two hired hands busy. Didn't used to be work for more'n one man there."

Clint said nothing. He could bend a bottle over Peddar's head if he started anything, but there was no percentage in that, not if it meant being tossed into a hick jail by a relative who packed a badge.

"The way I look at it," Joe said, "you've kind of moved in on my territory. I don't like that. I want you to keep clear of Devvy Callahan."

"She's my boss," Clint said. "She told you so herself, remember?"

"Uh huh. You always buy clothes for your boss?"

He didn't think for a minute the old lady would have told Peddar. The guy must have been tagging him, just as he'd tagged them at Martinez.

"Get around, don't you?" he said.

"I can see through a store window well as the next. Or maybe you were buying a skirt for yourself?"

"Maybe you were wrong," Clint said. "Maybe she isn't your territory. Ever think of that?" He stared hard into the pale eyes; it was strange to be sitting here as friends sit with someone out of the fog, one of those who had tried to keep him there, and who still might kill him.

The thought, piercing his cold anger, shook him. He said, "Smarten up. I don't like to work the same punk over twice."

Peddar said, "I didn't look you up for that, Farrell. Doc Morse sent me in with a message. He wants to know if you've thought over what he told you this morning. He says if it's the job you're worried about, he can give you work at The Retreat for a spell."

"What kind of work?"

"On the *Helene*."

"I thought your uncle owned her."

"He does. But it's okay with Mike. Tourist season's just starting. We'll need another hand."

"When you go back, tell them what they can do with their job."

They stared at each other across the table. The old hotelman was fussing nervously with a tray of glasses behind his bar. Peddar's face was yellow under his tan. He said thickly, almost pleadingly, "Get it straight. She's my girl. We've had our fights, sure, but she's always kicked around with me. Leave her alone. Get off the island, Farrell. I'll help you get off."

"And if I don't?"

"You won't be the first I've stopped."

"I like my job," Clint said. "I think I'll keep it."

He finished his beer and got up, still staring into the pale eyes. "I don't scare, and she's not your territory. Get in my way, or hers, and you get hurt."

The hotelman gave him a scared look as he passed the bar. "You better git," he muttered, "and keep going!"

At the general store, he found Devvy sitting on the steps with the packsack beside her. She'd had a shampoo or some such as well as a trim; her hair shone in the late afternoon light.

She said crossly, "You took your time. What have you been up to?"

"I had a beer with one of your friends. The big blond. He's in town, in case you didn't know."

"I saw the station wagon from The Retreat. You'd better keep away from Joe." She said, "I was looking for you—I wanted you to get a haircut."

"Yes, Mama. Shall I get it now?"

"We haven't time. I'll have Paddy do you with the horse clippers tonight."

"That'll be fun," Clint said. He wanted to grin at her, change the fierce look to a smile. Too bad he wasn't going to be around when she got her party dress. He'd like to see her face then.

The packsack was heavy, and he grunted as he hiked it into place on his shoulder. They left the town, trudging up the long dusty hill that climbed south toward where the logging side road hit the highway.

No sign of the truck when they got there. Clint dropped the packsack and sat on it. Devvy stood over him, poking at the dust with her toe.

"What did Joe want?" she asked after a while.

"Wanted me to keep away from you, told me you were his girl. How'd he know we'd come in?"

"He'd find out from Aila. I think he pays her to spy on me. Anyway, she keeps getting money from somewhere."

"Joe said something else. Told me Doctor Morse has fixed a job for me. How do you add that up?"

"I don't. Did you take it?"

"Nope. I like working for you. It keeps me on my toes." She was worried; it was strange how he could sense her moods.

She said, "Joe will be along soon."

Clint passed her his cigarettes. She hesitated, then took one. She didn't ask where he'd got the money, and he didn't tell her. They were smoking, not talking to each other, when the station wagon boomed over the crest of the hill. Joe Peddar didn't slow or even look at them. Devvy frowned after him through the roiled dust.

"Just what did you say to him?" she asked. "I don't like that. Something's happened or he'd have offered us a lift. Me anyway."

"You want him to give you a lift?"

"I don't like being brawled over. Keep out of my affairs, will you?"

"I'll try to. But they're hard to duck."

It was another quarter-hour before the logger in the pink rain-test hat ground his truck out of the side road. Devvy was still worried; Clint could feel it in her as she sat stiffly beside him, watching the highway ahead.

At the fir-log pillars that marked the entrance to the farm road, Clint hefted the packsack out of the cab. Devvy's tenseness had got into him now, and he walked softly, eyes and ears alert. As they neared the bend above the survey post where she'd cached her rifle, Clint offered her another cigarette, but she said, "No."

Then, frowning, "There wasn't any dust on the highway ahead of us. It wouldn't settle that soon. I don't think he went on to the mill."

"Who cares?" Clint spoke with an offhandedness he didn't feel. "Come on."

They walked around the bend. Beside him, Devvy

drew a sharp breath. A couple of hundred feet on, the dusty station wagon was parked in the bracken.

This was it.

He took a last drag at his cigarette and trod it into the lane. He was scared as he'd always been before a fight; there was the familiar tingle along his arms and shoulders and the hollowness in his stomach. Now, when it was too late, he wished he'd jammed Peddar into a showdown back there at Halem after all, even if he'd landed in their calaboose.

He glanced down at Devvy. Scared too—it bleached the tan of her cheeks and widened her eyes.

She said, "Go back, Clint. I went around with another boy for a while. He beat him up terribly. He—I don't know what he did to him."

"I'm not another boy," Clint said. "Look, you know what this monkey's got on his mind. Don't hang around." He slipped the packsack strap to the edge of his shoulder where he could be rid of it in a hurry. They walked on, slowly, toward the station wagon.

Joe opened the door and climbed out, taking his time. It was very quiet. Clint could hear the wind in the trees, and the Boss-Foreman talking far away, and the light scuffing of Devvy's sandals on the road. He said to her, not looking at her, "Go on. Do as I tell you. Beat it."

Joe walked toward them. He moved with the lazy deliberation of a cougar . . . and he was big, too damned big.

He said to Devvy, "No gun, sweetheart?"

Clint shucked the packsack. He didn't wait for Peddar but went in fast with his hands low. He faded with his right, short to Peddar's jaw, and rammed his left under the big guy's ribs. Peddar's mouth flew open and for an instant there was only complete astonishment on his face. Clint nailed him again, right and left smashes under the ribs before Peddar's hands could come down. His jaw was wide open, the dope didn't even know how to take care of himself. Clint jabbed his head back, stepped in on the balls of his feet, and uncorked his left.

He felt that one jar home from knuckles to heels, solid and good, with a *whunk!* like a butcher's cleaver coming down on a slab of meat. Joe went back three steps, then buckled as if someone had kicked him behind the knees.

He was bleeding at both corners of his mouth, but he got slowly to one knee. He shook his straight yellow hair back, and spat blood, then he came in with a shambling rush.

Clint pivoted away and chopped him hard on the side of the neck as he blundered by. He caught Peddar turning, and flattened his nose, and heard the blood-strangled grunt as Joe rushed him again. He'd been fighting all his life. He wasn't helpless now, he was working coldly at a business he understood.

They were off the road, and he was drifting back with slick madrona leaves under his shoes. Joe staggered. Clint slugged him twice, good eye and mouth, cutting his knuckles, not caring. Peddar would be something less than handsome when this was over.

He was licked, he couldn't take much more of that. Clint stepped in with both hands working, and his left foot skidded on leaves, and on the instant Peddar was upon him, whipping both long arms around him. They went down together.

Clint drove with both fists, but he couldn't break loose. Peddar's free hand was clawing for his eyes. He should have kept away, chopped him up, never given him a chance to clinch; he knew now, too late again, that he'd played it wrong.

He strained his head back, but the hooked fingers kept coming for his eyes. All his strength in it, he lunged sideways, but Peddar rolled with him.

Keep rolling, he thought flashingly, don't let him pin you!

He got a knee up as they rolled and drove it hard into Peddar's belly. That broke him clear, but while he was still on his knees, Peddar was on top of him again in a sobbing, scrambling dive. Blood from his mashed nose was a bubbling froth on his mouth. Clint cracked him twice in the throat, but kneeling, he couldn't get the power into it, and Peddar toppled him, pinning his arms as they went backward. His head smacked against the madrona trunk, and the strength was draining out of him, and Peddar's weight was a mountain on his chest.

Blood trickled off Joe's chin. His other eye was swelling shut, but his face was twisted into a blubbery grin.

He muttered, "You got away last time. Not now, you don't!"

He reached back to his haunch, and his fist came forward with something black in it. Clint heard a snick and saw the shine of steel. The slip knife. The fist came down and he snapped at it, feeling his teeth sink in. Peddar wrenched free. The hand with the knife was coming down again, inching down, the contorted grin and the pale eyes behind it, inhuman between their ridges of puffed and darkening flesh.

He heard, through the fog in his brain, a spiteful crack not much louder than a twig snapping. Peddar's fist opened, the fingers spreading and stiffening. The knife dropped among the golden leaves.

There was a tiny, far-off double click, and he heard Devvy's voice in a toneless whisper.

"Get off him. I'll put the next one through your head."

The weight shifted.

Devvy whispered again, "Get off, Joe," and he saw the worn brown steel of the rifle muzzle a foot from Peddar's temple. It held there unwavering.

He could breathe again now, and the fury and fear in him were better than strength. He writhed sideways, throwing Peddar clear, and bounced to his feet. Joe stood clutching his right wrist. Blood seeped through his fingers. Devvy faced him with her rifle cocked and halfway to her shoulder.

Clint lurched past her and slugged Peddar again, right and left in the face, no science in it but only the black and bitter killing rage. Joe turned and stumbled toward the station wagon.

"Let him go," Devvy said. "Clint, come back!"

"I'll kill the bastard."

"Clint!"

Her voice cut through to him and he stood glaring and shaking while Joe staggered across the lane to the car. He thought for a moment the big yellow-haired guy would pass out over the wheel. Then Peddar tramped on the starter and fumbled the wagon into gear, and reversed it crashing into the brush. Clint didn't know whether he was trying to run them down or not; but he yanked Devvy back by the shoulder, and a fender scraped past him. He saw Joe's face, a pulped and bloody mask, as the station wagon jolted back into the ruts.

With a savage triumph he thought, Mine. I did that much to him!

The car roared out toward the highway, and he wobbled off into the woods and threw up.

He felt better after that. Something was wrong with his left arm and shoulder, the back of his head was numb, and his knuckles were raw. Nothing broken or sprained, though; he'd come out of it a damned sight better than he deserved. He scooped the slip knife off the leaves and turned it over in his hand. The blade was whetted and thin, five inches long at least. He wondered where he'd have taken it, and shuddered, and flung it violently off his hand into the deep brush.

Devvy still stood where he'd left her on the road. There was no color in her face, and tears ran out of her eyes and down her cheeks. Gently he took the rifle from

131

her and lowered the hammer.

"I shot him," she whispered. "I had to. He was going to kill you."

"Devvy," he said. He put his hand on her shoulder and shook her, gently at first, then harder. "Devvy, come on. We'll go on home."

She looked up at him then, and the shock drained out of her face. She said, "I couldn't find the rifle. I never thought I'd get back in time. Did he hurt you much, Clint?"

"Mauled me around some. I'm okay."

He lit two cigarettes from his crushed pack, and they sat together among the bright brittle leaves.

Clint said, "He was a lot tougher than I thought."

She turned her head, studying him in faint surprise. "You almost licked him."

"Almost," Clint said. He hurt like hell now, from his ankles to the back of his head. But there was a lightness in him, a cockiness that wouldn't be suppressed. "I'll take him next time, Devvy."

Her shoulders twitched. She said, "There won't be a next time. If I'd had to kill him …"

Clint said swiftly, "Forget it. You just put a slug through his arm. Don't think about it any more."

He should be dead. He was alive, able to watch the smoke from their cigarettes lifting into the quiet air, to listen to the shuttling drone of hummingbirds in the glossy leaves above, and the distant mutter of the Boss-Foreman through its pass. This was the second time he'd been lucky. He knew suddenly that he was very close to remembering that other meeting in the fog. His mind was on the edge of it, peering over, and soon the fog would lift. Only the fear wasn't there to pounce on him and drag him down now. It was gone; and he knew with a curious certainty that it would not return.

Devvy said, "You could have gone back. You didn't have to fight him."

132

"Yes I did. He burned the troller and there's other things he's done. I'd have tangled with him sooner or later."

She was quiet, looking down at her hands, thin and brown on the knees of her faded jeans. Her hair smelled nice; it was smoother, and whatever the barber'd put on it had lightened it. He thought what it would be like under his cheek, and put that sudden hunger away. Nothing was different, nothing was settled. He still knew what he had to do.

"I didn't know you'd gone for the rifle," he said.

She said, "Let's go home." Her shoulders twitched again. "There's blood here, on the leaves." She got up and walked across the lane to where he'd tumbled the packsack.

"Let me," Clint said. It wasn't his blood; he didn't want to move away from this quiet place with its filtered sunshine and dry madrona music overhead, but he'd better start walking or he'd be plenty stiff tomorrow.

"No. You're hurt."

She was frowning, thinking again. In the mile to the farmhouse they had little to say. Once Devvy told him, "You aren't as helpless as I thought. But you like trouble. You thrive on it."

"Trouble likes me," Clint said. "I told you that, Devvy." The timber opened, the gate was dead ahead. Out of a ten-minute silence, Clint said abruptly, "You still think I dreamed up that ring?"

"I saw it too," Devvy said. "On his left hand, just before I shot him."

SHE LEFT HIM on the other side of the gate and walked on toward the house, lugging her packsack. He was tired now—bone-weary and aching. The big guy had given him his lumps all right, more so than he'd thought at first. But one thing sure: Peddar wouldn't be taking that face to any dance on Saturday night.

He limped on down to the barn. Paddy Burke was whistling inside, but he stopped now, and called, "Is it you, Clinton?"

He came to the doorway of a little room partitioned off from the main barn, and stood there staring.

"Holy Mother!" he said. "Has she taken a club to you at last?"

"We ran into Joe Peddar."

"He licked you, of course... No, begad, if he'd done that, I doubt you'd come strutting home on your own two feet with that chest on you."

"Strutting, hell! Sure he licked me. I let him grab me and he pulled a knife."

No use to say anything about the shooting. He supposed word of that would get around soon enough through Aila, if Devvy didn't tell Paddy herself.

"*Cherchez la femme*, as the French say. It was over Devvy, I take it."

"I thought so at first. Partly that, I guess. But there was more to it than just a punk with a girl on his mind."

The bright black eyes were searching his face. "What more was there to it?"

He liked Paddy, but he wasn't sure of him. There'd been that whistling in the dark woods down by the basin, and there were other things, too many of them, that didn't jibe. Better play it safe.

"I don't know," he said. "Got any soap, Paddy? I'll get cleaned up."

"He outweighs you by forty pounds," Paddy said reflectively. "You have shoulders on you, though, and a certain something in your walk. Yes, and a name that will work for you, if you let it. It is a name of fourteen units, d'you see, seven in the first or Christian name ..."

"Don't start on me with that," Clint told him testily.

"I asked had you any soap."

Paddy sighed. "Soap and welcome," he said. "I've revised my estimate of you, Clinton. I had you pegged for a carnal-minded gamecock at the very least. When you're washed I'll look you over. I'm a good hand with a sick creature."

Clint went out to the pump with Paddy's soap, and Paddy's towel pulled through his belt. They must have a deep well here—the water was icy, and it felt good on his back and aching head. The kitchen door was open and he could see Devvy's fair hair and white shirt, and the top of Brian's head where he stood close by her at the stove. He soaped down and rinsed off, and trailed back to the barn carrying his shirt and Paddy's towel.

"Step into my parlor," Paddy said, and Clint followed him into his box of a room.

Harness, much-mended but with its brasswork well-shined, dangled from nails in the whitewashed plank walls. A camp cot with gray army blankets stood alongside the end wall. One pair of greased work boots and another of black oxfords were laid out at the foot of the cot as if for inspection. There was a toothbrush between two nails, and on the shelf above, a glass and a neat row of books. Over the shelf, a hunting rifle rested on wooden pegs. It was a bolt action job, fitted with mounts for a telescope sight, its steel beautifully blued, its forearm and pistol grip diamond-checked. The room carried a pleasant smell of saddle soap and metal polish; its atmosphere was vaguely military.

"The light harness there," Paddy said. "The set with the noseroll. It was bought when Callahan decided to bring trotting horses to the island. There is a sulky some-where about, with a wheel stove in."

"Was the gun his too?" Clint asked.

"It was. He would not hunt with a thirty-thirty, the weapon of the land, but must have a Springfield Sporter with a stock of black walnut and a butt-plate of African buffalo horn. A king's ransom it cost him, but it's a marvel of a piece, Clinton. I've had it down to the bluffs in the scraps of free time she allows me, and I've brought judgment to hair seals at three hundred yards."

"Two hundred," Clint said.

"A measured three hundred, and through the head." Paddy's voice was muffled as he delved and groped beneath his cot. "It's this way with the seal, Clinton. A brain shot and he floats. Wound him just, and down he will go. We're different, us humans. A wounded man will float and fight while the life's in him."

"You talk as if you knew."

"Why, I've had a deal to do with firearms," Paddy said, and straightened with a bottle in his fist.

Clint asked, "What happened to Callahan, anyhow?"

"He was drowned in the parson's employ," Paddy told him. "Sit there."

Clint lowered himself stiffly to the edge of the cot, and lit a cigarette. The sunburned little man began to poke and prod with fingers that seemed to know what they were about. Clint winced as they explored the back of his head.

"New bumps and old," Paddy said. "Your noggin has the look of a Donegal murphy. It is no wonder your wits are scrambled, Clinton. Here's a fresh one, a beauty. A touch of liniment …"

It stung fiercely on his cut scalp, and Clint jumped and swore. He said, "You'd better keep that for the horses."

"It is horse liniment, right enough," Paddy told him. "A recommended brand." He was busy again, fingers knowingly occupied around Clint's shoulders. "Your collarbone is sound. I was doubtful, Clinton … There was a knife in it, eh?"

"There was. It's in the bushes now."

"You might have fetched it along. I could use a good knife."

"This was a fighting rig. I saw all I wanted of it."

"Um-hmm. Steady now." He slapped hard on top of Clint's left shoulder, and the persistent numbness lifted in a tingle. "What's the word from town?"

"Didn't hear any. I ran into one of Joe Peddar's relations down by the ferry. The local cop."

"Indeed so. Down by the ferry, you say."

"Yes. He turned me back, damn him."

"You were leaving us, Clinton?"

"Sure. Why not?"

"Why?"

"The boss has enough to worry her."

"She likes to worry. It's a habit she formed with her father, wondering which way he would next be jumping. Constable Beamish turned you back?"

"You know him, eh? Yés, he flashed a badge on me. Told me not to leave the island."

"He was within the law. I would do the same myself, if I were in his place. You're a suspicious character, Clinton."

Paddy had given over his massaging and stood now looking down with his pipe in his hand. "There's some talk of murder, the old Chinaman from the mill told me today."

"That's all it is. Just talk. I haven't killed anyone, Paddy."

"No … I think not. I would say from your knuckles, though, that you've half-killed Joe Peddar. It's as well for her sake up yonder you did. Maybe for your own too."

"What do you mean?"

"Begob, I'm not entirely sure myself. You puzzle me. Your status keeps changing, Clinton. How does it stand now?"

Clint grinned up at him. "Why don't you ask Devvy?"

"Do your own asking," Paddy told him. "There. I'm through with you, Clinton. You're a mended horse. Put on your shirt or what's left of it, and we'll go up for supper. There will be meat tonight, praise God."

"I'll kill a smoke here first," Clint said. "I need time to get over your treatment. She be sore if you asked her to save me something?"

"She will storm at you and upbraid me, and save it," Paddy said. His voice was suddenly, oddly kind. "She's told me of your trouble. I've seen men so taken before, in war, or when they are clean worn down by worry and hard lying. It passes. You did damned well by the blonde Electra today, Clinton."

"Come again?"

"Sometime, read a book," Paddy said. "It will improve such mind as you have."

He put the pipe in his shirt pocket and, humming softly, ducked out of the room. The barn was dim with evening, and Clint sat smoking, thinking over this cock-eyed day. He tried to recall when he'd last been praised, and couldn't; it was a good feeling, and he smiled, happy and sad together. He'd like to stay.

The thought was dangerous. He got up and walked to Paddy's bookshelf. Shakespeare. Something by a writer called Yeats. He pulled that one out, and it was poetry. Hand raised to slide the book back, he caught the shine of metal. He reached to the rear of the shelf and brought out a clip of cartridges. The clip was not for the hunting rifle on the wall, but for a .45 automatic, and it was fully loaded.

Clint weighed the clip in his hand, thinking hard, getting nowhere. Then, carefully, he slipped it back and replaced the book. He liked Paddy, but he'd had hunches go sour on him before. Ten minutes ago, he'd known what he had to do ... now, though, he was less sure. Maybe Devvy was a little closer to the dangerous vortex of this business than he'd imagined.

They were almost through supper when he came

into the kitchen. The children were there, Brian with a scratched nose from a day of woods ranging, and a bib tied under his round chin. His tongue went out at once in amiable salute.

No Aila. Clint said to Devvy, "Where's the duchess?" Paddy answered him. "On the town again. She left here a lady, and she will come back a—something else."

"You shouldn't talk like that in front of them," Devvy told him sharply. "Clint, you can get your own plate. It's in the oven."

Steak tonight. He tackled it hungrily, knowing she was watching him. After a while she said, "Well? Is anything wrong with it?"

"Way I feel," he said, "I could eat shoe leather."

She burned him with a look, and Paddy said, "There is no gratitude in the boy. It's a fine dinner, Devvy, and we'll wash up for you between us."

Devvy went out when they'd finished eating. Elsie took Brian squalling upstairs to bed, and Paddy began to clear the table.

"Where's she off to?" Clint asked.

"A place she has for brooding. I've learned what that look means. It is not a place for one to be alone." Paddy reached under the sink for the dishpan. "There is a trail past the head of the basin. It goes east over the bluffs. The walk would limber you up, Clinton."

"You go after her if you want."

"I've another errand tonight."

"Okay. But she'll just run me off."

"A chance you must take. I don't want her alone up yonder."

"If you mean Peddar, forget it. He's taken care of."

"Half taken care of, only. Remember that. Now, will you go?"

"What about the dishes?"

"Get out and leave me to them. She has me well house-broken."

❖

THE WOODS BEHIND the pasture were dim with dusk, but when he came out at the head of the basin, the moon was riding. Tide had backed into the creek so that he had to cast well upstream for a shallows. He waded and worked south along the other side till he picked up the black-earth trail again. It was a stiff climb, his lungs were laboring when at last the woods thinned and earth gave place to rock under his feet.

Abruptly, the timber fell away. He was close below the crest. The mutter of the Boss-Foreman, which had deepened as he climbed, swelled now to a roar. He toiled up the last hundred feet. No sign of Devvy.

He stood on the knob of a rock promontory bald except for one big old madrona, last of the trees. The moon was just off the full; moonlight sprayed through the branches to lay a bewildering pattern of light and shadow on the rock. The narrows were below.

Even here, with solid rock beneath him, he knew a quick unease, a sense of insecurity that had nothing to do with reason. It came from the Boss-Foreman down there, battering at the rock, a mad salt-water river tumbling and boiling through its gut between the island masses. The tide was running strong tonight; there was a feeling of unleashed power, of madness and speed.

Cautiously, he moved to the lip where the rock pitched over. His stomach tightened. He knew where he was now—on the prow of the wing-dam point that shoved into the Boss-Foreman at the bend.

Below, hundreds of feet below, was the whirl that had sucked the boom stick down by its butt that morning. Its steep-sloping walls were smooth, and they gleamed a polished black under the moon. There was no spray, no breakers; but you could drop a city block with its houses into that dizzily spinning hole in the narrows.

Beyond the whirl, north of it, two rock teeth jutted out of the run of the tide a little to port of center, ripping the narrows to foam. They leaned close together. The tide boiled between them, lashed at them and battered them, assaulting them with a howl that never slackened or ceased. "You'd better not stand there too long."

Her voice came from behind and above. Clint turned away from the edge, the cold hand loosing its clutch on his midriff. He peered up. She was sitting on the lowest limb of the big madrona, her back to its twisted trunk.

He said, "This is a hell of a place."

"Is it? I like it."

"You would." He tilted his head back, one hand against the smooth bark. "I come up?"

"No. And I don't like being followed."

"It wasn't my idea. Paddy sent me."

"Why?"

"Seems I'm your bodyguard or something."

"He needn't have bothered. I've got my rifle."

He was tired of squabbling with her; he said, "I'd hate to pile up on that reef in the middle."

"A survey ship did once," Devvy said. "She was a hundred and ninety feet long. The ebb pulled her off into the whirl."

"What happened to the crew?"

"They took to the boats at slack water while she was still on The Chair. Two men got clear. They couldn't tell how they did it and no one else ever found out for sure."

"Paddy told me your father swam it."

"He did. Farther up, though, one high-water slack. It nearly drowned him."

"Why'd he pull a fool stunt like that?"

"Joe's father bet him he couldn't."

"I didn't know that guy had a father."

She glanced down at him, moon spray silver on her face. "He hasn't. He's dead."

"What was he, another rumrunner?"

"Yes. He got shot in a hijacking."

"Nice crowd, those Peddars."

"Most of them are all right. Joe might have been if he'd had a chance."

"Nuts!" Clint told her. "Look, come down or I'm coming up. All you need is a banana in your fist."

"I told you, I like it here."

"Are you coming down? After all, you've got the rifle."

She turned sideways on the thick limb, and jumped. He caught her, steadying her, and for a heady, dangerous moment she was inside his arms as she'd been in the long grass by the Martinez orchard.

She said quietly, "Let me go, Clint."

He stepped back. She moved out of the shadows to the bare, moon-bright rock, and sat there, arms wrapped around her knees.

She said, "I'm not mad at you any more. I shouldn't have been at all. You were honest enough with me."

"Too damned honest," he said.

"Maybe. I saw something in you at Martinez that wasn't there. You can dream up all kinds of things if you're lonely enough."

He stood over her, frowning down at her bent head. "Such as what?"

"You had your black-haired girl. I had a boy who was tough with everyone else, but not with me. You're just—tough."

"I can't help what I am, Devvy. Nobody can."

"I guess not. Joe can't, I know that now."

"Joe doesn't take much figuring. He was born a rat."

"Of course." She turned her head and glanced up at him. "Everything's plain black or white to you, isn't it, Clint? You can settle any trouble with your fists."

"Boy, if I could!"

"I'll tell you about Joe Peddar," she said. "His people

have been on the wrong side of the law since he was a baby. He saw his father shot to death when he was only a little boy. When we went to school in Halem the nice children weren't allowed to talk with him or play with him. His teachers were scared of him. He hadn't any friends but me. When he quit school he couldn't get any decent kind of job on the island, and when he went to Seattle to work, he got mixed up with a longshore gang and spent six months in jail. After that, he came back here."

She said soberly, "I still thought I could help him, but he was past that. He started going out on the *Helene* with Mike Peddar, running aliens."

"How old were you then?"

"Fourteen."

"Old enough for him to make passes, eh?"

"He'd started before. But he was different after he came back. He broke my arm that year, twisting it. The bone came through. You've seen the scar."

"Couldn't your father take care of him?"

"Dad was still overseas. I was living with them, in that three-story house north of my road. I told Mrs. Peddar I fell off a log. She knew I was lying but she was afraid of him too."

"But you kicked around with him. You hired him to work for you. You've just been making excuses for the guy."

"I didn't want to believe he was all bad," she said. "Even now, I can't. He's been part of my life ever since I can remember."

"You grew up alongside the Boss-Foreman," Clint said. "But hell, you don't go swimming in it."

He stood over her, thinking of Aleko and the China-man, remembering the slip knife and the killer's eyes behind it. "You're wrong," he said. "He's all bad."

"He isn't. There's that queer, mean streak in him that always frightened me. His father had it. Mike Peddar has it. But Joe might have kept it under if he'd been given a chance."

"Maybe." He hadn't thought of Joe like that before. Some ways, he and the yellow-haired guy weren't so very different. "But after today I'm not getting softhearted about him. You'd better not either, Devvy."

"I'm through with Joe," she said. "At least I hope I am."

"What's that mean?"

"I can't properly explain. If you were a girl you might understand it. Perhaps there's something rotten in me too. He's like the Boss-Foreman, pulling at me all the time."

"That doesn't make sense."

"No, I suppose not. I hate the Boss-Foreman, but I have to go into it. It's worse when things pile up on me. Even if we hadn't needed money I'd have gone in this morning. Did you know I was as scared as you were?"

"You didn't look it."

"But I was." She put her head on her arms; her voice was low and brooding. "I came up here one full-moon night after Dad was drowned. I stood on the edge and wondered what it would be like to jump off."

Maybe this was what Paddy had meant. He'd felt something of that dark pressure himself, looking down from the drop-off, the whirl dizzying him, the long howl of the tide numbing his brain.

"It was strange, Clint. Something wouldn't let me. I thought it was him."

"That noise could make you think anything." The cold of what she'd told him was still on him, making him gruff with her. "When you die, you die. People don't come back."

"I was half crazy. After—that—I sat in the tree and thought. That's when I decided to run the farm myself. Aila wants to sell it, but she can't."

144

"What's to stop her?"

"The papers are in my mother's name. She left it to me."

"Did your father ever get wise to Aila?"

"I don't think he knew what she was till he'd brought her here. Aila's a wonderful actress, I'll say that for her. You heard her being a lady today."

"You mean she can turn it off and on like a tap?"

"Yes. Dad was always being fooled by people. He married her the way he did everything else. He'd rush into things; he wasn't happy unless he was taking a risk. He fished in the Boss-Foreman with a rod and line for sport. Dad always meant to run the narrows in a rowboat—we spent days up here, studying the whirl. He told me it could be done."

"Aleko said it couldn't. I'd take his word for it."

"The two men off the survey ship did it. There's three or four minutes on some spring tides when the whirl flattens out. All kinds of things come up then. Old drift and broken logs and queer fish. We found one under the bluffs that looked like a baby sea serpent. Dad pickled it in rum and sent it to a museum. They couldn't tell him what it was."

"Was he drowned in the narrows?"

She was quiet for a moment, then she answered in her low voice, "No. Outside somewhere. He was lost off the *Helene* not long after Doctor Morse came here."

"But if he was such a good swimmer ..."

"They said he got a cramp. He went down before they could find him in the fog."

"Do you believe that?"

She pushed against the rock with her hands and got up in one swift movement. "You aren't to ask me." Her voice was frightened, suddenly, and wild. "All I know is what Doctor Morse told me."

"Do you believe it?"

She turned and started away from him, toward the timber, but he caught her in three quick strides and spun her around, shaking her, digging his fingers into her arms.

"You've got to tell me. All the time I've been here, you've held out on me. What's wrong with this layout anyway? What goes on?"

"I can't tell you!" Her hands were over her face, and she was shivering. "Clint, let me go!"

"What really happened to your father out there?"

Her voice was a broken whisper. "He was murdered." He took his hands away, not knowing what he could say to her. She was crying, and she told him shakily, "Now you know. If you want to help us, all of us, you've got to remember. It's the only thing I ever want from you."

"I'll remember," he said. "Soon, Devvy … Come on, let's get the hell out of this place."

She kept ahead of him, going down the moon-laced trail. They forded the tinkling shallow upcreek from the basin. On the other side, where the path widened, he caught up with her. He asked her, "Is Paddy Burke with them?"

"No."

"Then who is he? What is he, Devvy?"

"I can't tell you."

He said, "Okay. You don't have to. He's some kind of a cop."

She didn't speak, and he said, striding beside her, "He is, isn't he?"

"I promised not to tell."

"You didn't tell. I'd guessed it before. What about Doctor Morse?"

"I don't know. Even Paddy isn't sure about him. Clint, I can't take any more. Don't ask me … please."

They walked on; and his mind was working swiftly now, fitting the pieces together, leaping ahead of the little he knew. He said, "You couldn't have kept me here.

146

I was planning to lam out tomorrow. Pinch your boat or swim to Martinez if I had to, grab the steamer there. Now, I think I'll stick around."

He felt lighthearted and young again, as if a very heavy load had been lifted from him. Playing it noble was okay for an actor in a movie, but on a plain Joe it didn't sit so well. He said, "You still think you're going to that dance with the Swede?"

"Yes, if I go." She said quietly, "Don't try, Clint. It's no use. I'm over you, you took care of that this morning. When this is settled I want you to go away for good."

"What will you do?"

"Just what I have been doing. Run my farm. Plant my fruit trees. Marry Gunnar Lund or someone like him in a few years."

"Listen," he said. "Maybe I'm as bad as Peddar. But you're my girl. You have been since Martinez. You're going to stay my girl, Devvy."

"Am I?"

"Yes."

"You can't settle that with your fists," she said, and he reached for her, but she was away like a shadow into the moon-flooded timber. He glimpsed her once, running through a pool of moonlight, and called to her, but got no answer.

SHE HADN'T BEEN BLUFFING. If she'd been mad at him, had torched up and told him off, he'd have been sure she'd get over it. That mood he could handle; it was Devvy as she'd been toward him most of their time together. He could ride with her punches, give her back as good as he got, knowing it would be different once she was in his arms. But not this. He'd done too thorough a job.

Full of a loneliness more bleak than any he'd known

147

before, he walked slowly down the trail and across the wild pasture, between the tall fir snags that were monument to Callahan's gentleman farming.

Because of Devvy he'd been going to leave the island, and because of what she'd told him, up there on the rock point, he had washed that notion out. One thing she was right about, though: he had to bring the rest of it back, and quickly. But there was nothing he could do to hurry memory, no more than he could hurry the spring tide snoring through the Boss-Foreman.

He angled down toward the barn, wading waist-deep through fireweed. A white horse moved out with a sigh and a snort from a fence corner and watched him as he passed.

Anyway, his slant on Paddy hadn't been haywire. With what dope that tough little man must have, and what he himself knew, they might be able to piece the rest of the business together.

Clint grinned wryly. He'd never thought to see the day when he would go looking for a cop!

No light showed from the barn. But it was late, Paddy most likely in his cot and asleep by this time. He stepped quietly between the double doors, out of the moonlight, and stood listening for the sound of breathing from Paddy's room. If he had turned in, no point in waking him. Tomorrow morning would do as well.

He heard a gentle stirring and said softly, "Hey. You awake?"

At once the noise stopped. It could be anything—he'd slept in enough barns to know they were even worse than old houses for talking to themselves at night. But there'd been something furtive and purposeful about that rustle. He inched, hardly breathing, toward the doorway.

His eyes told him nothing, but the heavy perfume shouted who.

He said, "Looking for someone, Aila?"

She didn't move. "Yes," she said coolly. "For you."

She was sober, she was playing the lady tonight. She said, "I wasn't quite sure where I'd find you."

"But you thought I'd be here, eh?"

"Perhaps." She came toward him, deliberately, not scared or confused as he'd expected her to be. "There were two places. I tried the other first."

"A bum hunch."

"Really? After last night …"

"That was last night. What's on your mind, Aila?"

"You're rude, Clint. But I like it in you." She moved closer to him, and he could see the white oval of her face now, and knew she was smiling. "You were offered a job today. A good job. If I were you I'd take it."

"You mean on the *Helene?* I'm thinking it over."

"Doctor Morse is interested in you. He can do a great deal for you if you'll let him."

"Why's he interested in me, Aila?"

"He knows you're in serious trouble for one thing. He thinks he can help you out of it."

"I doubt it," Clint said. "What's the matter with the job I have?"

"It doesn't pay. And there's no future in it, Clint."

Her over-sweet perfume was heavy in his nostrils. She was almost touching him, smiling up with her long eyes and ripe mouth in the dark. He waited, touched by something sharper than dislike. There was something about the tall black-haired woman, drunk or sober, that chilled him.

He said, hands slack at his sides, "Suppose I take this other job? What's in it for me?"

"What do you think, Clint?"

He felt as he had when he balanced Joe Peddar's thin-bladed knife in his hand. It was the same cold instinctive revulsion.

"Nothing I want," he told her curtly. "Now, suppose you get out of here?"

149

"You're sure?"

"I never was surer, Mrs. Callahan."

"Too good for me, eh lad?" Her voice was soft, amused. She reached up, deliberately, and her nails slashed across his cheek.

"To remember me by," she said. "You'll 'ave other reasons, ducky."

She brushed past him out of the room, leaving him shaken and jangled as if he'd trodden barefoot on a snake.

He waited till he heard the kitchen door slam, then lit Paddy's coal oil lamp. The little steel mirror on its nail by the bookshelf showed him three parallel red weals from right cheekbone to jaw. He sat on the cot and lit a cigarette, and smoked it in deep drags, trying to kill the smell of her perfume. He was still tight inside as a fiddle-string; he'd never yet clipped a woman, but for the second time since he'd met Aila, he'd been very close to it.

He was still sitting there when Paddy tramped in from the barnyard. Paddy's hat was tipped forward in go-to-hell fashion, and the cheeks above the stubbly jaws were redder than sunburn alone could account for. He was whistling, but he broke off and said cheerfully, "It's something, now to be waited up for! You'll pardon my state, Clinton. I've been boozing in the town."

Drinking, but not drunk. The bright black eyes stabbed sharp as ever.

Paddy said, "I'll worry no more about that girl. She's dealt faithfully with you, I see."

"Get yourself a shamrock, you damned vaudeville mick," Clint told him sourly. "It wasn't her. It was the other one."

"Aila? You play the field, Clinton. I take it she repulsed you?"

"I caught her snooping in here. She said she was looking for me."

"It could be. You have the ugliness that fetches the sex quicker than fine looks."

"She said the parson had a job for me. I gathered she went with it. When I told her no dice she dug her claws in my face."

"Jezebel," Paddy said. "Or would it be Potiphar's wife … I disremember, but they were both bad lots. You're a devil amongst the women, Clinton. Still and all, there's the makings of a gentleman in you."

"She wasn't looking for me. If I hadn't caught her here I don't think she'd have mentioned the job. That was on the level though—I had it from Joe Peddar in Halem."

"You were cruel hard on Joe. His uncle tells me his face will not be the same." Paddy brought out his pipe and tamped coarse cut into it from his gum-rubber pouch. "There's the matter of a gunshot wound too, but I'll not inquire into that."

"Why were you drinking with Mike Peddar?"

"Why not? I drink often with Mike. We're both men with a past, and that makes for good conversation."

"Was Aila there?"

"Briefly. But she remembered her children and flew away home."

"Sure. So she could search your room."

Paddy's eyes narrowed ever so slightly. "Why should the woman do that?"

Clint got off the cot and reached to the bookshelf. "I thought I'd crack a book," he said. "This one." He slid the poems by Yeats out of the row, and reached in behind. The cartridge clip was gone.

He turned, and Paddy was grinning at him.

"You had disturbed the dust," Paddy said.

"All right," Clint said. "You can drop the act. I knew you weren't a labor stiff."

Paddy struck a match on the haunch of his blue denims. He said, "What am I then?"

151

"A cop."

"The word lacks dignity," Paddy said calmly between puffs. "It smells of the nightstick. I'm a staff sergeant of the Royal Canadian Mounted Police."

"Still a cop. Aren't you off your beat?"

"I am and I am not," Paddy said. The shrewd black eyes studied him over the pipe. "Our countries are close. There are times when they work together."

"What are you after, Paddy?"

Paddy did not answer at once. Watching him intently from across the little room, Clint felt as he had yesterday in the hayfield—that he was being sifted and weighed and measured.

"I'm in a cleft stick," Paddy said at last. "I've no power of arrest in these parts. But there are others who have, and will use it at my word. Now here are our choices, Clinton: I can have you wafted off and held safe for us. That would be proper procedure. I'm a devil for proper procedure, only less so than my inspector, and the courts love it."

"Yeah," Clint said, "only if you do that . . ."

Paddy's headshake checked him. "Quiet now, till we've reasoned the matter out!"

He groped in his pockets for another match. "But there are times, Clinton, when to effect an end we must let proper procedure fly out the window. We must then use such materials as come to hand. We must lean on broken reeds like yourself, and make our bricks with damned little straw. It's my belief we have come to such a time." Paddy straightened his hunched shoulders. The change in him was almost frightening. Behind the hired man's ragged clothes, behind the dry and easy humor, you could see the grim manhunter whom neither fear nor pity could swerve.

"How will you have it, Clinton? To be taken away, or to be staked out for the tiger yet a while?"

152

"I'll stay here."

"Then begin at the beginning," Paddy said. "Everything you can remember. I've had it from Devvy as she burped it out of you like wind from a baby, but I want it from you as well. One word, the right one, might tell us all that's needful."

The Saturday night walk at Martinez, Clint left out. That wasn't the law's business. But he told Paddy the rest, all of it, sitting on the edge of the cot with the hard eyes drilling him.

Paddy had smoked his pipe out before Clint was done.

"That's all?" he said then. "You can't carry it past the night you picked up the Chinaman and his cans?"

"No." Clint beat his fist softly into his palm. "That's the way it's been. A piece comes back, but not enough. Never the part that matters."

He scowled in a fury of concentration, trying to force his memory deeper into the fog.

Paddy said, "You did not know what Aleko was when he signed you on?"

"No. I still don't. He was just an old fish-boat skipper who gave me a break. But I get that part of it now, Paddy—it would look funny, a man fishing an offshore troller alone. He needed a partner to make it good."

"A tough limb with the law on his tail would do well enough," Paddy said. "We were informed you fell into his lap like a ripe plum off a twig, Clinton."

"Informed?"

"We've kept an eye on Captain Johannsen for some time past. It's known to us that he lost his last partner by drowning, a trip or two before you met him. Well, Aleko is ours now, what's left of him, shot full of formaldehyde and safe on a slab."

"I'm sorry about that. He treated me okay."

Paddy sat down beside him on the cot. He said,

"You've lifted one weight off my mind, boy. We take little on faith in my trade, but I'm disposed to believe you. It fits what we know like a hand into a glove. If you were one of them by choice you'd be a long time behind bars, always provided you did not burn or hang. As it is, I think you'll go clear—if you can stay alive to the end of it."

"What do you mean?"

Paddy said gravely, "You're on borrowed time, Clinton. You were not meant to come in from there alive."

"I was sure of that when they burned the troller. Who all is in this, Paddy?"

"The Peddars, uncle and nephew, up to their bloody necks. A few other dogfish. One tiger shark."

"The parson?"

"For all we can prove in court, Doctor Morse is just what he appears to be. A retired missionary of private means. A man made rich by the death of his wife. I'll have no guessing, Clinton."

"But he knew Aleko …"

"No guessing, I tell you." Paddy's voice was sharp. "Only what you remember, and can speak under oath to a jury."

"All right. But tell me this much. Joe Peddar was laying for me today and I don't think it was just over Devvy. How about that?"

"You have me there. A planned try at manslaughter, maybe. But you went halfway to meet him, I'm told, so we'll leave Joe out of it. There you're a biased witness, Clinton."

"What about Aila? Is she in on it?"

"I think she is. The woman's a walking evil. You've seen how she looks at Devvy?"

"I've seen. Devvy thinks they pay her for spying. I figure she's onto you too."

"It's a chance. This is the way of it, Clinton. There are

wheels within wheels here, as they say. There are things we know, and others we can guess and more that we're in the dark on. At the moment the wheel in the center of the works is yourself—and, begob, that wheel is jammed."

"I almost had it this morning when I saw the *Helene*," Clint said. "Look—they'll take her out tomorrow to meet the steamer at Martinez. If I could see her with them in her, that might do it."

"Anything might do it."

Paddy thought for a moment, cheeks sucked in, cold pipe between his teeth. "It is a long shot, but this is not a case to be solved with a fingerprint on a drinking glass or a bit of hair under a microscope. We'll give it a try. Take Devvy's boat in the morning and cut over. Keep your mouth shut and your eyes open—and your fists in your pockets."

"Okay."

"And stay off the *Helene*. You've been marked for killing ever since they knew you were alive and on shore."

"I'm hard to kill. You told me yourself, Paddy. I've got a lucky name." He grinned at the wide little man, liking him better than he'd liked any man before.

But Paddy's face remained sober. "Be careful. I've developed a fondness for you, Clinton, the Lord knows why. There's bloody murder in this, never forget it. You were meant to stay out there as Callahan stayed, in the deep water, you and the troller both. But the devil's own luck brought you safe in, with help from Devvy. One piece of evidence they've destroyed. I saw young Peddar fire the troller, lying up in the woods last night with Callahan's rifle by me. You're another piece of evidence, the key piece. We have our corpus delicti, Clinton, Aleko on his slab. We have everything but the witness, the lad who can stand in the box and point his finger and tell a jury, "This is the man. I was there. I saw him.""

155

He sucked at his pipe and said, "That and the cans you saw. We want those too."

"What was in the cans, Paddy?"

"Opium. A fortune in the stuff."

Paddy turned and stood listening, facing the doorway. It was only Devvy. She came in, looking sullen and tired.

"You're up late, my sha," Paddy said.

"I've been chatting with Aila." She carried two blankets folded over her arm. The glance she gave Clint was cold as her voice. "Here," she said, and dropped the blankets on the cot. "You can sleep in the loft tonight."

Paddy said, "What's the trouble between you two?"

Clint looked down at the floor. Devvy said, "There's no trouble. How much did you tell him, Paddy?"

"Enough. You knew she was down here?"

"Aila made a point of letting me know." She said to Clint, "You'd better smooth out your technique. You didn't need to get scratched."

She turned and went out as quietly as she'd come, and Paddy shrugged and sighed. "Another reason for remembering," he said. "I wish she were well out of this."

"If she thinks I'd make a play for that …"

"The evidence is against you," Paddy said, "and a woman will believe what she wants to believe." He put his pipe away; for the moment his face was oddly soft. "There walks a fine lady, Clinton."

"You're telling me," Clint said. He groped for a cigarette, frowning at the floor. "Paddy, was her father mixed up in this?"

"He was not. But he came too close to it, just as you've done, and brought his death on himself."

"How? Talk straight."

"He'd been a rumrunner once, as I've told you. That was a rough game, but a gentleman could be into it and come out with his hands not too dirty. Callahan lived by danger. It was food and drink to that man. He needed money for some new wild scheme and he thought when certain ones approached him that it was no more than the smuggling in of loot from Japan. They came to his wife first—it was Aila who persuaded him. She'd married him for money he did not have, d'you see, and came here thinking it was to a fine estate. There is nothing that one would not do for money, and she hated him for the lack of it. She persuaded him, and when he learned what he was into, it was too late. That was his last mistake."

"Did Devvy know?"

"She'd guessed something of what was up, and had fought with Callahan and against Aila for him to keep off the *Helene*. When he sailed and did not come back, she wrote a letter to the FBI. They passed it on to the Federal Narcotics Bureau, and my people had it from them. It meshed with a word or two had come our way in the drug squad of the Mounted. We put our heads together. For two months after I came here, I was no more than a bottle fighter, a matelot who'd chased U-boats with Callahan in the corvettes. She gave me a job out of her kind heart."

He said, "There you have it, Clinton. All I can tell you and much more than proper procedure dictates you should know. We've been stuck till she brought you in from the Boss-Foreman with the look of death in your eyes and the wits knocked out of you entirely."

Clint said, "Damn it to hell, Paddy, I'll do anything to make myself remember. It's like a name on the tip of my tongue. That shaking up Joe Peddar gave me today brought it closer. Maybe tomorrow will do it."

"I hope so," Paddy said. "It has to be soon. Pick up your blankets now and let me get to my sleep. I need my strength for the haying."

❖

GOING UP TO THE HOUSE after the morning milking, they met Brian and Elsie.

"You're early out," Paddy said. "Where off to today?" The little girl said in her careful voice, "We haven't decided yet. Devvy told me to tell you to get your own breakfasts. We've had ours."

"Good enough!" Paddy scooped Brian from the lane and tickled a squeal out of him.

"And you're not to use the big coffeepot because you burned a hole in the bottom yesterday, Devvy says."

"The injunction is noted," Paddy told her solemnly. He put Brian down and started him on his way with a pat on the seat of his red corduroy overalls. Both kids had new sneakers, Clint observed; Devvy, he guessed, had squeezed them out of her fishing money.

He said to Paddy as they went on up, "That Elsie's an odd one."

"Is it any wonder? But it's a fine healthy life for 'em, by and large, running the woods. . . There is our employer, Clinton, and the black dog still at her heels. Her mother was a Finnish girl, as I've told you. Suomi blood should not be mixed with Irish: they have too much of a sameness."

Devvy was busy with a hoe in her truck garden. She gave Paddy a terse "Morning," and started on another potato hill; she disregarded Clint entirely.

When they were in the kitchen, Clint asked, "What about the boat? Shouldn't we wise her up?"

"I will," Paddy said. "It's a trifling hole, that in the coffeepot, nothing to make a song and dance about. We'll spite her and drink tea. I'd best wait till you've gone before I tell her you're away to Martinez, I'm thinking."

"Why?"

"Because she will raise seven kinds of hell. Your present status has me baffled, Clinton. Just drop us a clutch of eggs in the teakettle, we will kill two birds with one stone." Clint watched skeptically, but Paddy rustled a good enough meal. There was a handiness about him that went with the military orderliness of his room, and with his straight-backed swagger. They were smoking with chairs pushed back from the table when Aila came down the stairs.

She was in her stained green silk housecoat. Her hair was a black tangle around her shoulders, and it seemed to Clint, watching her, that the lines at either side of her mouth were deeper, more bitter. Yawning, she took cup and saucer from the cupboard over the sink, poured herself tea, and crossed to the table with a slip-slopping of green mules. She lit one of her Turkish cigarettes and blew out smoke.

"I'll be 'aving a proper cup o' tea soon," she said. "Shan't 'ave to look at your ugly face mornings much longer, Mr. Burke. I'm going 'ome."

"Our loss will be England's gain," Paddy said. "You've come into money?"

"Like to know, wouldn't yer?" Aila said. "Always poking and prying about 'ere, aren't yer? Well, a lot I care!"

She smiled at Clint, and her voice was a purr. "Sleep well, dearie?"

"Well enough." She was fixing for a sneak punch of some kind. Puzzled and wary, he waited for it.

The door opened, and Devvy's sandals clicked on the flags. She said at once, "It's eight o'clock, you two. You're loafing on my time. You can gossip on the way to the field."

"W'y," Aila said, and loosed another cloud of smoke, "she's all in a pet. Sit down, Devvy, do. 'Ave a cup o' tea."

"I'm making coffee for myself." To Clint, she said crisply, "You'd better put some iodine on your face. Her claws may be infected."

"So that's it!" Aila's laugh had the same sleek-cat

purr. "I've said it before, Devvy, and I'll say it again. You 'ave to at least look like a woman before you'll get far with a man. If you could see yourself! 'Alf the farm under your nails. Mud on your nose ..."

She got up gracefully, holding the housecoat around her. "But I'm finished with your friend. 'E's all yours now, Devvy, and I wish you joy of 'im."

Aila moved toward the stairs. Clint gulped his tea, sorry for Devvy, itching to be out and away from the kitchen with its still-tingling air.

Paddy cleared his throat. "She's no longer the grand lady," he said. "She has dropped her act and picked up her accent. Why, Devvy?"

"I don't know. Or care."

"She is going home, she tells me."

Devvy snapped, "Feet first, I trust. Now, will you clear out?"

She slammed the door behind them. Jogging around to the lane, they heard the crash of breaking crockery.

"She's thrown a cup," Paddy said. "Ah well, it will relieve her feelings!"

Even this early, it was plenty hot. The sunlight had a coppery quality from bushfires somewhere north along the island chain. At the top gate of the hayfield, Paddy peeled off his shirt, a hired hand readying for his day's work.

Last night's doings seemed a little fantastic now. "I don't see why you can't just move in on them," Clint said. "Should be simple enough if the cans are hidden around the mill."

"Even if it were," Paddy said, "and we don't know that it is, mind, we could have the place apart a stick at a time and not find it."

"It could be on the *Helene*."

"And it could be in the middle of the bay, or here in Devvy's woods, or clean off the island. Our man at the mill knows every teredo hole in that place. He's found nothing."

160

"Lum Kee?"

Paddy nodded. "Cook at the mill for twenty years. When they closed it, Callahan took him in. He became another of Devvy's waifs and strays, someone else she was after worrying and fending for. I sent him back last month to cook for the parson. Lum Kee does not know you're with us. If you see him you'll not tell him. He has his own job to do."

"That business about the red cod was a signal, eh?"

"It was. He went away from here yesterday with a walkie-talkie in a sack of murphies. There was no use to excite suspicion by having him come to the farm—once a day, or oftener, he will inform me what goes on at The Retreat."

"You've really got it organized," Clint said. "But it still sounds screwy to me, this cloak-and-dagger stuff."

"See now." Paddy's tough blue jaw hardened. "This is no game for a fool. If you haven't had that beaten into your thick skull by this time ..."

"Okay, okay," Clint told him hastily. "You don't have to get hot about it. I was just wondering, that's all."

"Do your wondering later. Be home before sunset— and keep off the *Helene,* for the love of God."

Paddy picked his scythe from behind a log at the edge of the woods. He waded into the wild hay, a hairy-chested little man in frayed denims, and hat that looked as if it had stopped a charge of buckshot, but still kept a certain scarecrow jauntiness.

Clint walked on. He looked back once from the rise beyond the lower gate, where the lane curved west away from the creek. He could see Paddy deep in the hay, close to the black stumps and the purple-pink wilderness of fireweed. Beyond, he could see the farmhouse, and the glossy green helmets of the madronas that flanked it. He wondered if Devvy had broken any more cups.

His eyes caught a flicker of moving blue midway between hayfield and house.

Aila's thin little girl. The boy was not with her; she had darted out of the woods and was running like some woods creature, furtively, through the bracken at the edge of the lane.

Odd kid. He'd speculated, seeing her at breakfast yesterday and in the yard this morning, over what kind of a tangle lay back of those green eyes too large for the pointed face.

But he had more pressing thoughts to occupy him right now. He trudged on, over the rise and down through the sunlit timber.

At the landing, he slipped the dinghy's painter and stepped in. Deep below, he could see the shadow which was the *Maiija*'s burned-out hull. That first day had begun to seem far back and long ago, but it wasn't so long, not even forty-eight hours. One way, everything had changed. In another, his affairs had only grown more muddled. It was curious, though, that the fear should be gone—he'd slept deeply, bedded in the dry fragrant hay of the loft, not even dreaming.

It was odd, too, that he'd never once known what he was afraid of. Deep water had never scared him before. He'd always felt at home in it, unworried and free. He might learn today; and, he thought, it could be with him as it had been with Callahan, knowledge gained too late to do him or anybody any good.

Here in the sunshine, though, it was hard to believe that. He tried to see Devvy as she'd look rigged for dancing, but it wouldn't come. He could only see her as she'd been in the troller, looking down at him where he lay in his bunk, with the gold lights in her gray-green eyes like the sunwheels in deep water.

With a half-tide creeping among the saltgrass it was no trick to follow the kinks of the creek estuary. He putted out to the bay, and pointed the dinghy's nose for Martinez Island east four miles under a pale sky rimmed faintly with heat-bronze. It was cool here, with the wind whipping in from Martinez Channel to kick up a chop; he buttoned his ragged shirt and lit a cigarette, crouching against the breeze with the match cupped in both hands.

The sawmill burner lifted its rust-red dome on the bay's south shore. He quartered the dinghy in, watching for signs of life. A toy man sat at the end of the tumble-down dock. The old cook, Lum Kee, fishing for rock cod. Clint lifted a hand in a hail, and after a minute Lum Kee waved back.

The *Helene* hadn't set out for Martinez yet. She lay, low and long, at her moorings. The cruiser was like a gray shark, basking there in the sun. She must be all tanks and engines, she'd have the speed of a torpedo boat. Clint studied her, squinting astern as the dinghy ran on up the narrow bay. The *Helene* was nothing but sixty feet of wood and glass and metal. But he wondered, watching her, what cargoes she'd carried and how much blood had been spilled in her since her keel was laid.

Memory didn't stir. A boat couldn't be good or bad in the way that people were. Hell, she was just a fast cruiser, tied bow and stern in a sunshiny cove.

He cleared the bay, the lapstrake dinghy bouncing in the chop. It was a couple of hours yet before the steamer was due, even if she should come poking down Martinez Channel on time. No smoke trailers on the horizon; the only other boat out was a troller a couple of miles southwest, creeping between sea and pale sky with spring poles spread.

That would be Gunnar Lund or some other fisherman from Martinez, plodding after salmon.

The last of the ebb was draining out of the Boss-Foreman. He twisted the throttle, and the outboard checked and sputtered, caught hold again for a moment, then conked in a diminishing string of pops. He tested the plugs and fiddled with the feed, but she wouldn't start.

Belatedly, he unscrewed the cap from the fuel tank and plumbed it with a bottom-board sliver. He'd run her dry.

But it didn't matter, the oars were under the thwarts and he had time to burn. He tipped the outboard clear of the water, worked the oars loose and got them overside. There'd be no need to row home. He could buy fuel at Martinez.

He was better than a quarter way across when he saw the *Helene* slide out of the sawmill cove. They'd rigged an awning over the cockpit; she looked like a rich man's commuter, loafing along effortlessly like that. He'd like to see her running all out—he figured that she'd hit forty, maybe more. A fuel-eating shark of a boat, not sturdy and honest like a troller, but built for the narrow waters, to run in the dark of the moon.

The *Helene* appeared to be taking her time. But seeing how the south shoreline of the bay unreeled behind her, Clint judged she was logging at least twelve knots. Still too far away for him to see who was handling her.

Clear of the bay now, she sprouted a bow wave. The hull between those creamy fans of spray looked narrower than ever, and the sound of her engines was a far-carrying roar. High-speed jobs: she probably had eight-hundred horsepower packed into her.

She was eating up the distance between them. Clint hadn't been worried before. Now, though, rowing steadily, he watched the cruiser with growing uneasiness.

The *Helene* swung a couple of points north, putting the dinghy directly on her course. Clint could feel his palms starting to sweat against the oar handles. Hell, they wouldn't even have to ram him. At ten-foot range, that high-piling bow wave would swamp the rowboat or tumble her end for end. The outboard would pull her down like a rock.

He looked over his shoulder. When last he scouted his course, the red-roofed cannery buildings of Martinez

Cove had been a little north of the dinghy's stem. Now, puzzlingly, they stood well south.

Buildings don't move. With a jolt that was like a blow over the heart, he realized what he was into. Watching the *Helene,* he had let his landmarks slide.

He had rowed through the minutes of low-water slack. The tide had reversed itself—the rise was shoving him down-channel toward the Boss-Foreman.

He glanced north; and his rate of drift appalled him. For every yard gained toward Martinez he was dropping another yard toward the fixed breakers at the mouth of the pass. Flashingly, he thought of swinging the dinghy that way, searching as Devvy had done for a slant of current that would hike him toward one shore or the other. But the tide was talking all around him now, a hurried and secretive mutter, the water dimples were forming and the water devils were tugging at his oar blades.

He backed with his right oar and hauled hard with his left, spinning the dinghy through a quarter circle so that her bow pointed due south toward the open channel. Laying into it, stroking fast, he began to make way. The constriction in his chest eased—another five minutes and the press of tide would have been too strong, the Boss-Foreman would have had him.

A voice hailed, and he snatched his head around. The *Helene,* engines turning lazily, lay directly across his course. Joe Peddar lounged at the wheel. His face was patched with surgical tape and his eyes were puffed almost shut, but he was grinning.

Another head and a narrower set of shoulders appeared beside Joe Peddar's.

The parson.

Doctor Morse called cheerfully, "Come alongside, Mr. Farrell. We'll tow you out of this."

Keep off the *Helene.* That had been Paddy's final

word. Rowing still, fighting the tide, Clint shouted back, "I'm doing okay."

"You're not," Doctor Morse called. "Believe me! Quickly, my boy, while we still have time."

Another man stood in the cruiser's cockpit. He was taller than Joe, but he had the same dark, heavy-featured face. His hair was gray, and he carried a hawk look about him, in the set of his head between his high, square shoulders and in the lines that ran deep-grooved from nostrils to the corners of his thin mouth.

Joe's uncle, Clint guessed, the runner of hot cargoes. Mike Peddar said harshly, "Quit being a damn fool. Haul alongside, kid."

The cruiser had lost most of her way. Her northward drift had brought her almost upon him. Tossing in the pyramidal chop, Clint saw the parson take the wheel with a nod to Joe Peddar. Joe swung out of the wheelhouse, stooped for a pike pole bracketed at the base of the *Helene*'s superstructure. A heavy pad of gauze was taped around his right arm above the elbow, where Devvy's .22 short had drilled the muscle; Clint noticed with an odd detachment that Joe favored that arm.

The play was plain enough now. If he'd been farther into the pass, they'd simply have held to their original course and let the Boss-Foreman do the job for them. But they'd seen, damn them, that he wasn't going to drown without help. So it was going to be an accident, the kind of accident that had given Callahan, that strong swimmer, to the dogfish at the bottom of the Straits.

The pike pole was reaching down, spike and burnished hook; and Clint looked up the shaft directly into Joe Peddar's face. Joe's bruised lips were pulled back from his teeth in a fixed and curious smile.

Aleko and the Chinaman … Callahan before them … himself now, capsized in one swift heave, dumped into the tideway to battle a current that no swimmer could beat. Sure, they'd toss him a line, they'd go through all the motions of trying to pick him up. And in the end, the dogfish would have him too.

Not that way. Any other way would be better.

He lunged hard on the oars, driving the dinghy against the *Helene*'s flank. The pike pole grazed his shoulder. He swung himself off the thwart, grabbed the dinghy's painter in one swift automatic clutch, and leaped. He sprawled in the cruiser's cockpit with the painter still in his fist. The jolt must have knocked him silly; the only thought in his head was that he'd saved Devvy's boat, she wouldn't have to be sore at him for that, at least!

From above him came the parson's mild voice: "Well done, Mr. Farrell!"

Still moving automatically, Clint picked himself off his knees. He worked the dinghy aft and threw a hitch around a stern cleat, taking his time about it, feeling their eyes drilling his back. But when he turned, Joe was already in the wheelhouse and Mike Peddar was going down the shallow companionway to the cabin.

The *Helene* carried fishing-type swivel chairs, two of them anchored side by side in the cockpit. Doctor Morse said pleasantly, "I'd been hoping for a visit, Mr. Farrell, but I hardly expected to receive you in this fashion. Please sit down."

He took the other chair; he looked spry and dapper in a clerical sort of way, with his short, neatly trimmed beard and his black broadcloth jacket, the round collar gleaming white above his high-buttoned vest.

"You were bound for Martinez, I suppose?"

"Yeah."

"Under the circumstances, do you consider that wise?"

"Devvy sent me over for groceries. I ran out of gas."

"It's fortunate we happened along," Doctor Morse said. "The Boss-Foreman isn't to be trifled with, you know. I had some difficulty persuading Mr. Peddar to go in for you."

Doctor Morse settled back in his chair. His spectacles glimmered as he turned his head. His expression was grave, a little distressed. "I'm concerned about you, as you know," he said, "and I'm afraid yesterday's … ah … occurrence did nothing to set my mind at rest. That was a bad business. Of course, I've had only one side of the story, so perhaps I shouldn't attempt to judge."

"Your boy started something. I finished it."

Doctor Morse sighed. "Young blood … I like Devvy Callahan a great deal, but I blame the whole affair on her. She's little more than a child, and a very headstrong one. Flaunting you in Joe's face was anything but prudent."

Clint said nothing. The *Helene* was easing cross-channel now, toward the cannery buildings and houses on the Martinez shore. He stole a glance at Doctor Morse, feeling a bit sheepish, unsure of himself, his conviction shaken. On the face of things, they'd helped him out of a nasty spot. And Doctor Morse looked exactly like what he put out to be, a retired missioner, gentle and rather vague, a minor unpleasantness over and already dismissed from his thoughts. He didn't look at all as a murderer should.

"Mr. Farrell, so far in our brief acquaintance, you've made it very difficult for me to help you."

The voice, startlingly deep and mellow in so small and spare a man, was altogether kind. Doctor Morse turned, the swivel chair creaking, and took off his thick-lensed spectacles, and rubbed a hand across his eyes in an almost pathetic gesture, as if he'd been struck by a sudden headache. His peering hazel eyes were oddly blank, unfocused. Shortsighted, Clint thought. No better than a daylight owl without those cheaters …

Once … somewhere … once before …

He'd taken off his glasses so, and drawn a hand across his eyes, and he'd had the look of the owl about him. No guessing, Paddy Burke had said. Now there was no need to guess.

It came to him as suddenly, as treacherously as that.

Clint heard his own voice say, "Hold it a minute, will you? I want to see how my dinghy's riding."

He got out of the chair, and stared astern, not seeing the dinghy, or the *Helene*'s lazy wake, or the smoke-hazed islands. For a long sick moment there was nothing solid and real here, nothing he could tie to. He was back in the swirling fog again, offshore on the *Maiija* ...

The little man had sighed and rubbed a hand across his eyes. Then he'd put the glasses back on his nose, and nodded to Joe Peddar and the dark thickset man who never spoke, and his right hand had dipped smoothly into the front of his trenchcoat. No other warning. Just that, then the quick slamming of the shots, and men dropping and men in each other's way, and himself falling with fire in his eyes, blinding him, and going down and down in the deep water.

Clint turned. He said, "You can't help me. Nobody can. Look—I wasn't sent over for groceries. I pinched her boat, I'm lamming out of here."

He wasn't smart like Paddy, he couldn't think on his feet like Devvy. But maybe the parson would believe him, maybe the horror that had come back to him wouldn't show too plain on his face. At least, the parson's small-boned white hand, more like a woman's than a man's, didn't slide inside his jacket.

In her own lean length, the *Helene* surged into speed. Doctor Morse's chair creaked again. He called in a tone of mild annoyance, "Joe! What are you about up there?" Mike Peddar said from the top of the companion, "We've got a steamer to meet, Doc. Remember?"

He tilted his head ever so slightly. There was no sign

169

of a ship, not even a smoke wisp to flaw the southern horizon; there was only the troller Clint had spotted from Cultus Bay. She was less than a mile away now, too far still for Clint to catch her hull color or for the man at her wheel to be more than a black dot. But not too far for sunlight to wink on glass.

High-power lenses would twinkle like that. The trollerman, Gunnar Lund or whoever he might be, was watching them.

Doctor Morse replaced his spectacles. "Oh, yes," he said. "The steamer." He clicked his tongue. "Do you know, Mr. Farrell, I'd quite forgotten."

"Absent-minded, eh?" Clint said.

"I fear so. It's an ailment common to my calling."

Clint squinted at the distant fish boat, and he felt a rush of gratitude to the guy out there with the binoculars at his eyes. A rigged drowning, a killing without witnesses—that was one thing. But murder under the eyes of a watcher, that was something else again. They might drown him later, but until or unless they got another chance, he was safe. Wheels within wheels, Paddy had told him in the barn last night... It was odd how you could sweat and be cold clear to your bones at the same time.

Doctor Morse said amiably, "I'm a reasonably sound judge of character, Mr. Farrell. I suspect you may be more sinned against than sinning. Don't run away. You'll only place yourself in a worse predicament, I assure you."

He gave Clint his kind, vague smile. "As a medical missionary, I've encountered more than one such case as yours. A severe shock, a blow on the head could induce it."

"But sometime I'll get things straight, won't I?"

"I'm certain you will. As for Captain Johannsen, don't worry about him. He was a very heavy drinker. Such men are a danger to themselves and others, especially if they do business upon the great waters. I warned poor Johannsen repeatedly."

"You think he could have fallen overside or something like that?"

"Yes. Or, let's say, attacked you in a drunken rage, forced you to act against him in self defense." Even knowing, it was hard to doubt the parson's sincerity. "So please don't … ah … lam out, as you put it. When your memory is restored, then is the time for us to approach the authorities. You'll return to Cultus Island?"

"I guess so."

"Good! Now, my boy, try to put the whole affair out of your mind. One doesn't heal a wound by probing it continually."

The *Helene* was opening Martinez Cove. Joe Peddar idled her to a berth at the outermost float of the bobbing string below the steamer dock. Even here, Clint could sense the power of the Boss-Foreman; the water was troubled and the green and brown weed streamed north from the guard logs in the pull of the tide.

He fought back a shiver. He had staked himself out for the tiger, and he still was alive. Maybe they hadn't been fixing to give him the treatment they'd handed out to Callahan and Aleko and the Chinaman off the steamer, but he'd take a lot of convincing.

He fetched his handkerchief from his hip pocket and mopped his forehead. "Hot for June," he said.

"Quite," Doctor Morse said amiably. "Thunder weather, Mr. Farrell."

Clint unhitched the dinghy and dropped into her. He sculled on down the line of floats and nosed her in between a couple of cannery gas boats. Then he sauntered whistling to the gangway that pitched steeply from the dock.

There were people above, a lot of people. Indian klootches in shawls and full skirts, their hair tied in the violently colored kerchiefs you seemed to find only in the commissary of a cannery settlement. Loggers in stagged pants and caulked boots loafing in the heat. A busy little man in a striped shirt and green eyeshade, scuttling around with papers clipped to a fileboard. He'd be a cannery push maybe, or the Martinez freight agent.

People—and he loved them all. He looked down at the *Helene* where she lay at the float. Doctor Morse seemed entirely harmless and kindly, standing there with his short legs apart and his hands clasped behind his back. Joe Peddar had come out of the wheelhouse and squatted on the forepeak hatch. He was whittling at his ship's hull again—he must have rustled himself another knife.

Clint wanted to talk to someone, and it didn't matter much whom, just so it wasn't a killer out of the fog. He idled over to the busy man with the eyeshade.

"Steamer about due?" he asked.

The agent told him importantly, "Give her an hour yet, son. She's been late every trip for seven years, so I don't guess it'll be different today."

"Thanks," Clint said. "Thanks a lot!" He even liked the agent calling him son.

What came next he could only guess. He'd tried to play it cagey, but he might have tipped his hand, or even that brief flash of binocular lenses might have told the parson all he'd need to know. But he didn't think so; if it had been that way, he was reasonably sure they'd never have let him get off the *Helene*. Anyway, he hadn't let Paddy down, he had got what they needed, and for the moment he couldn't be any safer in church.

He lit a cigarette and leaned his shoulders against the freight shed, soaking in sunshine as if he'd come out of bitter cold. A boy passed with two spiny red rock cod dangling from a piece of fishline. Clint grinned at the kid and the kid grinned back. People!

Lounging here, he felt as if he were at last rid of an

obscure sickness. He thought of Devvy, and he knew, now, that he wasn't going to let her go without the biggest fight of his life. Stump-ranch girl, stump-ranch girl ... it was making a song in his head.

The wheels would start turning now, he supposed. They'd move in, brail up their dogfish and their tiger shark, and it would be all over. He didn't let himself think about the butcher's business out there in the fog. It was safe in his head like eggs in a basket; all he had to do now was carry it home.

The baffling, the strange thing was that he'd known all the time. His mind had turned away from it in panic, bucked against his will, refused to go near it for all his forcing. He'd get the lowdown on it from a doctor sometime, find out what happened in a man's brain to account for a trick like that. But the doctor wouldn't be the awful little man who killed with a pulpit air.

Smoke on the horizon. The steamer was waddling down the channel. He took his back away from the shed and walked up the dock toward the commissary. He needed cigarettes, and he ought to get a towel and razor. There were a lot of odds and ends he needed; he could think about those things again now.

When he jogged back down with his parcel under his arm and a full can of fuel swinging from his other hand, the steamer was close. Sitting on the fuel can, he watched her poke into the cove and make her fussy landing. They didn't waste much time at these island ports—he guessed she'd call at a dozen or so on her round trip. The gangplank clattered to the dock. Up forward, a cargo winch began to whine, and a boom swung a netful of sacks and boxes over.

A logger high-stepped along the gangplank with a packsack on his shoulder and a pair of newly soled caulk boots dangling by their laces from his hand. He'd be coming back from a city holiday to some gyppo island outfit. Then an Indian family, the buck walking ahead, wearing a stiff-brimmed black felt hat with a scarlet band, his wife behind him with green kerchief and purple velvet skirt, a brown baby peering over her shoulder from its nest in her crimson shawl.

Clint waited, sitting on his fuel can with the heat soaking pleasantly into his back. The next passenger off was something different. His clothes yelled big city. Tropical suit and tan shoes, panama and patterned tie. A thin little guy; he sported a thin black mustache and he was frowning, looking around as if he expected to be met.

The man behind him was wide in the shoulders as Paddy Burke, and a good six inches taller. He wore no hat, and his black hair was slicked flat on his skull. Swarthy face, thin mouth, and nose that had sometime or other stopped a fast one.

Clint stiffened where he sat. The thin dude in the panama was a new one, but that other face was part of the remembered picture. He was the heavy who talked mostly in grunts. He'd taken care of the Chinaman, and he'd put a second slug into Aleko as the old man folded at the middle and crumpled to the hatch cover with a bubble of dark blood bursting at his mouth.

Black-hair had been here before—knew where he was going. He crossed directly to the float gangway, and the fox-faced man in tropicals followed him with a pavement step that was almost womanish.

"You ... hey, boy!"

The line agent was hollering from the far side of the wharf. "Ain't you with Doc Morse? He's pulling out!"

"Let him pull," Clint said. "I'm not with him."

He took a last drag at his cigarette, then got up and walked to the edge. Mike Peddar had slipped the *Helene*'s lines. She was sliding away from the float, the parson at her wheel. Joe Peddar, cross-legged on her forward deck, looked up from his whittling. With his bruised and swollen face, he had the look of a man wearing a mask.

They wouldn't get another chance at him, Clint thought; he'd give the *Helene* a clear channel. He had been only three days on the blue island over there, but already it was home. Suddenly he was eager to be clear, impatient of the whole grim and tangled business. Nothing left now but the cleanup, and that wasn't his affair. The law carried it from here; they could stand aside, he and Devvy, and it wouldn't concern them any more.

He guessed, though, that they would have to testify in court. Paddy had told him as much last night. Maybe it was a rotten thing to be glad men were going to die, but he couldn't help it. He'd stand in the witness box and say what he had to say. Sometime after that, he would read in a paper or hear on the air that the law had killed them, and he'd have only one regret.

All through, there'd been something impersonal about his dealings with those others. He was in their way; they'd had to remove him to protect themselves and their investment.

But with Joe Peddar, it was different. As long as he lived, he would never think of the big yellow-haired guy without knowing the metal taste of hate in his mouth. That was something beyond the law, even beyond right and wrong. If he could have taken care of Joe himself. Someone tapped him on the shoulder, and he turned. It was the town cop from Halem, Johnny Beamish, in his blue shirt with his worn bright badge clipped to a suspender strap. The hick constable who'd told him not to leave Cultus Island.

But Beamish wasn't in his own yard now. Stall him off, bluff it out.

He said, "The law, eh? You're on the wrong island."

"Never mind that," Johnny Beamish said quietly. "You saw those two off the steamer? The gorilla in the sport jacket and the thin one with the mustache?"

"Sure. I saw them."

"Tell Paddy Burke."

"What's it got to do with him? Tell him yourself."

It could be a trap. But somehow he didn't think so. Wheels within wheels, the wide little man had said …

"Now get this," Johnny Beamish told him. "It's important. I saw Aila in Halem just before I came over. She figures on a trip."

"I know. She told us at breakfast."

"Tell Paddy she says it's tomorrow night."

He gave Clint the barest ghost of a grin, and turned and ambled off up the dock, solid and tall, the country cop with his badge.

Clint picked up his parcel and fuel can. He jolted stiff-legged down to the float, and fueled the outboard. The *Helene* was across already, and into Cultus Bay. Safe now to go home.

Chunking up the estuary channel, he saw Paddy first, where he sat on the edge of the landing. Devvy stood behind him, facing the bay. He waved, but Devvy didn't wave back. The dinghy went aground on a bar below the basin and he stepped overside, pushing till she rode in deep water again. He didn't bother starting the motor, but paddled the rest of the way with an oar.

Paddy, he saw, was hunched over his knees. He had a browbeaten look about him.

Clint called, "Hi, Devvy," glad to be back, achingly glad to see her again.

"Don't you talk to me," she snapped at him. Mad! She was shaking mad, glaring at him in her rolled-up jeans and old scuffed sandals and open-throated white shirt.

He said, taken all aback, "Don't be like that. What the hell, Devvy!" and her face puckered, and she began to cry.

Paddy Burke said, "Leave her be." His black eyes were

intense. "She was frightened for you. She was all for going down to the mill and doing God knows what. Shooting up that place with her great ugly rifle, I suppose."

"I'd have done it, too. Damn you, both of you, you fooled me. You stole my boat. Oh, if I'd known!"

She whirled, and the loose planks of the landing clattered as she ran still sobbing for the lane.

Clint started after her, but Paddy told him grimly, "Leave her, I say. Patch your quarrels later. You took long enough, Clinton."

"Ran out of gas. They picked me up halfway over."

"I know that. There've been two pair of glasses on you since you left the bay."

"It's just as well. Who was that in the troller, Paddy?"

"A friend of hers up yonder. He has been working with us."

His news would keep no longer. "Well," he said importantly, "I got it!"

"I know that too. It's plastered all over your mug. There was no guessing? You remembered?"

"All of it."

"Then who is our man?"

"Morse."

Paddy nodded. "We lacked only the proof."

"It was the damnedest thing. He took off his glasses on the boat and looked at me, kind of fuzzy as if he could hardly see me, and it hit me just like that. He looked the same way the night they killed Aleko and the Chinaman. I know about the Chinaman now, too. He was an agent for some Hongkong exporting firm. He took a bit of rice paper out of the back of his ring and gave it to Aleko. I figured it was a bill or a receipt or something like that. And I know now why they killed him ..."

"Wait," Paddy told him. "You've sat on it like a broody hen for days. An hour or two more makes no

177

matter. I'll not have it told me this way, all hind-end to."
He pulled out a dented dollar watch. "You'll give it to
me all orderly, Clinton, as you must do in court. I've an
errand or two first."

"One thing you'd better know," Clint said. "I ran
into that cop from Halem. He said Aila told him she's
leaving tomorrow night."

"So?" The lines tightened at the corners of Paddy's
eyes. "They've got the wind up. You're a thorn too deep
into the parson's side. Well, it means a quick end to it."

"Something else. Two men got off the steamer and
came over on the *Helene*. I saw one of them that night, a
black-haired guy. The other's thin with a little mustache.
He wasn't with them."

Paddy said, "More dogfish, Clinton. We've let them
slip in. We'll take 'em all at the one cast. It saves bother
for the law, and taxpayer's money."

"That Halem cop," Clint said. "Johnny Beamish. I
didn't know he was with you."

"You were not meant to know," Paddy said. "He's
on the side of the angels, Johnny Beamish. I had him
turn you back. You were badly needed here, boy."

"You could have told me, couldn't you? And how
about that trollerman?"

"You were a suspicious character, to be told nothing
and watched close." Paddy chuckled. "Gunnar Lund
is a good lad, not over-bright, maybe, but willing. We
leave no more holes than need be in our net. I heard
it from him when Devvy near drowned you in the
Boss-Foreman yesterday. We sweated you clear of there
together."

"Is he a cop too?"

"No. His status is unofficial. He's a fisherman, just,
with a walkie-talkie in his cabin and a pair of binoculars
and the eyes to use 'em. We've talked often across the
water, Gunnar and me. I tolled him up soon as ever the

Helene had her snout out of the mill cove this morning."

"I almost didn't come back from that ride."

"It was a risk to be taken. You took it, and I let you take it." He said gravely, "You've helped us and yourself more than you know."

Paddy walked with him as far as the indistinct path that emerged from the timber between the hayfield and the farmhouse.

"What's up there?" Clint asked him.

Paddy said, "Tools of my trade. They are one reason her haying has gone so slowly."

Radio, Clint guessed; but he was learning not to ask too many questions. Anyway, although it couldn't be past midafternoon, he was tired as if he had put in a hard day's work.

Paddy said, "There's humor of a sort in this affair. It's discernible to me, although those in high places are not able to see it. Do you know you've been the anxious concern of two governments whilst you sat brooding on your precious egg?"

"I haven't done much sitting," Clint told him through a yawn. "If you don't need me for a spell, I'll go do some sleeping now. I'm out on my feet."

"Go on along up," Paddy told him. "For all you fleer at the sciences, Clinton, I'm well enough pleased with you today."

Devvy was shelling peas on the kitchen stoop with Brian helping her, but when Clint came in from the lane, she picked up her basket and saucepan and went inside. In that mood, she was best kept away from. He walked on down to the barn.

It was cool in Paddy's whitewashed box of a room, and already dim. He dropped his parcel from Martinez into Paddy's chair and kicked off his shoes. Lying on the cot, arms under his head, he felt the odd, persistent happiness still at work inside him. Paddy's backhanded praise had something to do with it. So did the knowledge that he could stop running away now, that, thank God, he wasn't on the lam any more.

Close to sleep, the day's trouble and tension draining out of him, he let himself think about Devvy.

Perched in the barber's chair yesterday, with her light hair combed out, she'd looked like a sulky high school kid. Then the barber must have teased her about something, because she'd tipped her head back, and her face had lightened the way it sometimes did, making her lovely of a sudden, and gay.

His mind continued to work on her with a quiet wonder. She'd stood over him with two cigarettes between her fingers that first night in her room, and he'd realized then what had come to him two weeks before, and had stayed with him, growing in him, ever since.

Still plenty to worry about, even with cops his friends instead of his enemies. Maybe Devvy meant it, maybe she really was off him for keeps. Something else too, a small thing which he knew he ought to deal with, but he felt peaceful and unconcerned, and very sleepy.

He turned on his side and slept deeply, and the fire and the fear and the drowning water were far away, no more than an echo, like the mutter of the Boss-Foreman remembered in his sleep.

It was dark when he wakened. Someone was moving quietly in the little room. Devvy said, "Just me. All right if I light the lamp?"

"Sure, Devvy."

The glow deepened softly as she turned up the wick. He rolled over on the cot, feeling more rested than he had for many days. She was standing by the door with the blue dark of the night behind her.

"How do you feel?" she asked him.

"Good."

"Hungry?"

"Nope."

"I put a plate away. You can have it later. I'm going for a walk now."

She was as she had been when he'd first seen her, except that her fair hair looked softer and smoother.

"By yourself?" he asked her.

"No. I want you to come."

"Okay. Paddy was going to give me the horse clippers tonight though."

She didn't smile. "That can wait. Paddy went off somewhere after dinner."

He tugged his shoes on. There was a stillness about her, an indrawn quality that puzzled him. He started to slip his cigarettes into his breast pocket, but Devvy said, "No. Leave them here."

He couldn't understand her, and she didn't help him. They went down together, along the dim lane that ambled toward the hayfield. Hot weather was lowering the creek; its voice was almost inaudible. The night was cool and the land breeze was only a faint breath on his left cheek.

He said, "Devvy, what is it?"

She didn't answer.

Clint opened the hayfield gate and held it for her. "Put the bar back," she said. "I don't want the horses to get in here."

He had a feeling of a scene repeating itself. They'd walked this way yesterday dawn, although it seemed a great deal longer ago than that. They'd stopped where Devvy halted now, and she had turned toward him like this, hands in her pockets. He waited, wondering.

"I'm still trying to figure things out," she said.

"I don't get it."

"Some clothes came from town today. There was a note with them."

He hadn't thought of the business in the store

since morning. But there shouldn't be any note, there couldn't be. He'd taken care of that.

Facing her in the dim lane, looking down at her, he felt stupid and clumsy. He said, "I still don't get it. The clothes, sure. I did write sort of a letter too, but I tore it up."

"Why, Clint?"

"That wasn't part of what I'd meant to do."

"What did you mean to do?"

"Give you a break. I was pretty sure I'd killed Aleko."

"I wanted you to stay. I'd told you that."

"I know. I guess I was kind of sick in the head, Devvy."

"You've done a lot of stupid things. That was the stupidest."

"All right. So I'm stupid. But I still don't see how you got the note. Unless that old she-squirrel at Halem …

"Don't you call her that. Mrs. Nesbitt sent me the pieces in an envelope. I put them together."

"There'd been no need if you hadn't run out on me last night. Damn it, I was doing my best to tell you."

"I wouldn't have listened." She hadn't moved, and her low voice went on. "The note told me what I wanted to believe about you, Clint."

"I asked you to stay with me. If I weren't a bum I'd have run you off."

"I asked you first. What does that make me?"

It was a habit, arguing with her. He said stubbornly, "Talk to Paddy. He's been around, he'll give you the score on drifters like me."

"I've talked to Paddy. He told me the score."

It was an argument he didn't want to win. He said, "Okay, Devvy. I'll bust a gut trying to be what you think I am. But I'll be in other jams, and you know it."

"I'll take that chance," she said.

He sighed. It was as if the last of a heavy load had

slipped from him. He told her, "I'm glad Aila came in the other night. I ... oh hell, I want a lot more than that."

"I've been rotten to you. I gave you an awful ride, Clint."

"You did. I'll admit now I was scared silly in the pass. That place gives me the creeps."

A heron flew up-valley from the direction of the tide flats, invisible but trailing its strident voice after it like a nail across window glass.

"Sounds like Aila," Clint said.

They were quiet for a while, standing in the cool dark with the hay-scented night around them. Then Devvy said, "We still have to get it straight. About what hit us."

"It's straight now," he said. "Devvy, don't kick it around. I know what hit me."

"I want you to tell me."

"I haven't got the words."

"Tell me, Clint."

"All right. I love you, Devvy."

The heron cried again, distance smoothing the edge of its harsh voice. Devvy said, "Are you sure?"

"Yes, I'm sure." She was close to him, almost touching him. The happiness was something alive and bright now, like a fire burning. He said, "How about you?"

"I love you, Clint. I knew it that night. Even before then, I think I knew."

He said, "God knows why, Devvy. Whatever the parson is, I still think what he said about you was right."

"It wasn't," she said swiftly, vehemently. "It would have been the same no matter who was around, how many friends I had. Even if I weren't dirt-poor and a tomboy, Clint. Believe that."

"Tomboy!" He wanted to reach out to her, touch her. "I didn't mean that. Aila'd ripped you up the back. I was trying to get your mind off her. You're more a woman than she could ever be. Believe that too."

He took her wrist, the wrist he'd twisted on the black trail above the basin. "I'll never have the words, Devvy. When I woke up in your room, and saw you standing there ..."

The happiness surged into his throat and choked him. She said, "Will you take me to the dance on Martinez Saturday night?"

"How about Gunnar?"

"I'll give him one dance. The boys will have bottles cached outside. You can have a drink with him. He's kind and good ... I'd like you to be friends with Gunnar."

"Just so he knows you're my girl."

"Gunnar will know," she said. "They'll all know it, Clint. I've been thinking it over since I patched your note together in my room. But it still sounds strange, hearing you say it." Her face was only a pale blur, but he knew she was smiling. She lifted his hand to her neck, and he felt the thin silver chain of the totem he'd bought her at Martinez. "I want people to know I'm your girl."

He said carefully, "What will you wear?"

"You knew I was lying about my clothes, didn't you?"

"Sure. I've lied like that often enough too. You aren't mad at me for what I did, Devvy? I had some fishing money."

"*Mad?*" She said it softly. "Did you pick those things yourself?"

"No. I hadn't any notion what you'd need or want. I didn't even see the old lady pick 'em."

"There's a white chiffon with a high waist, Clint. I'll take it in just a bit. It's made for dancing. It's got little puffed sleeves with black velvet ribbons in them." Her voice was low and dreaming, as it had been in her room, when she held his hot face between her breasts. "I'll have white satin slippers without much to them except straps and heels. High heels. And I'll have Nylons, but you won't see them, Clint, and it's too bad, because I've got good legs."

"I know," he said, and laughed, her wrist warm and slight in his hand. "You'll be the prettiest girl there, Devvy."

He should kiss her, and he wanted to, but this thing they shared lay like a spell on him, deepened by night and quiet and the cool sweetness of cut hay. The spell was on her too; and she knew what he was thinking. She said, "No, Clint. Please, not yet."

She took her hand away, and brought the pack of fine cut from her hip pocket.

"I knew you wanted a smoke that morning. Roll one now?"

He took the package from her, and built a cigarette for her, and another for himself. Her eyes were softly luminous in the match flare. They walked back up the lane together, not touching, not talking. The voice of the Boss-Foreman was only a murmur; the moon was over the bluffs now, and a silver mist lay light on the wild hay.

He opened the gate for her. She said, "You'll never make a farmer. You didn't put the bar back after all." Her hair brushed his cheek as it had on his first day here, in this same place. He said, "Still my girl?" and she repeated it softly, "Still your girl."

She was in his arms then, and her mouth was under his in a long, yearning kiss.

PADDY WAS SITTING on the farmhouse front steps when they came in across the lawn, his pipe a dull spark in the night. He got up and waited for them, standing above them, a blocky, darker shadow among shadows.

"Aila is on the prowl again," he said to Devvy, "Did you run into her?"

"No. We'd have heard her if she'd been near us."

"The woman's a snake in our Eden. We would shift her out fast enough, except it would mean flushing our birds untimely." Paddy said around his pipe, "I'd have you two out of here as well. You're on my conscience. This is no game for children."

"She wouldn't go into Halem this late," Devvy said. "I suppose it's The Retreat."

"For spiritual counsel, I don't doubt," Paddy said. His voice was casual. "What counsel have you been taking?"

Clint felt Devvy's small hand tighten on his. She said, "We're going to get married, Paddy. Is that what you meant?"

"It is." There was a subtle sadness behind the humor in the little man's voice. "I'm glad, Clinton, to be through with puzzling over your status. It's been up and down like a ship in a gale." He knocked out his pipe on the veranda rail and came down to them. "I could wish you both had a few years more on you," he said. "But you're not children. I was wrong there. You have grown up fast, too damned fast. I'm for it, though, and good luck to you."

"Thanks," Clint said. "We're going to need it."

"Another day," Paddy said, "and we'll be out of the woods. If you'd had me in mind at all, you would of course have waited till then." His voice came from farther away, lighter, as if he'd thrown something off. "But such matters don't wait on the law's convenience. You're not a bookman, Clinton, but I'll quote you a verse anyway:

> Howso great man's strength he reckoned,
> There are two things he cannot flee.
> Love is the first, and Death is the second ...

The rest does not apply. When you've eaten, come down to the barn. There's a statement to be taken, just in case."

"In case what?" Clint asked him. But Paddy was walking away from them, silently across the moonlit lawn.

"What'd he mean by that?" Clint asked Devvy.

"I don't know." A shiver went through her as of sudden cold. "I don't want to know." She said softly, "Poor Paddy," and moved away from him, into the dark house.

In the kitchen, she lighted the lamps and brought Clint's plate out of the oven. The roast was tough and the fried potatoes were withered, and she said, "You were right about my cooking. Nothing ever comes out the way I want it."

"Not your fault," he said. "It's been sitting there for hours. Anyhow, it's a change from eggs."

Devvy poured coffee and rolled herself a cigarette, sitting at the end of the table. Her chin was between her hands, and she watched him, lamplight kind on her fair hair, turning her eyes almost black in her triangular face.

He grinned at her, loving her, still not quite believing what he'd heard her say out there in the dark to Paddy. "You're thinking," he said. "It shows. I can always tell."

"I'm worrying."

"What about?"

"I wish we knew what Aila's up to. I think she's suspicious."

He said, "She doesn't know anything. Quit being scared."

"I won't let myself be. I'm sorry. But don't let anything happen to you, Clint. I'd be lost forever then."

"Nothing's going to happen." He said it crankily. "I wish you'd lose that notion… Look, you want to show me your party dress?"

"No. Not till Saturday night." She got up, and

187

crossed to the stairs. "Stay here. I won't be long."

His cigarette had burned out. He lit it again. The cuckoo clock on the end wall, dark wood with fancy-carved gables, ticked quietly, and he heard the soft sifting of wood ash through the grates. It was a happy house in spite of Aila; you could tell about a house best of all at night, when it was quiet like this.

He'd finished his smoke before Devvy came down-stairs. She stood where Aila had stood the other day, one hand on the banister. She was wearing the pleated tan skirt, and a high-necked sweater of pale green that brought out the lights in her hair. In girl's clothes she seemed taller, maybe because the new dark-brown san-dals had higher heels. The old lady at the Halem store must be fond of her—she'd really done a job.

She looked doubtful, almost shy. "It's been so long since I had nice clothe. Am I all right?"

He said, "Like a million bucks." She came on down, slowly, into the soft lamplight, and he went to her at the foot of the stairs and put his arms around her. "I wish I'd stayed in school longer. Maybe I'd have the words then."

"You don't need them," she said. "We'll go down to Paddy now."

But he still held her, chin against her hair, the quiet wonder working in him. He said, "We'd better get mar-ried soon, Devvy."

"I know," she said. She raised her face, looking at him, something of the night still in her eyes. "It's the same with me, Clint. If I weren't happy tonight, I wouldn't be frightened. Now there's so much to lose." Her low voice was passionate suddenly, and there was a fierceness in the way she pressed against him. "Clint, I never thought it would happen, not to me. There never was anyone but you. There never will be anyone."

He kissed her, a quick, rough kiss, and put her arms away. "Make it soon, Devvy," he said; and they went out together to the cool, late night and the high-riding moon, and the distant, constant thunder of the Boss-Foreman in its pass.

A thin edge of light slanted from the barn doors. They went in. Paddy's lamp was lit, and he lay face down on his cot, head on his arms. For a moment Clint thought he was asleep, then Paddy lifted his head and sat up, swinging his legs to the floor. The butt of an automatic stuck out of the waistband of his pants. It was strange to see it there; it didn't fit in with the rest of him at all.

"What's up?" Clint asked. "Expecting something to pop?"

"Ready if it should. Aila has not gone to The Retreat at night before. It's a departure from the norm, Clinton." Paddy said briskly, "You took your time. Now, to business."

From under his cot he tugged a scuffed brown fiberboard suitcase. He opened it and took out a writing tablet, and fished around till he came up with a fountain pen. He shot ink at his toe, then said, "Sit yourself by the door, Devvy. If you catch anything louder than the squeak of a mouse, hush us ... Clinton, let's have it."

"Okay."

Clint crossed to where he'd left his cigarettes. He lit two, and passed one over Devvy's shoulder. Then he stood in front of Paddy, feeling kind of important, wondering how you gave out with a statement to the law.

"You took the cans on board," Paddy said. "Then the Chinaman." He flipped a page in his tablet. "There was the business of the ring, and yourself the soul of virtue with Captain Aleko Johannsen. Proceed from there."

"Well, I was boxed. There wasn't anything I could do about it. We had breakfast. I cooked it. The Chinaman wouldn't drink coffee, so I made him tea and put canned milk and sugar in it, and he wouldn't drink that either. Aleko laughed his head off; he thought it was a hell of a joke."

Paddy had started to write. He asked, "The cans. Where were they stowed?"

"In the forepeak. Aleko put them there. I wouldn't touch them—I thought maybe if I didn't have anything to do with the deal I'd still be in the clear. When we'd eaten, Aleko dug out a bottle of some stuff he called aquavit and we knocked off a couple of drinks. He was jumpy as a cat, he kept sticking his head into the wheelhouse to make sure I was on course."

"How was the weather?"

"Hazy. Real flat, hardly even a ground swell. I figured she'd fog up by night. We kept heading in, and by evening we were within sight of islands. I guess they were this group."

"One does not guess in court," Paddy said.

"All right, I'm sure. When it started to get dark, a light came on. It was an eight-second light and there's only one in these parts. It's on Martinez Cape."

"That's right," Devvy said. She'd turned Paddy's kitchen chair around, and sat with her bent arms resting on its back. "Could you hear the bell buoy too?"

"No. We were still pretty far out."

"I'll have all your attention," Paddy said. "You saw an eight-second light. Then?"

"We headed in for another hour. Aleko'd taken the wheel, and I could tell the way he kept squinting at the binnacle he was real fussy about our course. We were slowed to around four knots."

"Were you running under lights?"

"Yes. Aleko took out his watch and hung it beside the binnacle. At nine-thirty he slowed us till we were hardly making trolling speed. He was sweating, and after a while he took off his rain-test coat and I saw he had a gun in his hip pocket. I'd never seen him with a gun before, didn't even know there was one on board. It was a revolver, and it had walnut grips."

"Where was the Chinaman at this time?"

"Lying in my bunk. I think he was asleep. He'd been seasick even with just that much swell."

"Go on."

"It began to get foggy. The stuff came down on us from the northwest. In ten minutes it was inshore of us, real thick, and we lost the light. Aleko told me to go out and keep hitting our fog bell. I'd figured just before the fog came that we were maybe five miles off the light."

Paddy asked, "Five miles from any land?"

"Yes. I don't know what time it was when I heard something; I thought at first it was an airplane. I remember I wondered what a plane would be doing out there at night in a fog. It got louder, and I knew it was a boat. It passed us off the port bow, and Aleko came out and shoved me away from the bell. He started to make a signal, the same one he'd used with the steamer, a short then a couple of longs and another short. The boat headed back. She must have circled us, because she came in from starboard. They'd throttled her away down, and she was hardly making any noise. She was running dark. I didn't see her till she was close in. Aleko'd gone back to the wheel. He killed our engine, and they ran alongside and shut off their own power. Mike Peddar was handling her."

"How do you know it was that one?"

"I didn't then. It was Mike though—I knew for sure today. He didn't board us. I saw the cruiser's name, *Helene,* and knew I'd spotted her at Martinez Cove two weeks before. The parson, Doctor Morse, was in the cockpit with Joe Peddar. I recognized Joe; I'd tangled with him at Martinez. The *Helene* was lower in the water than the troller. We had our fenders out, and Aleko told me to hold the boats together with a pike pole. I did, and the parson came over, and Joe Peddar, and another man. He was the black-haired one with the broken nose who got off the steamer today."

"Hold it," Paddy said. He turned a page and flexed his wrist, then settled the tablet on his knee again. "I've no love for paper work," he said. "Slower now, and leave nothing out."

"Nobody said a word. Aleko'd put his coat back on. They all went down to the cabin. There was some kind of argument going on—I could hear Aleko and the parson. Aleko sounded mad."

"Could you catch their conversation?"

"No. Just a word here and there. Once I heard Aleko say something about a big risk and a fair price. I don't know what the parson answered him, but a minute later I heard him laugh. Then I heard Aleko getting out glasses and that aquavit stuff, and I figured whatever they'd been arguing about, it was all settled now."

"Slower, for the love of God!"

"After maybe ten minutes, they came out of the cabin. The black-haired man had two of the cans, and Joe Peddar had the other two. They set them on the hatch cover. Aleko came up after them, and the Chinaman was behind him."

"Where were you?"

"Starboard, holding the boats together."

"I'm caught up with you. Proceed."

"Aleko asked the parson when would be the next trip. Morse said, 'There will be no next trip, Captain.' He took off his glasses and wiped his hand across his eyes. I was watching him; he looked like a skinny little owl."

"You could see him well?"

"Yes. Aleko had an electric lantern in his hand he'd brought from the cabin. The parson put his glasses back on and nodded to the man they called Blacky, and reached into his trench coat. Everything came so fast then that I couldn't keep track of it. Aleko tried to get his own gun out, but Morse shot him while he was still pawing under his coat. Blacky shot Aleko again, and he doubled over and dropped on his face. They were still shooting, and the Chinaman yelled once, high like a woman. Joe Peddar came at me across the hatch cover. I don't know whether he had a gun or a knife. I dropped the pike pole and slugged him in the neck, and a gun went off right in my face."

"Slower!" Paddy told him. "You're telling it all in standing leaps like the devil going through Athlone!"

But Clint scarcely heard him. It was too close, too real again.

"Joe must have had me picked for his meat. He was between me and the other two, and the parson was telling him to stand clear. He drove at me with whatever was in his fist, and I went backwards over the side. The boats had swung apart maybe four feet at their sterns, and I hit my head an awful crack on the *Helene*'s gunwale. I was three-quarters knocked out, but I knew when I broke water they'd finish me off. So I let myself go deep down, then started to swim. I came up under our stern. They speared around with a flashlight for me in the fog, then I heard Joe Peddar say, 'That bastard won't come up.'"

"Was it Morse who fired at you, d'you know?"

"I think so. But I can't be sure. It was one hell of a mixup. I trod water under the stern with just my face clear, and heard the parson say, 'Take care of those two.' From the sound, he crossed to the *Helene* then. In a minute there was a splash on our portside like a body going over. It was really two splashes. A little one and a big one right after."

"We found no ballast," Paddy said. "But the dogfish had been at him, and a leg was missing. Somebody bungled there."

Clint said, "That's what Morse thought too. He called something to Joe about a botched job. Those were his words. Joe said, 'He's down for keeps. Quit worrying,

Doc.' Morse was still mad, though. He said, 'I expect clean work from my associates. Remember it. See you dispose of our other friend properly.'"

Paddy asked, "What did he mean by that?"

Clint nodded at Devvy. Her head was on her arms, and her fist beat softly on the chair back, as it had on the dinghy's gunwale when they played tag with the tide in the Boss-Foreman. She'd know what had happened to her father now—this wouldn't be easy for her to take.

"Get on with it," Paddy said. His black eyes glittered in the lamplight. "Comfort her later."

"They went to work on the Chinaman like they were gutting a fish, and they were laughing and talking while they did it. I heard enough of what they said to give me the score. Aleko'd wanted more money for running the stuff in from the steamer—he'd asked Morse for more that night we put in here, and they'd turned him down. So he held out on them when they came to meet us and pick up the cans."

"Greed killed him," Paddy said. "But we'll be grateful to Aleko. He's put the parson into our hands."

"I heard Joe ask, 'Wonder how much Doc saved on this deal?' I figured they'd killed both of them, the Chinaman as well as Aleko, just to save paying off."

"Sound business," Paddy said. "If it was the parson's last trip, he would not scruple so to do. He would save the price of his cargo and remove two who might bear witness against him, all at a single stroke. What next?"

"When they were through with the Chinaman they weighted him and heaved him over. A ship was somewhere near, coming out of the Straits. I could hear her fog horn, and her propellers thrashing. The parson told Joe to take our ax and smash the *Maiija's* tender, and I heard Joe lighting into her. Then the *Helene* pulled away. When I couldn't hear her engines I climbed back on board. Water was pouring in. I crawled down to the hold and found where they'd unscrewed a drain plug. The water was up to my ankles and I couldn't find the plug, so I got our emergency sail and pounded all I could of it into the hole. Then I went up to the cabin—I thought maybe a shot of Aleko's Swede whisky would help me think straight. But one slug and I passed out proper."

Paddy looked up from his writing.

Clint said, "Well, that's the works." He was sweating, he wiped his face on his arm.

"Sign it," Paddy told him. "Each page ... Devvy, you too."

When they were finished, Paddy scrawled his own signature on each sheet, dropped the wad into his suitcase and the tablet and pen on top. He said, stooping to shove the suitcase under his cot, "It's the lucky name brought you clear, my son. You'll be on borrowed time for the rest of your days."

"Yeah," Clint said. "I know that."

They stood close together, looking down at Paddy where he sat on the edge of his cot. Devvy said, "He's clear now? He won't be in trouble any more?"

"He will be," Paddy told her. "He will never be long out of trouble. It's the nature of the beast." He studied them, the odd half sadness softening the tough planes of his face. "But we're not without gratitude, Devvy. In this affair his slate is wiped clean. The British Columbia police have torn up their warrant, and the matter in Oregon can be forgotten. We'll see to that. Call it a wedding present from the law."

He went on, still smiling, still with his bright, hard gaze on Devvy. "It would not surprise me if there aren't other tokens of gratitude later, when we've sorted our fish in the net. We've still to find out just who the parson is, and what. All we have are a few odds and ends of facts, and a theory of sorts."

He took out his blackened cherrywood pipe and

began to load it from the gum-rubber tobacco pouch. "I'll tell you what I can of him. He's a killer as you've both had good reason to know. If we've pegged him right, he's a master thief, one who was a thorn in the side of the English at Singapore and a friend of the Japanese."

"Then he was never a missionary?" Devvy asked.

"He may have been, once on a time. But if he's the rogue we have in mind, he's been long lost to grace." Paddy struck a match on the sole of his boot and puffed his pipe alight. "If he is that rogue, he was until three years ago a small trafficker in narcotics. Now he's grown big. He would henceforward have taken no direct part in the dirty work of his business, but sat back as a company president should, and let his dogfish handle it for him. He's run great risks, shifted opium out of China and Iran not by the pound but by the hundredweight. He has made great profits."

"How much would those cans be worth?" Clint asked.

"Hard to say. Prices vary, and there's no fixed scale. But processed and on the retail market, something between one and two million dollars."

Clint whistled softly. "That much? The way they handled it you'd think it was just what it looked like—four cans of gasoline."

"Raw opium," Paddy said. "Brown lumps of it, wrapped in the leaf of the poppy. I've handled a deal of the stuff. Mud, it's called in the trade."

"I can figure the system," Clint said. "An offshore boat to make a pickup in open water and a fast job to run it in. It was pretty slick."

"He's a wily bird, the parson," Paddy said. "And as you've seen, he dislikes to leave witnesses. There was an excellent pirate lost in the little man at the mill."

Paddy grinned at them. "It's a curious thought. You'll be the better for this, you two. It will give you something, to remember in your old age—perhaps it will keep you from fighting."

Clint didn't know he'd taken Devvy's hand. It was just there in his, and it belonged there. He said, "What happens now, Paddy?"

"I am ashamed to tell you, it's so easy. There's a police launch at Fox Island. She has been waiting for two nights. She's powered with a twenty-two-hundred-horsepower aircraft engine and she's good for an easy fifty knots. If they try to run, the *Helene* will be taken before she's around Martinez Cape, and it's all over but a fair trial and the frying of our catch. You've given us our case."

He leaned forward, pipe in his fist. "It will be to-morrow night, the chances are, since we know from Constable Beamish that Aila plans a trip. Their game's up—they have to run. The parson's left a live witness against him this time. Yourself, Clinton. We'll give 'em till tomorrow dark to make a move. If they have not stirred by then, we whistle the police launch in from Fox Island and take 'em at the mill."

"How do you know it won't be tonight?" Devvy asked him.

"It might be," Paddy said. "But we're ready for that. Gunnar Lund's nighthawking in his troller, watching the channel. They can't creep past him unseen. Let 'em wiggle and twist, we've got 'em."

"There's one hole," Devvy said.

Just for a moment, Paddy's eye corners tightened. "What's that?"

"They could try to run the Boss-Foreman."

"We've a watch dog there too, Devvy. Listen and you'll hear him roaring."

"Dad said it could be done."

"Your father might have tried it," Paddy told her. "But not Mike Peddar. We've discussed the Boss-Foreman over our beer more than once. Mike knows that pass as well as any man on the coast. He insists it's death to put any boat more than half a mile below the first reef, any tide." He said with an abrupt chuckle, "Mike has told me he'd sooner hang than try it. I'm inclined to take him at his word."

He got up, yawning and stretching. "We've had a devil of a day," he said, "and I'm feeling the weight of my years. Get out now, and leave a man to his sleep."

Clint walked with Devvy to the house. She was quiet and indrawn again, and when he kissed her at the door, her lips were cold.

He said, "Not worrying still?" and she said, "I can't help it. It's been going on for so long, and Paddy's so sure. My father was always like that. It isn't lucky."

"If he wasn't sure," Clint said, "he wouldn't tell us so. He knows what he's doing."

She said, "I keep trying to think about how it will be with us. But it's no use, Clint. I'm scared—I think I'll always be scared."

"Devvy …"

He reached for her hands, but she stepped back and away.

He saw the tears start out of her eyes, silver on her cheeks. She said in a choked voice, "We'll never be married. We'll never be clear. I know we won't."

"We're going to get married," he told her harshly, angry with her fear. "Devvy, you're not to think anything else."

"It's no use," she said. "I thought after tonight I'd never be afraid again, not of Joe or the Boss-Foreman or anything. But I am, and I know what's going to happen …"

She turned swiftly, and the door closed behind her.

He didn't like to leave her that way, but maybe she was better alone till the mood wore off. Halfway to the barn, he heard someone coming along the lane from the direction of the highway. The moon was low; he waited, standing quiet in the long tongue of shadow cast by the house. Aila, coming home. She walked with a lurch, and she was talking to herself; she hadn't got that glow from beer. Aila saw him and stopped, swaying a little, peering at him.

She said thickly, "You, is it? Wot a start you give me!"

He didn't speak, and she said, "Too good for me, eh lad?" and giggled, and walked on, lurching, toward the house.

Clint shook his shoulders. Walking evil, Paddy had called her.

He'd thought to find Paddy in bed, but he was sitting on his blankets with his pipe between his teeth.

Clint said, "You were right about Aila. I just passed her coming back from the mill."

"She went inside?"

"She was headed that way. Drunk as a hoot owl."

"A common state. Callahan should have left her in her music hall." Paddy got up and went to the barn door and looked out, listening with head cocked. "Gone in," he said. "She'll be raising hell with Devvy, I expect."

"What about Devvy?" Clint asked him. "She's still worried. She thinks you're too sure of yourself."

"Nerves," Paddy said. "You have much to learn about the sex. She's handled herself better than most men would through all this, but now it's over she will treat you to a week of hysterics. Mark what I say."

"What do you know about it?" Clint asked him. "You're a bachelor, aren't you?"

"I am," Paddy told him, "and I will continue so. But women have always flung themselves at my head. When I was a young constable at Regina with the scarlet tunic on my back and my leather well-shined and a fine horse under me, I near had to beat 'em off with a quirt." He turned, and Clint knew the little man was ribbing him. "I'll tell you this too. You're better thought of than you deserve to be. All while you were on the water today, I was heckled and shrewed and cursed at as no drill sergeant ever used me. The life you'll lead with her!"

They stood side by side, lounging in the doorway, and there was a warmth and a kinship between them. Clint said awkwardly, "She's the best thing ever happened to me. Only she could have done better for herself—I'm sorry about that."

Paddy laughed. "Forget it! That was a fool's notion. I'm an old badger with the sap wrung clean out of me. You'll be good for her. Yes, and begob, she will be good for you. She'll knock the chip off your shoulder when it needs knocking, and bend your stiff neck a little, as you'll bend hers. You're babes in the woods, the both of you. You'll be church-mouse poor, and your troubles will multiply with your family."

He paused, and then said quickly, "Get up to your hayloft now, Clinton, and let me be."

WHEN THEY WENT up to the house for breakfast, Devvy was back in faded blue jeans and white shirt.

"A whistling woman and a crowing hen," Paddy said, and she turned from setting the table and grinned at him, the gold lights awake in her eyes.

"It's that song of yours, Paddy," she said. "I wish you'd put English words to it for me."

"I will," Paddy told her. "When you're safe married, and not before."

He went to the sink to wash. Clint waited by the range, his new towel tugged through his belt.

There was a gayness about Devvy this morning, as if she'd pushed the night and more than the night out of her mind. Clint watched her; she was teasing Paddy now, holding his towel just out of reach of his fingers while he groped for it with wet face screwed into a knot.

"What you need," Paddy sputtered, snatching again and missing, "is a husband that will beat you. Often, and to leave a mark."

Devvy let him grab the towel. She said to Clint, paying him some attention at last, "Will you beat me?"

He'd been a little anxious; this new mood was something for which he hadn't been prepared. But her smile told him all he needed to know. He said, "I'd be scared to. You'd probably shoot me. You're tough."

"Wait till you see me in my party dress," she said.

He wanted to kiss her, but this thing was still too new. Maybe she felt the same way.

She said, talking like a boss again, "I'm making hotcakes. You'd better eat hearty, because that haying has to be finished before dark."

Clint looked past her to the stairs. He hadn't expected to see Aila this early, but she was coming down in her green housecoat, with her cat walk, and the small secret smile on her mouth. She said, "Good morning all," and Paddy answered from the sink, looking into the mirror and not turning, "Good morning to you, Madam Callahan."

Aila disregarded him, but gave Clint her sleek smile. " 'E's a joker, that one." Then, purringly to Devvy, "W'y, you're almost pretty, my dear. Give love a chance and wot it won't do for a girl!"

He'd have slugged her cheerfully; he watched Devvy, urging her in his mind, Don't let her get you. Don't torch up. But she didn't; she flashed Clint one surprised, half-warning glance, then said calmly, "Brian and Elsie were out early. Are you eating this morning, Aila?"

"Coffee, if it's made. I thought once out of men's clothes you'd be glad to stay out of 'em, Devvy."

Devvy poured her a cup of coffee. If she was fighting her temper, she gave no sign of it.

"Takes a little getting used to, I suppose," Aila said. "Any'ow, you shouldn't dip into your trousseau before the wedding, ducky. Bad luck, you know."

Fixing for a sneak punch of some kind, Clint thought; but he wasn't worried now. Aila couldn't hurt her again like that.

"It's as well 'e bought 'em for you," Aila said. "Even if you'd 'ad the money you'd just 'ave put it all in taxes." She poured cream into her coffee and said amiably, "We wouldn't do it that way at 'ome, of course. Wouldn't consider it respectable, like. But I suppose in this country such things don't matter."

Devvy said, "Sit down, Aila. You'll feel more human after your coffee."

He saw the faint lines deepen at Aila's mouth corners, and the look she threw them was spiteful and puzzled, and for an instant altogether vicious.

She said nothing more, but lighted a cigarette and smoked it with her coffee in quick, nervous puffs. They were still eating when she butted the cigarette in her saucer and went back upstairs.

Devvy said, "I'm going to be busy today, so clear out. I'll bring you your lunch."

"Busy at what?" Clint asked her. She said, "Taking in my dress. It's Saturday tomorrow, or had you forgotten?"

"I haven't forgotten," he said, and saw the quick color come up in her cheeks.

Paddy said, "Come, Clinton. Saturday will keep. For now, there's work to be done."

No wind stirred in the creek valley. The heat held, and the bloated thunderheads were piled high in the south. At the hayfield, Paddy fetched his scythe and hone from behind the log. He told Clint, "If you're to be a stump rancher it's time you were learning. See can you run this machine for a spell without taking off a leg."

"While you sleep under a bush?" Clint asked him.

"In a manner of speaking, yes. I'll be up on my hill talking to this one or that." Paddy tossed him the hone, and began to peel his checked workshirt over his head. He still packed the big gray .45 in the waistband of his patched denims, Clint saw. "If they plan to run for it tonight, there's the cans to be put on the *Helene*. Let Lum Kee tell me they've done that, and in comes the launch from Fox Island with more law than these parts have seen since Prohibition."

He draped his shirt over the log, and plunged into the brush. Clint hefted the scythe; he'd never held one before, and he found it an awkward thing to handle, ugly and lacking any proper balance. But it was fun to be doing just an ordinary job of work again, and he whistled as he tramped down toward the creek corner where Paddy'd left off yesterday.

The fireweed dripped diamonds from last night's heavy dewfall. The chuckle of the creek was good company for a man alone, and the scythe became less clumsy in his hands after the first few swings. He started to get the hang of it; and he felt peaceful and right with himself, sweating here with the sun hot on his bare shoulders.

North half a mile, he could see the gray roof of the farmhouse, flanked by its madronas. He thought of Devvy up there, and he tried to think about the doings at the mill, and of Paddy waiting to haul his seine. But that wasn't important any more—much less important than finishing this quarter acre of wild hay.

The quiet, persistent happiness stayed with him as he worked. He'd take her back to that bluff over the Boss-Foreman next full-moon night. They'd be married by then, and he'd hold her there in his arms till the tide was only a whisper and the moon was down. They'd talk their lives out and make their plans, and even if

Paddy was right and they never more than scrabbled a living for themselves, it wouldn't matter.

Once, before he'd got sense, he'd imagined that having to live in a place like this would be the next worst thing to being in jail. The way he felt now, though, anyone who wanted cities could have them. People among the islands lived better.

They'd need a car. A light truck first, and if things worked out well, maybe a convertible later. And something better in the way of a boat than Devvy's outboard rig. Steamer days and Saturday nights, they'd run cross-channel to Martinez Cove. He guessed they'd do most of their shopping in Halem. Buy their groceries in the big, cluttered general store above the dock, pick up their mail from Mrs. Nesbitt—he liked that old lady. Then knock back a couple of beers in the tavern with the beat-up red leather chairs, and head for home like a young married couple should.

Clint grinned to himself, swinging the scythe. In spite of what Paddy had said last night, he didn't think they'd do much rehashing of these days. Murder and dope-running didn't belong in a friendly, quiet place like this. They were things to be shoved out of mind as quickly as possible, overlaid with the pleasant happenings of every day.

Thoroughly into the rhythm of the job now, he lost track of time, letting his mind range lazily where it wanted, paced by the swish of the scythe and the whisper of cut grass falling away from the long blade. He didn't stop till his arms were weary and the sun was blazing straight overhead. Then he loafed off to the creek, and when Devvy came down he was smoking on a flat rock, watching a water snake minnow hunting in the opposite shallow.

It was a big snake, three feet long anyway, and heavy-bodied from good feeding. He saw it catch a trout minnow and start for its den among the water-worn boulders, the minnow still alive, wriggling crosswise in its mouth.

Devvy set down her lunch bucket. Clint watched her, cigarette butt cupped in his palm, while she threw rocks at the snake, straight and hard as a boy would, until it was writhing with jaws wide open and back smashed.

"You didn't have to do that," he said. "It wasn't hurting us."

"They kill trout," Devvy told him. "Anyway, I hate them."

"Well, you hit it, go finish it off."

She said, "Why? It's as good as dead now."

"Nuts!" He hopped from rock to rock across the pool's exit riffle, and dropped a heavy stone on the snake's head.

"Those things can bite," Devvy told him when he came back. "Joe dropped one down my neck once."

Clint picked up the lunch bucket. "That why you were so tough with this one?" he asked her.

"Maybe. I don't know. I dreamed about that last night."

"No wonder, the spooky fit you were in. What came over you, Devvy?"

She scrambled up the creek bank, and turned and waited, looking down at him. "Dad used to say there's no one crazier than a Finn except an Irishman. I'm both."

"Over it now?"

"Pretty well. But I don't like the way Aila's acting. She's gloating over something, fairly hugging it to her."

"Forget her," Clint said. "Look—here's where I was working. How'd I do?"

"All right," Devvy said. "You know, Aila thought she'd hooked a rich man. She thought she was coming to an estate. I'll always remember the look on her face when Dad brought her here. She hated him and she hates me."

"Quit talking about her." Clint set the bucket on Paddy's log. No sign of the little man yet; chances were he'd stick with his radio now till he got the message he was waiting for.

"We might as well go ahead," Devvy said.

They ate their lunch, bacon sandwiches and cake in waxed paper and a thermos of coffee, sitting on the log in full sunlight. Paddy didn't show up. When they were finished Devvy said, "I'm not going back to the house. I've had all of her I can take for a while."

"I don't think she'll be around much longer," Clint said. "Not after tonight."

"I hope not."

She stood up, and he said, "I thought I was doing pretty dam good with that scythe."

"Better than I expected," Devvy said. "But you blistered your thumb."

"It's nothing."

"You can't work with that."

"For God's sake!" He grinned at her, wadding the lunch paper in his hands. "If you want us to play hooky, why don't you come right out and say so?"

"I wanted you to ask me." She might be kidding him; but her face was sober. "I'm trying to learn how to be a girl, Clint."

"You'll get by." He stowed the lunch bucket and the other thermos in the shady lee of the log for Paddy. She had something there—in a way, they were both starting from the wrong side of scratch. "No taking the boat out, though, we might find ourselves in the middle of a battle."

She said, "I hope it's over today. I want to be through with it." She turned her head and smiled at him, and he knew she felt about that as he did. "We'll be able to worry about other things then, Clint. Things like taxes. I haven't made last year's yet."

"We'll make 'em," Clint said. He took her hand and they walked on like that, down toward the estuary basin. "I've been thinking too. A trollerman does all right for himself. If I could knock off twenty bucks a day handlining for a spell, that'd soon get us a gas boat …"

"You'll keep out of the Boss-Foreman," Devvy said. "We'll never go in there again. Anyway, trolling is a job for a single man. I want you home nights."

"Suppose I went fishing just for a while? Maybe I could save enough to buy into a truck-logging outfit."

"You don't have to go fishing. 'Ric Henderson needs a bulldozer man. He'd take you on if I asked him, and that job pays well. 'Ric's got more contracts than he can handle."

She'd had a lot of this kind of figuring to do—she'd always had to carry other people, look out for them. He said, "I can make money when I have to. That way I'm lucky. You can quit worrying and start thinking about those trees you want to plant."

She said, "It's going to be wonderful, Clint, working it out together. I keep thinking about things we'll do. Just ordinary things. Like filling out mail-order lists from catalogues winter nights. And going in to town Saturdays. We'll take a trip to Seattle once a year and stay in a big hotel."

"No kids," he said. "Not for a long time, anyway. Just you and me."

"Kids," she said. "Two, maybe three. I can see a fight coming up about that."

The basin looked as it had on his first morning here, except there was no troller at the landing. Tide was lower too—they could see the *Maiija*'s hulk clearly, bedded on gravel. Clint emptied his pockets, kicked off his shoes, and flipped in. He came up halfway across the basin; it was good not to be afraid of deep water any more.

Devvy had a bathing suit on under her clothes, a

two-piece yellow rig that left most of her slim body bare. He whistled at her, and she laughed, stepping out of her jeans at the end of the landing.

"You did me proud," she said. "I've been dipping into my trousseau again, Clint."

He wondered, watching her, why he'd ever wanted a black-haired girl. She was the long-legged, lovely girl he'd put together those lazy days on the offshore banks, to the music of the little spring-pole bells and the throb of the Diesel below. She was all the girl he'd ever want.

He called to her, mimicking Joe Peddar, "No gun, sweetheart?" and she grinned at him, and arched off the landing in a clean, shallow dive. She was a good swimmer; she tagged him the length of the basin, and they trod water, facing each other, hanging in the gentle current.

"I don't need a gun," she told him, and flung her wet hair back. "Wolf season's over now."

"Like hell," he told her, and chased her back to the landing and caught her there and kissed her till she locked his arms and sunk them both in the warm green water.

When they hauled out, the sun had untangled itself from the trees and was beating down on the planking with the concentrated heat of midafternoon. They lay side by side, drying, heads on arms, faces turned to each other.

"What was your father like, Devvy?" he asked her lazily.

"He was seven feet tall and he looked like God." Her eyes were closed; she spoke softly. "That's what Charley Jukes at the Plaza said about him once. He had no more money sense than a child, and everything he touched went wrong. After my mother died he was worse. He didn't seem to care any more. He went rumrunning— Mike Peddar got him into that. Of course he got caught."

"You had it worse than me, I guess. It's harder for a girl."

"Maybe. It was good when Dad was here. Tell me about you."

It made him restless even thinking about those days; he rolled over and sat up, frowning at his hands pressed flat on the planking, new scabs on his knuckles over old scars. "About all I had was these and they never got me much but trouble. It's funny—you're pushed around enough, you start hating everyone. Even good people. I didn't want to like anyone till I met you."

She said, "We'll know all about each other sometime," and smiled up at him. "It was quicker with us than with my people. They'd known each other three weeks. He was logging in British Columbia. She lived on Sinfala Island where nobody lives but Finns. He crashed one of their dances on a dare and they beat him up. It took a lot of them to do that. He came back the next Saturday night and fought her two brothers and the man she was engaged to, and ran off with her in her father's gas boat. I wasn't much older than Brian when she died, but I remember they used to laugh about how he kidnaped her. They laughed a lot."

"We will too, Devvy."

"Will we? I hope so."

...Thinking again, kicking it around. He could always tell by the way she seemed to draw into herself, the small frown between her eyes. She'd had a Finnish girl for her mother; it showed in her high cheekbones and her light hair. When she was little she must have run these woods pretty much like the skinny redhead, Aila's Elsie. Devvy'd be skinny too, a spider monkey of a kid with green-gray eyes too large for a pointed face.

It was deeply good to be here with her, the sun beating down on them and the drowsy madrona music in their ears. It would be better later. He'd go after the bulldozer job. Work hard, maybe make enough to pay wages for a hired hand. If Devvy wanted the farm whipped into shape, she'd have it that way. It would be tough, but very good.

He had no wish to leave the island, but a girl had a right to a proper honeymoon, and he thought he knew how he could swing that. Seattle, maybe even San Francisco if he could bring the deal off. The *Maiija's* seventy-horsepower Diesel ought to bring the price of a honeymoon. She'd get a kick out of Market Street. He could see them there as if they were two other people, him in a new outfit …

She said, "Did you ever sleep with a girl?"

He stared at her; he could feel his face getting hot. "You come out with the damnedest things."

"Did you?"

"No. Not quite. Suppose I had?"

"I'd be mad. I knew Aila was lying the other night but it made me mad just the same."

"Hell with Aila. Don't talk about her, I said."

"Joe has. He told me about it once."

"You let him tell you?"

"I couldn't help it. He was holding my wrists."

"Was that while you were living there, Devvy?"

"Yes."

"That was tough for you."

"Tough?" Unsmiling, she looked him in the face. "Sometime I'll tell you all about it. Only I want your arms around me when I do. The second time was worse because I was older and so was Joe."

He scowled down, and she laid her hand lightly on his fist. "Don't. It's crazy to get mad about it now."

Clint said, "I should have killed him."

He got up, prodded by sudden bitter anger, and stood over her, hands in his belt. She watched him, golden face turned and still, while he fished around for words. As always when he wanted them, the right ones wouldn't come.

All he could find to say was, "That guy's wrong in the head. It won't be like that with us."

She didn't answer, and he said challengingly, "Well?"

"No." Her voice was soft. "It won't be. That's something else you've given me, Clint. I wanted a boy who wouldn't be tough with me. Now I've got him."

"I'll be tough when I have to be." It was the first time he'd really felt older than Devvy; the way she looked up at him had something to do with that. "I can see you're going to need a lot of straightening out."

He reached for her hands and pulled her up. She stood close to him, inside his arms, and he knew these days had changed her, too. Made her younger somehow, lovelier.

She said, "You're taking on a terrible job, Clint. If I weren't selfish I'd send you away till we're both older."

"Would you?" He tightened his arms, looking down at her, hungry for her as he had been in the half-dark of her room, but sure of himself now, and of her.

"No. Who'd keep you out of trouble? Anyway, you might find another girl or one of us might die."

He wanted to kiss her; but he wasn't that sure of himself. He ruffled her hair over her eyes and said, "You know, you like to scare yourself. Go get dressed. We'd better hunt up Paddy."

THEY FOUND THE WIDE little man in the hayfield, swinging the scythe as if he were just what he looked to be—a casual laborer sweating out a casual afternoon's work. He broke off singing and jogged up to them. His sunburn was peeling, and with his wreck of a hat and his wiry blue bristle, he looked disreputable and altogether shiftless.

"Clinton," he said, "this scythe will not be the same. You've had it among rocks." He brought out his pipe and hunted through his pocket for a match. "Where'd you vamoose to? I've been worried for you."

"We went swimming," Devvy said. "Has anything happened yet, Paddy?"

"Nothing that signifies. Lum Kee talked with me a while back. He has no way of being certain, but it's his belief they put the cans on the *Helene* last night."

"Then you don't have to wait," she said. "Paddy, call the launch in. Get it over."

He said, very kindly, "Steady now, my sha. We'll leave no loose ends untied. There's Aila. Let me just know she's out of your house and gone down to them and we'll move fast enough. We want 'em all together." He said to Clint, "Give me a match, I'm out of them entirely. Then go up yonder quietly, and if she's flitted, back and tell me."

They left him sitting on his log. It was very still in the valley, and sultry, with the feel of rain in the air. Their feet made no sound in the dust of the lane, and they went up quietly, hand in hand, held by the same curious tension.

The white horse and the two cows were far down in the wild pasture, and the house was asleep behind its sun-browned lawn.

Devvy said, "Someone's been here from the mill."

"You sure?" Clint asked. "It could have been the milk truck."

"No. It's a different tire tread. I think it was the station wagon."

The kitchen door was open, and they thought at first the house was empty. Then they heard a mouse-stirring upstairs, and the boy, Brian, was peeking down at them through the banisters. He'd been crying, the tear channels showed on his chipmunk cheeks. On the left side of his face was a dark bruise.

Devvy made a little, low sound in her throat, and ran

up the stairs to him. He began to cry again, full-bodied howls as she gathered him into her arms, and Clint could hear her soothing him, mothering him.

The range was smoking badly, and the firebox door was ajar. He crossed to it, and yanked the door open. One of Devvy's new sandals dropped to the floor. The leather was crisped and charred. Farther inside was a half-burned white bundle. The party dress. He lifted off the back lid, and the smell of smoldering wool wrinkled his nose. Aila's farewell act of spite.

Bitch! He set the lid back on and kicked the firebox door shut.

Under the kitchen table, as he turned away from the stove, he saw something that stopped him. She'd smashed Devvy's rifle too, probably set the butt against the floor and stamped on it till the stock cracked at the narrow wrist below the forearm. She, or Joe Peddar—Joe, most likely. That looked more like the kind of job he'd do.

He called to Devvy, "How is it up there?"

She didn't answer. Brian had stopped crying, and the only sound in the house was the ticking of the clock.

"Devvy," he called again, anxious now, vaguely alarmed, and started for the stairs.

Sunshine patterned the worn carpeting of the upstairs corridor. She stood looking into Aila's room, still as if she were frozen there in the doorway. Brian was pressed against her legs, and she was holding him tight to her, his face turned away from the room.

"What is it?" Clint asked, and went to her, feeling the hard thudding of his heart.

He looked past her, into the sunshiny room, then took her by the shoulder and swung her around, seeing her blank face, all color drained out of it, her eyes darkened by shock.

"Get out of here," he told her harshly, and when she didn't speak or move, he pushed her away from the open door. She took Brian's hand and moved like a sleepwalker to the head of the stairs, still with the blank, dazed look on her face.

He stepped into Aila's room, not wanting to, but drawn in spite of himself. She lay face down across the rumpled bed in her blue-and-white checked housedress, as if she'd passed out or gone to sleep. The blue ribbon had come loose from her black hair, and one arm trailed over the bed's edge, long white fingers brushing the floor.

Blood made a gay, dreadful pool between rug and bed, and between her shoulders the dress was soaked with blood. He forced himself to touch her. Her cheek under his fingers was cold.

Knifed. Dead for hours.

Except for the body and the blood pool on the floor, the room looked much as it had three days ago. Clothes scattered where she'd dropped them, clutter of bottles and makeup gear on the dresser, toilet set with a scrolled A on the backs of silver hairbrush and mirror.

He backed out of the room, and closed the door after him.

Devvy was still at the head of the stairs; Brian was whimpering again, clinging to her hand.

Devvy said, "She's dead, isn't she?"

He nodded, and took her other hand, and they went down together, across the stone flags of the kitchen, and out of the house. Devvy was very pale still, and she looked dazed and sick, but he knew she was over the first shock of it.

"She was in with them," Devvy said. "Why would they kill her?"

"I don't know."

He saw Elsie then, watching them from the lane. She still had the look of a furtive woods' creature, and she came toward them slowly, as if ready if they moved or spoke, to whirl and run. On her thin sharp-boned face was bewilderment and fear. No kid ought ever to wear a face like that, Clint thought, sorry for her suddenly, feeling shaken and sick.

Devvy said, "Clint, go and tell Paddy. I'll take them out to the highway. 'Ric Henderson will be passing in an hour; he'll drive them in to Mrs. Nesbitt at Halem."

"You're not going down that road alone," Clint told her grimly. "You're staying with me till this is over." He said to Elsie, "Who came here? Can you tell us?"

She only looked at him. Devvy said gently, "Was it Joe Peddar?" and the little girl ducked her head and began to cry then, tears without sound.

Devvy said, "You're to go out to the highway, Elsie. When you get there, wait for 'Ric and ask him to take you to Mrs. Nesbitt. You'll stay at her house tonight and I'll come for you in the morning. Will you do that?"

Elsie whispered a *"Yes."* They watched the two cross the lawn and start up the lane, small figures alone in the heat of late afternoon, trudging toward the timber belt between house and highway.

"Nothing we can do here," Clint said. "We'd better go."

He didn't know why they'd knocked her off. That didn't make sense. Devvy'd thought the woman was suspicious of Paddy, and he was certain she'd been searching Paddy's room that night. One thing—they'd never learn from Aila.

"That was a hell of a thing to walk into," he said. "Feeling better now?"

"I'm all right." Devvy didn't look at him. "He must have come in not long after I left."

"If you'd been there …"

She shook her head. "Don't let go of my hand. I'm scared, Clint."

They found Paddy Burke where they'd left him, sitting on the mossy old fir log with his shirt across his knees and the scythe leaned beside him. Clint told him. Paddy listened, not interrupting.

When he got off the log he seemed bigger somehow, and there was nothing casual about him. "They're cleaning house," he said, "so we'll take no more chances. If the parson's so pressed now that he leaves a body behind him, he'd not boggle at others. We'll go on up and finish this business."

Devvy said, "But why would they kill her? She was supposed to go with them."

"Perhaps." Paddy knocked out his pipe against his heel. "Or we may have been running a false scent there. She married your father for money he did not have. She brought him to his death, pushing him into a devil's game for money. We know she's had money from somewhere." He pulled the automatic from his waistband, checked the clip and slapped it back into the butt. "Aila may have made Aleko's mistake, set too high a price on her services. Or she may just have got the wind up and been ready to bargain with the law. Anyway, the woman's dead and you're free of her, Devvy—let it go at that."

"I'm glad she's dead," Devvy said. "That's what makes it so horrible. But I've hated Aila ever since Dad brought her home. It was the one thing he ever did that I couldn't forgive him."

Paddy pulled out his watch. "Six-forty-five," he said. "The launch will be into the mill cove twenty minutes after they have the signal. By the look of the sky, they may have a squall to help."

He told Devvy gently, "When that's out of the way, we'll talk up Johnny Beamish. She and everything of hers will be out of your house when you go back to it. I'll leave in the morning, Devvy, and sorry to do it. Tomorrow night, you'll go dancing."

He walked between them, up the empty lane between

216

the fir and the red-limbed madrona. His cherrywood pipe was between his teeth again, and he looked tough and calm, and a little sad.

"Sell me an acre sometime for my old age," he said. "I'll a small cabin build there—it is from a poem by an Irishman, Clinton—and I'll fish for cod and bring the science of numerology to each benighted soul on your island."

"We'll give you an acre," Devvy said softly, "and Clint will build your cabin. You'll be missed, Paddy."

"I will not," he said, and a grin creased his blue-jawed, peeling face. "You're good children in your way. Babes in the woods and too young for marriage, God knows, but you've got spunk. You've had the devil like a roaring lion amongst you, and you've helped us beat him."

He was in a talking mood, like a man who has finished a hard and weary day. "I've planned me a vacation," he told them. "I'll have myself posted to guard duty at the front doors of the Bank of Canada in Vancouver. I will stand there in my red tunic and boots you could see your face in, and let the she-tourists ogle me as they pass."

"No horse?" Clint asked. He wondered if the little man was making talk for Devvy's sake, and glanced at him curiously and with a great liking. He fished in strange waters, he played a deadly game where there were no rules to guide a man; and even knowing what he was, it would always be hard to think of him as a cop.

The heat held, but a fitful breeze brought the smell of new-cut hay. Paddy walked ahead of them now, with a lengthened stride. Clint took Devvy's hand and swung it lightly. Her fingers were cold in his.

"I'll see about that bulldozer job tomorrow," he told her.

She said, her voice almost a whisper, "I'm scared, Clint. Terribly scared."

She'd taken the full, unparried shock of this last of

the parson's murders; and even without that, she'd had it tougher than he, and for a lot longer. All he could do was take care of her from here on out, try to make it up to her. Nothing he could say to her now, though, would help.

Paddy ducked off the road into a path that Clint could scarcely see. It was the same dim trail out of which he'd stepped to whistle at them two mornings ago. He shouldered ahead through hardtack and spirea. They followed him; the farm woods must be threaded with these paths, made by deer, or by Brian and Elsie at play. Clint wondered again what Devvy had looked like when she was the redhaired kid's age, and he hoped she'd have some pictures. It wasn't as if they'd been able to grow up in the same town, go to school together and run with the same after-school crowd. They'd have a lot of catching up to do.

Paddy stopped where a mossed-over cedar stump humped out of a tiny clearing. He knelt and scooped at a litter of brush in its lee. When he leaned back he held an oblong bundle in his arms, wrapped in what looked to be parachute silk.

It was very quiet here. A whitethroat was singing somewhere in the deeper woods, and they could hear the mutter of the Boss-Foreman like a humming in the evening air. Paddy unwrapped a small and compact radio in a green metal case. Clint watched him tug an aerial out of its slot and untelescope it.

Still kneeling, Paddy bedded the radio among the roots of the stump. He looked at them, and his grin was merry and wry. "We will set the great wheels turning," he said. "Then home to milk the cows."

A twig stirred with a tiny rustle in the masking spirea. A wren could have made that sound, or another whitethroat settling for his evening song.

Clint felt Devvy s hand harden in his, saw Paddy's head jerk up. He saw pale orange flame puff from the spirea, and heard the flat slam of the shot.

Paddy swayed backwards on his heels, grunting as if all the wind had been beaten out of him. Shoving Devvy down, Clint saw Paddy's hand stab at his belt and come away with a fistful of fire. He was on his feet now, bulling forward, the shots almost running into each other. The gun in the spirea slammed again, twice, and he gave a small, tired sigh, and crumpled slowly to his knees.

The big gray automatic dropped from his hand as if it had suddenly grown too heavy to hold. He pitched forward on his face, his hat fell off and he sprawled there across his radio like a man asleep.

Clint heard the brush rustle behind him. A mild, familiar voice said, "We'll continue our discussion, Mr. Farrell." He whirled, ready to slug, hearing Devvy's scream going on and on in his ears. Then the weight of the world dropped on his head, pushing him down with fire in his eyes, down and down.

There was no one to reach for him this time, no hands to help him now.

HE WAS ON A BOAT AGAIN, he could feel the faint and languid pulse of her engines.

When he wakened—when he could bring himself to that great effort—a girl would be bending over him, a girl with light wind-roughened hair and a still, sullen face with high cheekbones, and gray-green eyes with golden flecks in them like the sunwheels in deep water.

He dragged himself up from the fog and the quiet, and it was night and he could scarcely see her. But she was there beside him, her face a dim triangle above him.

He said her name, "Devvy," and she said, "I'm here."

Her voice was as he'd last heard it, low, almost listless. She said, "You shouldn't have wakened. I hoped you wouldn't, ever."

"Where are we?" he whispered dully.

"On the *Helene*. They shot Paddy."

"Why didn't they kill us?"

"I don't know. I don't think we'll be alive long, Clint." He lay on the floor of the *Helene*'s narrow cabin. She was crouching beside him, and he groped for her, and her arm was under his hand.

"They knew about the radio," she said. "They were up there waiting for him."

"How'd they find out?"

"It was Elsie. She was playing in the woods when Paddy moved the radio to a new place. She saw him and found it, and told Aila."

So it was as small a thing as that. He'd seen the skinny little redhaired girl running through the bracken, something furtive about her, something of urgency and caution in the look of her, and his own caution had been deep asleep. He'd walked on with his head in the clouds, a boy on a man's errand, and Paddy was gone and they were here, and all the wheels were spinning in reverse toward disaster.

"I spotted her," he said. "I should have known."

"How could you? How could any of us?"

He asked, "Are we offshore yet?"

"No. I think we're just outside the bay. They're waiting for the next squall."

The window ports were open, and he could hear the light whisper of rain, and the Boss-Foreman growling between its islands north away. He listened for the heartbeat throb of a gas-boat exhaust, the sound that would tell him Gunnar Lund was prowling the channel, but the only sounds were of rain and tide.

He'd been slugged, with a gun butt, he guessed. The hair on the back of his head was matted with blood. More bumps than a Donegal murphy, Paddy had said, busy over him in his box of a room. Strange a thing like that should come into his mind now.

Devvy said, "He got two of them, Mike Peddar and the man with the black hair."

Even though he knew the answer, he had to ask her. "Joe?"

"He's here. He and Morse and the other one off the steamer." She said, "Don't take your hand away, Clint. If you do I'll start screaming again. I won't be able to stop screaming."

"We've got a chance," Clint told her. "Gunnar's out here somewhere. There's the police launch at Fox Island."

The sky through the port was dark. The whisper of rain had ceased, and the *Helene* was barely moving. He listened again, mouth open, sifting the night for the pulse of a troller's exhaust. That sound would carry far—clear across the channel. But it wasn't there.

Devvy said, "I wish it were over. There's a lot of things I wish now. That Aila hadn't come into my room. That I'd made Paddy let you go."

"I didn't want to go, Devvy. I'm glad we got that straight, anyway."

She said, "It's strange when we fight so much. I didn't want to be in love with you, Clint. All I wanted was to pay them for my father and get rid of Aila and make something out of the farm. I never thought of anything else till you put in at Martinez."

He said, "You helped me. You've always done things for me. I've never been able to help you, not the way I wanted."

"You have, Clint. Oh, you have."

"Not enough to matter. I told you I was trouble— you should have believed me then."

She was quiet again, and he held her wrist, the wrist she could only turn halfway over. The *Helene* had almost stopped. She was hanging in the tide that sucked down to the Boss-Foreman. The talking of water against the cruiser's skin was a light overlay of sound above the voice of the narrows.

Clint said, "We aren't dead yet. If they meant to kill us, why wouldn't they do it in the woods?"

"Joe wanted to kill you then. Doctor Morse wouldn't let him."

"Why?"

"He said something about the wrong time and place." The cabin door swung softly open. The man above them was only a shadow. He came down with a soft, heavy padding; he must be barefoot as he had been when he stood on the *Maiija's* companionway in the estuary.

Clint, heard the lazy voice, "Don't try anything. You haven't any gun this time."

He said to Clint, "I've been looking forward to this. Get up."

Clint came slowly to his knees, and Joe Peddar crossed to him and hauled him off the floor by the front of his shirt.

"I'd take longer with you if I could," he said. "But we're pressed for time." The grin was in his heavy voice. He said, "You should have brought your new clothes, Devvy. We're going on a trip. It won't be a tourist cruise, but we'll have fun."

He told Clint, "Walk slow ... I'll be back, sweetheart. You can stay here and listen."

The knife was in the small of his back, prodding him out of the cabin and up the companionway. Outside it was lighter. He saw the thin man with the mustache, the city type, lounging in the portside fishing chair.

"You won't have to worry about Devvy any more," Joe said. "There won't be a thing to worry you, not where you'll be."

The thin man said without interest, "Quit playing around. Take care of him."

"Keep out of this." Joe's voice was thick with a curious

222

hunger. "This is my party ... Farrell, turn around."

The knife was in his left. He'd switched hands since the .22 slug drilled the flesh of his right arm. With his left he might be a fraction slower.

Clint turned, and threw himself forward, cuffing down at Peddar's knife hand, crashing him against the gunwale. He drove again, all his weight in it, and Peddar gave one cry, and they plunged over the *Helene*'s side together.

There was no sensation of striking water, just of sudden cold, and the light dwindling as they went under. Clint let air out of his lungs, sinking them deeper. Weight didn't count here, or reach or strength. He wasn't helpless here in the deep water.

He drove hard with his knee, into Peddar's belly, and shoved away and drove again. Get his mouth open ... strangle him ...

Peddar broke loose from him and Clint kicked himself toward the surface, seeing the darkness lighten above him. He let his head come out, and gulped air, and hung there wary as a seal or an otter. The *Helene* was fifty yards away; she'd circled and her shadow of a hull was creeping down toward him.

Twenty feet off, the water humped and Peddar lunged head and shoulders out. His arms flailed and his mouth was a black hole in his face, and his voice was a crazy bubbling.

Clint turned and stroked toward him, then, like an otter in a stream, flipped under. He caught Peddar's ankles and trickled air from his lungs and took Peddar down as an otter takes a fish. He pulled Peddar's body down, and turned him and locked his forearm under Peddar's chin, all his hate in it, crushing and tightening. Peddar's left hand, the knife hand, threshed at him, and he caught it and twisted up and back, not feeling the knife, only the bones breaking. The hand and the arm and all the long heavy body lay slack now, but he held till he knew he must come up or be drowned himself. Lungs near to bursting, he opened the vise of his arm, and Peddar was sinking past him. He set his feet against Peddar's shoulders, driving him deeper, kicking himself toward the surface.

He lay like a seal in a tideway, and watched for Peddar's head to come out, or his back to roll clear, or bubbles to break the slick water skin. The *Helene* was very close, but still he hung there, waiting for what might come up.

The *Helene*'s bows were over him, and he pulled himself aside with a weary stroke.

Peddar would not come up. The tide would roll him, tumble him down with the rest of its flotsam into the roaring funnel of the Boss-Foreman. Maybe some later tide would release what the dogfish left of him, toss him on a beach somewhere, with the drift and the brown slimy kelp at tideline.

That much at least he'd done for Devvy. That score was paid, for both of them, in full.

His fist was clenched tight on a smooth, hard oblong; and he knew he held the green jade ring, stripped from a dead man's hand under the sea.

He saw the lights of Martinez, distant over his left shoulder. From above, the parson's mild voice said, "Bring him aboard."

The thin man sounded tired, uninterested in the whole business. "Why louse us up with a couple of kids? Get rid of them, Doc. We can't hang around here."

"I'm still your employer. I said to bring him on board."

"Okay. But where there's one law there's others." The thin man leaned overside and caught Clint by the wrists. With wiry strength, he hauled him inboard to sprawl in the *Helene*'s cockpit.

Morse called from above, "Come up here, Mr. Farrell. Perhaps now we can talk without interruption."

He sat in front of the dull-gleaming instrument panel, his hands light on the wheel, relaxed and at ease like a parson in his study. By the faint glow from the binnacle, Clint saw that he was smiling.

"You've done me a service," Morse told him. "Unintentionally, of course, but nevertheless it's appreciated. There's no room in my organization for a man who bungles twice." He added with a gentle chuckle, "You handled that matter very efficiently. I take it you drowned him?"

Clint said, "What do you want with us?"

"I was reasonably sure of the outcome," Morse told him. "Otherwise I'd not have forced you to display your talents." He said briskly, "So much for that. Now, Mr. Farrell, please think of me as a businessman. One older than you, and a great deal wiser. You've chosen so far to work against me. It was not profitable, I think you'll agree. Bluntly, I'd prefer to have you with me."

The rain set in again, bouncing off the wheelhouse roof and hissing into the sea. Another squall. Morse reached forward to the instrument panel, and the loafing engines quickened their tempo.

He said in his deep, pleasant voice, "My operations here are finished. Perhaps my choice of a location and associates was unfortunate, but there's an element of risk in every business." His hands shifted on the wheel. "Immediately I suspected Mr. Burke's identity, I made certain changes of plan. We'll be picked up off the Straits by an Orient-bound cargo vessel. She's not under the American flag, and since she's clear of territorial waters it's most unlikely she will be interfered with. I hope before we reach her you've decided to accept my offer, Mr. Farrell."

The *Helene* was driving smoothly ahead now, and the rain was a blinding sheet across the raked wheelhouse windows. "As for Devvy," Morse said, "she's a charming child, and I hope you can persuade her as well as yourself. I imagine she's worried about you—I'd suggest you go down to her now."

Clint ducked out of the wheelhouse. Rain lashed into his face, and he was glad of the chilly shock of it. It would be easier if he could write the mild little man off as crazy, but he knew that wasn't the answer. Morse was outside the ordinary run of humans, no more to be labeled and bracketed than the strange sea creatures Devvy'd told him the Boss-Foreman whirl tossed up on a spring tide.

The *Helene* ran very smoothly. Face screwed against the whipping rain, Clint peered south. This squall wouldn't last long, but it didn't have to. Give her half an hour more and she'd be clear of the islands, in the open Pacific. He thought of the police launch over at Fox Island, and, anger returning, of Gunnar Lund. But even if that damned bonehead Swenska trollerman weren't asleep in his cabin or drunk ashore, it wouldn't be any different. Morse had the weather with him. Slipping along without lights, blanketed by the squall, the *Helene* could have passed him at a quarter mile, unheard and unseen.

Southeast, off the port bow, he caught a rain-dimmed flash. He counted to eight, and it came again. The Martinez light. They were farther, a lot farther up the channel than he'd guessed.

He hadn't had time yet to get scared again. That would come later. For now, they were both still alive, and they weren't bucking a gang any more, just two crooks with their minds set on escape.

The thin man was huddled in the fishing chair, shoulders hunched against the rain, hat pulled low. He'd pack a gun, it would most likely be in a holster under his left shoulder. Jump him … he'd have to be quick and quiet about it … then take the parson from behind. It would be something to run the *Helene* around to Fox Island, turn her over to the law.

He moved a casual step toward the stern, and instantly, like a snake disturbed, the thin man lifted his head. Rain trickled down his narrow face, and Clint heard the snick of a gun hammer tipping back. The thin man said in a bored tone, "Don't try it. You won't be lucky twice."

The drum of rain dwindled to a tapping, then, as suddenly as it had come, the squall swept astern of them. Clint saw the Martinez light clear now; only it had gone haywire, it was low to the water and its beam was whiter, stronger.

The thin man got up from the swivel chair. He still held the revolver, but it dangled at his side; he was bent forward, staring, straining against the night.

"Doc," he called. "You see that?"

There was a new sound in the air, very far away, like the distant drone of an aircraft engine. It grew in volume second by second, swelling in on them from the south. No troller power plant ever sang like that.

"Doc!" the thin man shouted. "Get going!"

Morse, in the wheelhouse, did not answer, and the *Helene* still ghosted south with no acceleration of speed.

White light glanced along the water from the southeast in an intense, narrow shaft, prodding and searching, sweeping the mouth of the channel. Clint saw, just for an instant, fir trees in a black huddle silhouetted on the south horn of Cultus Island. Then the searchlight glanced away, slashing a new path across the dark water.

They'd been waiting, ten miles off, for the word that would set the wheels spinning …

Only there'd been no word. The parson had shot Paddy before the word could go out. Unless there were more strands to the net, unless the grim merry little man had more cogs in his machine than he'd revealed even to them …

The white beam swept diagonally across the channel, and the *Helene* was caught in it, pinned by it. Clint heard her engines wake to a full roar, felt the shiver and lunge as the cruiser leaped into her stride. She was out of the searchlight beam, then it reached for her again and held her.

Let him twist and run and fight the net. He was boxed now, he hadn't a cat-in-hell chance of clearing the islands, and even if he did, they had two-thousand horsepower and fifty knots to run him down in open water.

Cops! Once he'd hated cops. Now, he loved them.

"Heave the cans over," the thin man shouted. "Get rid of them!"

The *Helene* lurched and spun, and shook the searchlight. But for seconds only. It fingered across the channel again, closer now, blinding white, passing them to bounce from a shore bluff of Cultus. She couldn't escape them. They were quartering the channel, probing it foot by foot as they ran. The white light crashed against his eyes again, and he ducked away from it, toward the cabin.

The thin man's voice broke in a yell. He clawed past Clint and darted for the wheelhouse steps. Clint saw Morse half turn from the wheel, saw the orange blossom sprout from his hand. The thin man's arm jerked up. His revolver flew in a high arc over the side. He took a backward step, and another, and let go at the knees and rolled down into the cockpit.

Above them, the clouds had lifted. The *Helene* was running all out, roaring through a pale wash of moonlight. The searchlight lost her, and found her again, and settled. Up-channel, a woodpecker hammering jarred the night. The cruiser swung violently, and somewhere to starboard, hornets hummed in an angry swarm. Machine gun. It was hammering again, lobbing tracer in lazy violet arcs, and forty feet beyond their bows, the water flaunted a sudden edging of lace.

Morse had turned her almost in her own length. He was driving straight north now, and the din of the engines and the hiss of the high-climbing bow wave muted the clatter of the machine gun up the channel.

He couldn't break away, and he knew it. Then what the hell was he trying to do?

Clint heard glass shatter, and dropped to the cockpit. He crawled to the cabin door, batted it open and tumbled down the steps.

He could see Devvy's white shirt in the gloom. She was kneeling, he groped forward to her, hearing glass crash again, and pulled her down. She clawed at him and he shook her, shouting at her, "It's me. God damn it, lay off!"

He felt her gasp, her body live and warm under his hands, and held her close for a moment, some of the cold of the sea going out of him.

She was sobbing at him, trying to tell him something, but with that din shaking the cruiser he couldn't hear. He yelled, mouth against her ear, "The cops came in. They've got him, Devvy!"

He still couldn't get it, the thing she was trying to tell him. She was pushing at him, straining away from him now. He let her go. The launch had stopped shooting. Devvy was up and moving toward the steps.

Clint followed her, puzzled, less triumphant now, out to the *Helene*'s cockpit.

For a moment he had no notion where they were. The lights of Martinez Cove should be east somewhere across the channel, but he couldn't find them. He turned, peering over Devvy's head, searching the shoreline. Then he saw the sparse cluster of lights, to starboard and far astern. They'd run north beyond the Cove, and the Martinez shoreline was close. He shot a glance to the other side and saw the bluffs of Cultus Island, close too.

The triple crescent of fixed breakers was south of them, and the *Helene* was racing as if with some life of her own. There was a new sound in the air, a sustained roaring that drowned the noise of her engines, beating all other sounds down. He knew now where they were, what Devvy had been trying to tell him.

Morse had tossed them into the funnel. They were

in the Boss-Foreman with engines and a spring tide hell-bending them on down for the wing-dam point and the whirl that stood ninety-foot boom swifters on end and dragged them under, that had swallowed a survey ship entire.

The searchlight licked into the cockpit, weaker now, from somewhere south beyond the breaker crescent. It showed the face of the dead man where he lay between the fishing chairs, staring up without approval or interest at the full moon.

Ahead, down the searchlight beam, the narrows ran tumbling white like a rapid in a river. The *Helene* crashed through a boil. For an instant her propellers lost their grip and she yawed violently east till the Martinez cliffs hung almost above her.

Maybe Morse could still beach her. Pile her under the bluffs. There might be ledges ...

But he'd swung the wheel again, shearing away, out to the mad main current.

The dreadful mild little man at the wheel might really be crazy. But Clint sensed a purpose and a plan in what he was doing. If he made it, if he ran the Boss-Foreman, he might still keep his date with the freighter offshore. The cops in the launch wouldn't expect him to come out. And if he did make open water he'd be hard to catch as a hunted wolf, free to sneak down Redoubt Pass or west around Cultus Island. He had a fortune stowed in the *Helene* and his neck to lose if the law got him. For him, it was a chance worth taking.

If he did it, though, if he put the *Helene* past the bend in one piece, he'd be doing what no man had ever done before.

Clint looked at Devvy. She was staring ahead, where spray and moonlight mixed in a shining curtain of terrible beauty beyond the rock snout of the wing-dam point.

The searchlight wasn't on them now. The *Helene* was

driving to starboard, quartering toward the Martinez shore again. Morse could skirt the whirl perhaps. There might be an inshore slot beyond the grip of the whirl, a narrow alley of deflected current down which he could slide her.

They were into the bend—hell, they were going to make it—then the bows swung as if a hand had closed upon them, and a power beyond all horsepower had her. The whirl had reached for her lazily, clenched its fist around her and drawn her in. She coasted gently at first, then faster. They were looking down the slope of a moon-polished water wall, riding its rim, smoothly but with a steepening list. The dead man rolled over and settled against the base of the portside chair. Clint stood braced, hand locked in Devvy's belt, staring with a frozen fascination into the vortex where the spinning walls converged.

The whirl carried them almost full circle, from Martinez to Cultus and back again. Down-channel, Clint glimpsed black rock under the curtain of moon-shot spray. There was a check in their smooth gliding, a lurch and a directionless hesitating. Then the whirl tossed them like a flung stone into breakers that caught the *Helene* and bounced her, crashed on her and battered her, burying her almost under.

They struck with a grinding crash. The bows reared and the slim long hull tipped and tilted, plowing forward and upward. Clint fell hard, taking Devvy with him, feeling the subsurface teeth of the reef slicing the *Helene*, gouging the bottom out of her. Then the grinding stopped and there was only the sustained, crazy howl of tide, and the cruiser hung between the rock teeth, a third of her sixty feet bedded on the rock seat of Paul Bunyan's Chair.

They'd hang here till the tide changed, till the salt-water river reversed itself and ebbed south between Cultus and Martinez. Then the *Helene* would slide off the sloping ledge, go the way of the survey ship, back into the whirl and this time, for keeps.

Morse stepped out of the wheelhouse. Flying glass or a slug had grazed his temple; he came down to them, dabbing at the cut with a white handkerchief. He looked dapper still, soberly clerical, and the prim mouth above the little beard was quirked in a smile.

The parson shouldn't look like that. When a man was at the end of his string, when he'd lost a fortune and was going to lose his life, it should show on him. They stared at Morse; and Clint could feel Devvy shivering.

"Still with us?" Morse called to them over the hurly-burly. "I'm glad! We'll go below."

The broken hull absorbed some of the water thunder. The cabin slanted steeply from the cruiser's heavy cant to starboard. Moonlight flooded through the ports to gleam on the litter of broken glass on the floor. Clint settled his back against the edge of a bunk, and they watched Morse tug at the galley door, wrenching till the shock-warped frame released it.

He came out with a bottle and glasses. "Not broken," he said, pleased. "Everything was well-secured, but even so, it's a miracle."

He poured precisely; his spectacles were still in place, and he was frowning a little, concentrating on what he did. His hands, Clint saw, were entirely steady.

"Mr. Peddar—senior, that is—had this from Prohibition days. Imported Scotch. He tells me it's the best obtainable." He offered the first glass to Devvy with a tiny bow. "Told me, I should say. I forgot for a moment that he's no longer with us. In fact our company has dwindled remarkably in the last few hours."

Clint took the precise three fingers the parson poured him. He wasn't scared, not in any way that he'd ever been before. Maybe in a spot like this, part of your brain went numb. He listened while the mild and pleas-ant voice ran on.

"It's regrettable that Mr. Burke can't be with us. He was a man to appreciate such a situation as this, I'm sure."

Clint didn't drink. He said, "What are you, anyway?"

"A businessman," Morse said. "A speculator who has just lost the biggest gamble of his career." He drank, and slipped the white handkerchief from his cuff, and patted his mouth. "I realize now that it was lost at our first meeting, Mr. Farrell. One can't let evidence accumulate, and I was never quite able to rectify that error."

He was like a defeated general outlining why and how his campaign had failed. He said, "I've always tried to reduce the element of chance to a minimum. But that minimum remains. Peddar, junior, bungled badly. And you, Mr. Farrell, were lucky."

"Sure," Clint said, feeling Devvy's hand quiet in his. "I've got a lucky name." He drank, and the stuff was tasteless, no heat in it. This was like a conversation among dead people—maybe liquor would be like this in a ghost's mouth, if there were ghosts, and if they had mouths to drink.

"On one point I'm curious," Morse said. "Since it no longer matters to any of us, perhaps you'll be kind enough to inform me. Our friends up yonder"—he gave his chin a casual tilt—"how did they know? I was satisfied that no message had gone out."

"None did."

"Well then?"

"You know as much about it as we do. Maybe it was luck again."

"Yes ... Yes, I suppose so. The one factor which we can't eliminate. Too bad. I dislike the loose ends it forces one to leave."

"I've noticed," Clint said. "Like loose bodies lying around, eh?"

"Unfinished business of any sort." Morse sighed and smiled. "My judgment was at fault about Joe. I thought he was a likely lad. But he's gone now, poor fellow, and I'll not speak ill of him."

Devvy said, "He killed Aila. Why?"

"Because he lost his head." A faint shade of annoyance tinged the parson's voice. "She had supplied us with certain information, for which she asked a fantastic price. I believe she mentioned the possibility of a bargain with the law if we failed to meet it… " He finished his drink and said reflectively, turning the glass in his slim little hand, "When she refused to leave your house except at that price, Joe took the most obvious solution. He quite failed to realize she was in a poor position for bargaining."

"What would you have done?" Clint asked. He'd seen rattlesnakes behind glass once in the Seattle zoo; he'd watched them like this, repelled but at the same time fascinated. "Coaxed her out to the ship and killed her there?"

"Of course!" Morse twinkled at him, pouring himself another drink.

"That's what you'd have done with us too, isn't it?"

"Not necessarily. Your attitude would have decided that. Believe me, Mr. Farrell, I was completely sincere in my offer. You possess something which would have been useful to me—a notably short time lag between thought and action. There are occasions in a business such as mine when an aide with that quality is invaluable."

"You mean I'd have made a good heavy," Clint said. "It's something to know, anyway."

Devvy said, "What would you have told him, Clint?"

Still watching Morse, he said, "I'd have gone along with him till you were in the clear."

"Then?" Morse asked.

"Then I'd have wrung your head off."

"Charming!" Morse said. "You're a sentimentalist, Mr. Farrell. Young people usually are."

He was into his third drink now, but his hand remained steady. He said gravely, "One achieves a certain wisdom. I went out to China, Mr. Farrell, as an earnest young man not many years older than you. My wife went with me—we were very newly married. I lost her there, and although it was a very bitter blow it was for the best. It permitted my mind to function with a clarity lacking before. Think long enough and one sees to the other side of very many things."

Except for the glass, he could be a parson in his pulpit, speaking solemnly and rather sadly now. "One realizes the true worth of human values, one learns to laugh at the stupid emphasis the Occidental places on the sanctity of life and the dreadfulness of death. One learns the complete inefficacy of prayer, Mr. Farrell. There is no pity sitting in the clouds, none whatever. I learned that earlier, of course, when my wife was first taken ill."

He drank, and wiped his lips, and said, "Fortunately you two will not live to learn those lessons. They're much better never learned."

His voice, with its mad, twisted logic, was a meaningless sound going on, like the slamming of the Boss-Foreman's crazy tide around them.

But there was one thing he'd said that made sense. That's where we are, Clint thought. Over on the other side of things. They'd passed beyond fear this night, they were like ghosts here in the gut of the Boss-Foreman, spirits talking together.

The howling outside was in a lower key; they hardly had to raise their voices now. Tide must be nearly at the flood. Clint said, "You know all the answers, so tell us this. Aila wasn't with you just for what you paid her. What had she against Devvy to hate her like that?"

"She was a low creature," Morse said. Then to Devvy, kindly, "I suspect she saw something in you, my dear, which she'd never had and never could hope to have.

Honesty. Virtue of the classical sort, which is to say chastity with courage."

He emptied his glass and set it carefully beside the bottle, tilted against the inner edge of a bunk. He took off his spectacles, drew a hand across his eyes in a tired, vaguely pathetic gesture; and instantly Clint had him by the wrists.

Devvy said quietly, "No. There's no need. He's dead already."

So that feeling had been on her too. He looked at her, and she was very calm. It wasn't hope, the quickening in the back of his mind, but something akin to rebellion, an instinctive, contemptuous striking out against Morse and his denial of all things human.

He said to Devvy, "Sure. He's dead. But we aren't."

"No," she said, studying him with the familiar, weighing frown between her eyes.

He let Morse go, and the parson replaced his spectacles. "I wish you wouldn't be so suspicious," he said. "There's no need, really. If you'll pardon a jest, we're all in the same boat now." He twinkled at them, and said amiably, "I wish I could marry you. I have the service by heart still, in the shorter version. But there's the matter of witnesses, and anyway the legality of such a ceremony might be questioned." He chuckled merrily. "Forgive me. I forgot that we've passed a little beyond the law."

Devvy said, "I'd sooner be married by the devil. I don't want even to drown with you. Come on, Clint."

They left him there, back turned, pouring himself another drink. The breakers in the tailrace from the whirl were much lower, and there was a choked, muffled note in the voice of the tide.

"Look," Clint said. "It's a chance. Better than waiting here."

"We aren't going to wait," Devvy said.

Clint scrambled to the cabin roof. The *Helene*'s tender was still lashed and chocked in place, a tidy ten-footer. As far as he could see, it was undamaged. The oars were lodged neatly under the thwarts. Mike Peddar must have had a feeling for the *Helene;* he'd kept her well.

Morse came out of the cabin and stood watching them, the bottle in the side pocket of his black broadcloth jacket, glass in his hand. There was mild disappointment in his tone.

"I'm not to have your company?"

From above, Clint called to Devvy, "Can you ease her down?"

Morse said, "Permit me ... but Devvy told him sharply, "Keep away!"

She stood ready below, slim and lithe in her short-sleeved shirt and rolled-up jeans, while Clint worried the lashings free and boosted the dinghy out of its chocks. It came with an easy slide. Devvy caught the bow as it dipped, and went back a pace, easing it down. Morse stepped across and helped her the rest of the way with it.

He said, "It's no earthly use—I'm sure you must realize that. But it will be a very interesting experiment."

"It's been done," Devvy said. She was looking south up the pass, studying the tide.

Clint came down to her, and she said, "They had a spring tide too, that other time. Dad said he'd wait for a spring tide to try it."

Morse clicked his tongue. He said—and, oddly, his words were Paddy Burke's—"Babes in the woods! But if you insist on leaving me, I'll give you a remembrance."

He climbed agilely to the wheelhouse, and came out lugging two gasoline cans by their handles. He brought down two more. "Take these," he said. "I'm anxious to convince you that I bear no ill will. I like you. For a time you were a hazard to my business, but that's over." He said, eying them gravely, "These could make you rich. There's a king's ransom in each of them. But if you do reach shore, I suppose you'll turn them over to the police." The spray rain had lightened to a drizzle, and the howl had sunk to a mutter. The race divided smoothly, parting on either side of the Chair to join streams again in a snarling rip below.

Devvy said, "It's almost slack water. If it's going to happen, it has to be soon."

She continued to watch the pass with fixed intentness. Clint fished for cigarettes. They were a wet pulp in his breast pocket, and it was queer a thing like that should irritate him now.

"You'd better get the boat in," Devvy told him.

He skidded the dinghy over the *Helene*'s stem. She bobbed in bristling, licking water. Devvy held the painter, keeping her fended away with her foot. Crouching, Clint worked the oars free, set them in the rowlocks and crossed the spoon blades on the stern seat.

The race from the whirl ran smooth as a lazy river. It was hard to estimate the speed or strength of its flow, but it seemed to be almost halted.

Devvy said, "I think it's high-water slack. It only happens on a few tides. If this is one, we'll have about four minutes from when the whirl comes up."

Two of the cans Clint set amidships, fitting them snugly under the rowing thwart. There wasn't as much weight to them as he'd expected ... they must have cost a lot more than their weight in blood. He shoved one under the stern seat, and set the last on the bottom boards. The dinghy was a gray lapstreak, broad in the beam. She'd be overloaded, but not too badly.

"I can't be sure," Morse said, "but I do believe you're correct, Devvy. The whirl seems to be flattening." Conversationally, he told them, "The Peddars spoke of this phenomenon, but frankly, I didn't believe them. There was a time when I would have been convinced the Lord had smoothed a path for us through the waters."

"Us?" Clint stared at the parson.

"Why, yes." Morse twinkled at them amiably. "I've never held with the foolish tradition that a captain should go down with his ship. And the thought of death by drowning has always distressed me. Since there appears to be a slight chance of avoiding death in that form … " "You'll hang if we make shore. You know that."

Morse sighed. "The lesser of two evils, my boy. It's a quick and tidy end."

"Don't take him, Clint." Devvy's voice was sharp. Clint stepped down to the dinghy and settled himself on the midthwart. The oars were light and short, their handles felt good in his fists. He said to Devvy, "You're lightest. Get into the bow." And to the parson, "Stern-sheets for you."

"Clint!"

"Shut up. If we haul out of this, I'm turning him over to the cops, him and his cans together."

The dinghy rocked, then steadied. He dipped the oars, shooting them away from the *Helene*'s stem. The parson's chuckle, jolly as if they were off on a picnic, was in his ears.

There was very little current. What there was still set to the north, the last surges of the flood through the pass. Clint asked, "Which way?" and Devvy said, "South. Row as I tell you."

He took three more strokes, and gently but with a strength not to be resisted, the dinghy began to swing cross-channel toward Martinez.

"Let her go," Devvy said. "Don't even try to steer."

He lifted both oar blades clear, and they moved in an easy arc, slowly, toward the Martinez cliffs.

They were on the rim of the whirl again. The water sloped away to a shallow center that had a burnished look to it, as if the moon itself was trapped and spinning down there.

He knew Devvy was kneeling, back to him, quiet as

if she'd even stopped breathing. The arc became a half circle. Downchannel, glancing across his shoulder, he saw boils forming, and a random chop as if a wind blew there that could not reach this place. Somewhere below the bend, the water was giving off a sound curiously like a snore.

They'd gone full-circle now, and the moon-bright vortex was lifting, broadening. Clint forced his eyes away from it. When they were midway between the Chair and Martinez again, he realized that the dinghy floated on an even keel. The whirl had flattened.

But the water was boiling under the Martinez cliffs, clucking and fleering. Devvy said quietly, "Turn out now. Straight across for Cultus. We haven't much time, Clint."

Where the whirl had been, the narrows lay like a millpond. But it was a millpond filled with treacle. The water itself seemed thick, resisting the oars, slowing their progress to a crawl. The dinghy hung in it like a fly in treacle, caught there, fighting her way ever so slowly.

Devvy had told him the currents went crazy here, that no one had ever figured them out. Maybe there were layers of current; he had the feeling that, down under, the water moved in heavy masses, directionless for the moment, but restless and waiting the signal that would give purpose to its strength.

Devvy said, "Give it all you've got."

They were not halfway across. The oars had felt light when they pushed off from the Chair; now they were heavy in his hands. He was tired—he'd been tired for months, and the tiredness was piling up on him, getting to him at last.

He could see the Chair again now, and the *Helene* hanging on the shelf like a gray shark stranded there.

"Harder," Devvy said. "Clint, row!"

They were past center. The dinghy's bows bumped

gently. Something scraped along her side. Seconds later, he saw what looked to be a fantastic sea monster astern, horned and staring. A drowned buck, a big fellow, antlers silvered by moonlight. Logs floated here, old logs that looked like no other drift he'd ever seen. They were splintered and chewed, mauled as if a giant had chumbled them in his jaws.

The water was uneasy. The Boss-Foreman had a life of its own, it was dozing in its pass. They were creeping across its chest, and it was sighing in its sleep, and it would soon wake.

He heard broken water chattering ahead, somewhere beyond their bows, under the Cultus bluffs. Close—he hadn't realized they'd pulled that close.

"Clint." Her voice was a whisper behind him. "Row!" His chest was on fire and his legs were numb, and his arms were muscleless strings between his shoulders and the leaden oars. The dinghy hung without forward way, held there, gummed fast. The parson's bearded face wavered before him, smiling, dimming from his sight. He brought the oars out raggedly, and dug them in and dragged them through, and dug and dragged again at the binding water.

The bow pitched, and the dinghy seemed to lunge ahead. She bounced into a rip. He caught a crab and toppled backward, and the dinghy reeled and water slopped inboard into his face.

The chill shock of it cleared his brain. He sat up, and reached wearily for the oars. They rode in a white blaze of moonlight, in an almost currentless cove.

"Excellent," Morse said. "Excellent, Mr. Farrell!"

He took off his spectacles, drew a hand across his eyes in a tired, vaguely pathetic gesture. The spectacles glimmered as he replaced them on his nose. His other hand, his right, dipped smoothly into his jacket.

"Keep rowing, Mr. Farrell." The voice was mild, but

the click of the revolver hammer had a cold authority. "In approximately a dozen strokes, we'll ground on a ledge. There, I'm afraid, we must part company."

Moonglow highlighted the gun and the little hand that held it. "It's a necessity that gives me great regret, but we must cut our cloth to suit our circumstances. And our circumstances, I need hardly point out, have changed." He chuckled merrily. "Business, I might say, has picked up!" Clint rested on the oars, staring dully into the smiling face. They'd come this far, they'd almost made it, but his will was as numb as his arms now; he couldn't fight any longer.

Behind him, Devvy said, "There's still someone to hang you. There's Lum Kee."

"Gone too," the parson said. "Lum Kee had been failing for some time, I regret to say. He suffered a fatal seizure just before we left The Retreat, Devvy. I believe it was hastened by a stoppage of breath."

Morse said pleasantly, "So I fear you're in error, my dear. There will be no one who saw me on board the *Helene* tonight. A certain suspicion will attach to me, of course. But suspicion and proof are different matters... Harder on your port oar now, please, Mr. Farrell."

There would be fire in their faces, but they'd feel nothing, not the shock of the bullet, or the sinking down and down in the deep water. The tide, reaching into this cove, would take them, and the Boss-Foreman would have them as it was always meant to have them, and that would be the end of it. Clint leaned forward and pulled once more, pointing the dinghy's stem for the ledge he couldn't see. A dozen strokes, Morse had said ...

Wind fanned his face in a sudden puff. He heard the smacking impact of the bullet before the explosion crashed against his eardrums. The shot had come from inshore, from somewhere close on the bluffs. He swung the oar handles forward, the motion automatic;

and smiling still, Morse bowed stiffly toward him. His revolver clattered to the bottom boards. He lurched sideways against the gunwale, a black hole starred upon his left temple between cheekbone and hairline. The dinghy rolled as Clint's port oar dug deep, and the bright silver water rushed up to meet them.

Devvy was only a stroke away when he shook the water from his eyes. They swam strongly, side by side, out of the moonlight into the black shadows of the bluffs. Clint's knee scraped rock. He hauled up the slope of a barnacled ledge. Filled suddenly with a panic fear that even now, rock underfoot, the Boss-Foreman would lazily reach out for them and haul them back, he reached for Devvy's shoulders and dragged her up to him. Moving like people in a dream, they followed the wide ledge in.

Tideline. Popweed crackled under their feet. There was a brushy draw in the limestone and a thread of a creek flumed down it, its voice a tiny, mocking echo of the Boss-Foreman's. They toiled up the creekbed. The brush thinned, and Clint slipped and slithered on a drift of leaves. Devvy caught his arm, and they climbed the rest of the way together, up to bald rock and a faint random breeze that touched his face like a welcoming hand.

They were on top of the wing-dam point, not more than a hundred yards from the tip of the headland. He didn't speak to Devvy, or she to him. But, wearily, they trudged along the crest of the point toward the drop-off.

It was dark up here, but the last of the moonlight silvered the narrows. They stood and watched, saying nothing, not touching. Clint could feel the beating of his pulse in his throat.

Below, the shining millpond dulled as if a quick wind had gone over. The water humped and shattered. Where the millpond had been was a vast circular boil. The center of the boil began to spin and sink. The water had purpose and direction—the whirl was forming, and the air was filled with a muted thunder, and the Chair upstream now from the whirl, reared out of a woolly carpet of foam. Clint could see the *Helene* still hanging on the shelf between the tall black pinnacles.

He half-turned, looking down toward the cove where they'd landed. The *Helene*'s dinghy hadn't capsized. Heavy with water, she was cruising sluggishly out to the main current as if drawn by her painter. The parson had rolled inboard. He lay in a small huddle, shoulders against the edge of the stern seat, beard cocked at the setting moon.

The dinghy glided into the outermost ring of the whirl. She began the great circle that had swung them almost to Martinez; but while she was still midway between Cultus and the Chair, she faltered and fell off at a tangent. She sideslipped faster and faster. They watched her dip into the black hole of the vortex as a beetle goes down a drain.

Clint said, his own voice coming to him from far away, "We licked it."

"No," Devvy said. "It let us go."

They drew back from the drop-off. The great madrona was down the point, the first of the trees. They couldn't see it, but they could hear its leaves singing very softly. It was the turn of the night, the dawn wind was waking in the madrona top.

DEVVY, TRUDGING BESIDE him, squeezed water from her hair. Her voice was exasperated. "I had it done just the other day. I don't know when I can afford to again."

He gave her frown for frown. "What are you beefing about? Is it my fault you got wet?"

"I didn't say that. But if you hadn't taken him off with us, if you'd done what I told you instead of being so smart ..."

"He had the gun. He would have made us take him. Anyway, you're not my boss!"

"Yes I am."

"Then I quit. I'd meant to, soon as we were out of this."

"Good! It saves me firing you!"

They glared at each other; and from the edge of shadow, a voice said, "Fighting still, like a brace of Kilkenny cats. Is a man to have no peace from it?"

Clint halted, stock-still and staring. The wide little man came swaggering to meet them, his hat tipped back jauntily from the blood-splotched bandage that ringed his head.

"Paddy." Devvy's voice was half a sob. "They shot you. We thought you were dead."

"Half dead only ... Don't be after hugging me now! Would you drive my splinters deeper?"

"You're alive, Paddy. You're all right."

"I am not all right! Three years I've had that pipe, and seasoned to my exact taste. Now it is scattered amongst my ribs. There's a new parting in my hair as well. He would have missed you for certain, Clinton, the kind of shot he was."

Casually under his arm, Paddy carried Callahan's hunting rifle. The foot-long scope, set in its mounts above the slender barrel, gave off a dull and wicked glimmer.

Clint said, "You didn't miss."

"With his head square into my cross-hairs?" Paddy chuckled grimly. "No seal ever gave me a chance like that. Still and all, it was a pretty shot by moonlight at two hundred yards, and a credit to any man."

"Three hundred yards," Clint said.

"We're liars both," Paddy said. "It was a shade over the hundred, but never mind. What of the others?"

"They're all dead. Now, you tell us something. What brought the police launch in?"

Paddy said soberly, "Luck, and Lum Kee. When he heard the donnybrook in the woods, he talked up Gunnar Lund on his radio from the mill. Gunnar could not contact the launch, the way the black squalls were cracking around him, so he ran his boat clear over to Fox Island after 'em."

"They killed Lum Kee, didn't they?" Devvy said.

"In his own kitchen," Paddy said, "with one squeeze of his sparrow's neck. But you'll not grieve for him, Devvy. He was a loyal man, and we've evened his score this night." Devvy sat down on the leaves, and Clint dropped beside her. He felt for cigarettes, and remembered, and muttered a "goddam."

"Here," Paddy said, and tossed his tobacco pouch. "Do as the heathen do, and roll a cigaro in a leaf. The taste is hellish, but there's some comfort in it."

He stood over them, and Clint knew he was smiling. But when Paddy spoke, the odd half sadness was in his voice.

"You're a dull gaboon as I've told you, Clinton, without sense or learning and given to scoffing at the exact sciences. All you have is the lucky name and a certain walk and way with you. But I'd give a corner of what soul I have left me to shed twenty years and stand in your shoes. I'll be off now ... there's your house to set in order, Devvy, and Constable Beamish's wife to be told at last why her man would leave her to go drinking with Aila in the town. She'll not take his naked word for it, women being as they are." There was a diminishing rustle along the point. Paddy's song of the Bat d'Af drifted back to them, whistled off-key between his teeth.

Devvy poked among her cigarette papers. She found a few leaves in the middle of the folder less damp than the rest, and held them out.

"Make me one, Clint?"

He built two cigarettes, and found dry matches in

Paddy's pouch. He drew Devvy inside his arm, and her hair was under his chin, and the madrona trunk was a rest for his tired back, something solid, rooted in earth, out of reach of the tide.

Once, a long, long time ago, he'd wanted to be a trollerman. But not any more. Gunnar Lund could have it, or any other damned fool that wanted it. He might get over the feeling sometime, but for long enough to come, he'd want rock and firm earth under his feet.

He could feel the drink he'd had down there now, as if its kick had been suspended till they should come up from the Boss-Foreman, claw their way back from the dead. He felt good, the powdery dry tobacco was better than any he'd ever smoked.

Gently, he rubbed his chin on Devvy's hair; he wanted to talk to her, but there weren't any words for the way he felt.

Her cigarette had gone out. She said, "I've never been so tired."

"Sleep then," he told her. "You can sleep safe now, Devvy."

The sun was up when he wakened. Devvy was still sleeping, her head in the hollow of his hip. He studied her, and all the storm and trouble was gone, and there was only the quiet wonder and delight. He was going to marry a stump-ranch girl, and they'd fight like hell, but they'd live happy ever after.

Gently, he shifted her head and got up. The Boss-Foreman was shaking the air. He walked to the lip and looked down at the pass, hands hooked into his belt. The two black, bare pinnacles reared out of a white smother. But the *Helene* was gone as if she'd never hung there, dragged off by the mighty suction of the spring-tide ebb, and the parson was gone, and he wondered, just for a moment, whether it hadn't all been a nightmare. Always, it would be hard to believe Devvy and he had been down there and had come back.

Clint lifted a hand to his shirt pocket. The ring lay against his chest. He brought it out and held it, turning it in his fingers. This was real enough. Maybe he ought to keep it, just to remind him. But they wouldn't spend much time remembering. It hadn't belonged here, any of that tangled and bloody business—it was foreign to the island, they'd chew it around for a spell in Halem, then it would all drift out of mind. And there were some things even the law didn't have to know, things not to be talked of or thought about, or even dreamed of at night. They were better left there for good, sunk in the deep water.

He smiled, and flicked the ring out to the thundering pass. No souvenirs.

Devvy was awake when he turned. Her fair hair was ruffled, and she sat rubbing her fists into her eyes, bare brown legs stretched out before her on the golden leaf-carpet.

"The children," she said. "Brian and Elsie. They'll have to live with us."

"Elsie? After what she did?"

"She couldn't know. Elsie can be sweet sometimes, Clint. She just hasn't had a chance."

"Okay," he said, scowling down at her, loving her. "But it's going to look funny. Strangers will wonder."

He reached his hands to her and pulled her up. "Come on," he said. "Let's go home."

The timber was lacy with sunshine, and the voice of the Boss-Foreman behind them was a din without menace or meaning. It signified less than the sifting fall of a leaf.